COYOTE

A NOVEL

G. Lawrence

4-20-05

VANTAGE PRESS
New York

This is a work of fiction. Any similarity between the characters appearing herein and any real persons, living or dead, is purely coincidental.

Cover design concept by Teresa Emerson of the *Philadelphia Sunday Sun*

Cover design by Sue Thomas

FIRST EDITION

All rights reserved, including the right of reproduction in whole or in part in any form.

Copyright © 2001 by G. Lawrence

Published by Vantage Press, Inc.
516 West 34th Street, New York, New York 10001

Manufactured in the United States of America
ISBN: 0-533-13420-X

Library of Congress Catalog Card No.: 99-97513

0 9 8 7 6 5 4 3 2 1

To those around "the way" who left early:

SUMMERSVILLE

Especially EZRA (BUBBIE) and PHIL (DOC)

CONNY (CHUGALUG)	VERLYN	ERIC
BUCKEY	STATESTORE	BUTCH MAJOR
DUST	STEWBUM	DICKIE NESBITT
MARSHALL	JOHNNY BARTEE	KNOCKIE
VEDA	MITCHELL "TWIN"	CORA
EENA	FACE	VAN
MATTHEW	JOEY	PRIMO
LARRY BOON	AUBREY	SANDY
TOMMY TROTTER	DAVE RICHARDSON	BOOKER
POPPY	WORM	LES
ALLEN JOHNS	PENNY (NAPPY-CHIN-PIN)	BUSH

Answers

I've lived, I've loved, I've longed to know just what it is
   I need
To do, to be, to solve what seems a mystery to me
I've looked, I've tried and I'm trying still to reach within
   myself
To find myself. To synchronize . . . myself with sanity.

I've lied, I've cried, I've tried to hide, I've run, I've
   blindly groped
for peace inside my mind; my soul; to fill a void I'd hoped
I've peered into my human being, looked as far as I
   could see
I've searched and inquired and I questioned. What is that
   power that be?

It's not unlike an endless maze or a corridor wide as time
A doorless room, eternity, an obscure and pointless rhyme.
An abyss so deep, a floorless sea, an overwhelming sense
   of infinity.

I know there's a way to find the way, to master, to
   overcome
the obstacles and setbacks life nonchalantly does. It's a
   lonely way
yet the only way and it's fleeting as time that was.

If it's a love gone sour, bewitching hour or just time to say
   good-bye

The party's end, a dying friend or the loss of a material thing
A failure here, a defeat there no matter what life may bring
There's a way to do it, to understand, the whole of life's facade
And it's as bright as the sun in the sky up above
The answer, my friend, is GOD.

—G. Lawrence (4/85)

"The coyote bitch, she get in heat, she take care of all the males first. Then she go to town and all the male dogs? They smell her. She lure them out to the desert, she get one alone. The other coyote? They circle that dog, they kill him, they eat him."

—Excerpt from the movie *At Close Range*

Preface

The animal society, and, I imply, others as well, seem to adhere to certain basic instincts that are crucial to the proliferation of that society. The behavior is accepted as a part of life and understood as necessary for the survival of the species in that society.

One of these instincts seems to affect a portion of that society in particular, a portion of that society that genuinely "cares," wholeheartedly, for all others in that society, and, somehow, seems to feel bonded and responsible for the survival of that society at a certain level.

They do for others, knowing that it "COUNTS." They perform their action purposely and precisely, and with the inherent knowledge that—it is necessary!!!

The human society as well as the society of the coyote are both MALE DOMINANT. There are a multitude of questions posed by this factor. Are the actions of the majority of females in our society so overpoweringly influenced by MALE DOMINANCE that they have chosen or accepted certain roles? Are females chemically designed (as opposed to choosing or accepting) to perform certain roles other than the procreative phenomenon? Is the physical structure of either sex the basis for their inherent/chosen/accepted roles in these societies? Is society responsible for this turnout? Or is our sprirtual understanding of self at the root?

This writing attempts to address a small aspect of this issue of MALE DOMINANCE through a storyline that revolves around the trials and tribulations of one woman and her relationships with several friends. Her early years forever affected by a teenage misconception, which resulted in her seducing her father, one time, out of pity. Afterward, her father forcefully continuing to pursue the incestuous relationship against her will. And the sorrow of the regretful act continuously impacting on her confused, lonely drug-strewn life.

This story follows her interaction with her friends and how their lives were thrown together by destiny, held together by sheer necessity as they struggle to survive in an African-American environment, replete with all the social and emotional problems that beset people. Even as they are inadvertently brought together on the wings of fate, their lives are further enmeshed by the murder of a central figure in all their lives. The residual effects of this atrocity have lasting effects on each member of the group. One member in particular. This particular character is at first enlightened by an encounter with a female coyote. Then, eventually, she realizes the lack of a crucial element of being that is at the very crux of this mortal coil called life, and that crucial element is GOD.

I will highlight how the subtelty of these phenomena, as perpetuated throughout this writing, very well impacts on life and the relationships that we weave in and out of throughout our lives.

GOD is good all the time, and HE makes no mistakes.

Acknowledgments

"In all thy ways acknowledge him, and he shall direct thy paths" (Proverbs 3:6).

Sincerest and eternal thanks to:

My Lord and Savior Jesus Christ for delivering me, my wife Harriet (Harri) for her unending love, faith, support, and confidence in me, her, and us; my mother Bernice (little birdie), my daughter Yvette (Vet), my son, Glenn Jr. (Snuff), his wife Terry, Debbie and Darryl, my Aunt Elaine, my brother Steve, my niece April and her husband Steve, my sister Rose (Angel), Pat, my mother-in-law Bernice (mom) Mathis, my cousin Carla, Linda Black (for her invaluable editing assistance and advice), Richard and Judy Whiten, Richard Whiten Jr., Sabrina (Breenie) Claude, Deloris Claude, Randolph (Randan) Minor, Leslie Eisdale, Fred Whiten, Maresy (at Pinkerton), Melvina (Beany) Armstead, Barbara Mccoy, Jean (at Elite), all my former co-workers at Bell, my church family, Rev. T.D. Jakes, and anybody else who gave me feedback, advice, encouragement, inspiration or help in any way for this novel to become real.

May God bless and keep you all.

I
REPROBATION

Kansas

The bus had just pulled into the station. The passengers were patiently beginning to exit the bus when suddenly a young girl, who had just gotten off the bus, passed out on the floor of the terminal. She had vomited and was lying in it. People stepped gingerly around her as though she were a puddle of water. She was unkempt and smelled bad as it were. Her clothes were also tattered and dirty. Not a very appealing sight. The onlookers were not rushing to her aid. The people near her had more or less given her room to fall and were moving slowly by her as they looked down on her with disgust. She had fallen in front of one of the passengers who did stop. It was a man. The same man who had boarded the bus in Chicago and had sat behind her but had never said a word to her during the entire ride. The man bent down on one knee, moved the girl's face out of the regurgitation, and wiped it from her mouth with his handkerchief. He appeared to know what he was doing as he moved her around on the floor so that she was lying flat on her back and out of the mess. He looked up at the others passing by, but no one else seemed interested in helping him. He checked her carotid pulse on the left side of her neck and tilted her head back to allow her to breathe easier. As he did so, she opened her eyes and looked into his. His eyes softened as he looked into hers. She knew she was safe.

"Did I fall out? Damn! I ain't never did that shit before," she said in a whispered voice. She was obviously aware of her situation now and he had moved away from her body a little to allow her to see and move more freely.

"You feelin' alright now? You okay?" he asked.

"Yeah. I think so. Where is this? I mean, where is we at?" She was struggling to sit up as she spoke.

"We in Kansas. Witchita, Kansas," the man told her.

"Where? What the fuck am I doing in some Kansas?" The girl was clearly confused. "I was supposed to be going to California. How the hell??...." She paused to gather her thoughts as she gazed into the face of the gentle, older man. "Who are you?" she suddenly requested.

"Oh, excuse me, ma'am, my name is Jason, Jason Freeman, an' I live here. I'm from these parts. It's pretty clear to me that you didn't intend to get off here," he smiled to her.

"Hell, no!! Well, not to stay anyway. I remember wanting to go to the bathroom and that's the last thing I remember. I musta' fell out then." She was suddenly overpowered by a strong stench. "Is that my spitup? She glanced at the mess she made. "Can you help me up please?" She appeared to be in full control now as she attempted to get up with some dignity. Jason stood and assisted the young lady to her feet. She was still a little wobbly, so he had to put his arm around her to steady her as he led her to an empty seat in the now empty bus terminal. A few people who had witnessed the incident were curiously looking at the couple, but the main body of onlookers had passed and the girl was looking at the remainders with a very intimidating glare.

"And just what is your name, young lady?" Jason asked.

"Damn white people! What yall lookin' at?" she muttered at the onlookers as she slowly turned her glance to Jason. "Oh!! Me? Oh!! My name Jessica."

The newly acquainted couple left the bus terminal and headed for an old beatup, blue, pickup truck that was parked nearby. Jason threw her bag in the back and helped the girl step up and into the cab of the truck. They didn't say much as they began the ride to Jason's home, which was about an hour and a half ride just on the outskirts of the prairie. Jason had offered the hospitality of his home to her, sensing that she really had no true destination. The girl slept as they drove. When they arrived, she awoke and looked around. She appeared to be annoyed.

"Is this where you live?" Clearly unimpressed with her surroundings.

Jason smiled and nodded his head in confirmation. He noticed the look of disapproval on her face as she spoke. True, it wasn't much to look at, but it was his. And he liked it just fine. Just on the outskirts of the prairie, he had lived there by himself since the death of his wife. He did what he could to keep it clean and livable. He was a Christian man. A man who served the Lord with every fiber of his body and every minute of the day. And he believed it was his faith that kept him strong, not so much the work, so he didn't put much value in material things. He put much value in the power of prayer.

Although the young girl was anything but impressed with her new surroundings, the sun was going down at the time and it caught her attention with its brilliant orange light on the horizon. It seemed to sit on the edge of the flat land in a distance. She had never seen anything like this before. She stood mesmerized for a few minutes just standing, looking. No buildings. No houses. No pavements. No streets. No trees. She seemed to be trying to assimilate differences between where she was standing now and what she was accustomed to. A different world, she thought. She stood there entranced when the howl of a coyote scared her back to reality and she realized she had been standing there for a while when she suddenly realized where she was. She was beginning to feel fear creep into her. It was getting dark.

"Mr!! Mr. Jason," she yelled. As she turned to run but stumbled on the edge of the porch after her first step.

"Hold on there, girl, where you goin'? You already here!!" Jason assured her. She didn't realize she was right in front of the porch all that time or that Jason had been sitting there in his rocking chair watching her. She felt foolish.

"Oh, ahm sorry. I heard that wolf out there and it scared me." Jason smoked a corncob pipe that he never actually lit. He took the pipe out of his mouth to allow him to laugh out loud.

"That weren't no wolf out there," he assured her, "that's a coyote. You ain't never heard them talk, I suppose?" he said jokingly to her. She looked at him with a grimace.

"Talk? They don't talk. Get outta' here." She really didn't know one way or the other what he meant.

"Oh, I don't suppose they talk the way we do, but I know for a fact, they talks," Jason responded.

"How you know so much about them?" she asked, more astonished than curious. She relaxed a little more and slid closer to where Jason was sitting. She was still on the floor of the old porch looking up at him as he began to speak. He put his pipe back into his mouth and held it there as he stared into the darkening stretch of land.

"Well, I suppose it's 'cause I been here so long. I kinda sense what they saying. Besides, I know a little about the way they lives. I knows that the coyote female goes into heat spells and when that happens, the male coyotes, well, they just gets all excited when they smells her scent. All night long you can here 'em out there howling. Talking, I calls it. First it be just one, then they all start. One seem to know what the other sayin'. I know for a fact that when they gets this close to town, they hongry. And it's the gal that's out there trying to get to the stray dogs."

The girl was all ears. "How you know that?" she asked.

"I know that 'cause I know that she the one that give off the scent that the dogs and the other coyote smell and she know that they follow it. And dogs and other animal is what they eats. Sometime they eats us too. Sometimes they eats they own kind. They do what they got to to survive out there. It's just God's way."

The young girl was amazed upon hearing this. She listened intently. Somehow this vaguely reminded her of her life in New York and Philadelphia. It was as if her life seemed to contrast so clearly with that of the coyote story. The female in particular. Her responsibility to the clan. She remembered how she used to skillfully lure the suckers, the unsuspecting drug dealers, and men with money into following her. How she would take them to various places all the while promising sexual satisfaction and a good time. Goading them into thinking they would be pleasured once there. But what usually awaited the unsuspecting, was pain and sometimes death, and loss of their money and whatever else they had of any value. Her male counterparts would invariably be there to greet them when they arrived or they would barge in after the couple arrived. The unsuspecting would eventually be robbed, beaten, tortured or killed. Their goods would be taken from them.

She fought back the horror of what she had done as she recounted to herself one or two specific incidences. She rationalized that like the coyote, she did it for survival. It was just a way a life. Certainly not God's way, she thought, more like "her" way. She forced these thoughts from her mind.

"Do you think that humans and animals are alike?" she posed this question while peering into the now moonlit prairie. Jason didn't respond immediately but rocked slowly back and forth as if pondering the question. She looked towards him when he didn't answer right away. "Huh?" she queried again. He peered down at her and smiled. Sensing the curiosity and need to know in the girl's voice.

"Well!" he said in a comforting voice. "In a lot of ways, I suppose, especially when it comes to food and," he hesitated. "That reminds me, I'm hongry. What say we go on in and get us somethin' to eat?" The girl agreed and they adjourned to the kitchen.

Jason had a large bowl of leftover beans and neck bones that he retrieved from the icebox and warmed it on the pot-bellied stove. Not much was said as they ate and afterward Jason spoke very little. He prepared a room for her and told her not to forget to say her prayers before she went to bed. Then he went into his room and closed his door. She had no idea what prayer to say. She went into the room that Jason had prepared for her and sat on the edge of the bed. It had dawned on her that she was in an ideal place to get high. She frantically reached for her suitcase, which Jason had tossed on the bed. Remembering she was a junkie, she quickly acquired the "junkie happys." She began to feel a sense of elation and control and was smiling to herself as she found the hyperdermic needle she had carefully placed under her meager belongings. And she continued looking until she located the small cellophane packet, which contained a small amount of heroin. She knew that a soup spoon could serve as the vessel she needed to cook the drug in, so she sneaked out of the room and to the kitchen area and searched until she found one. She was unaware that Jason was listening to her movement and had been peering through a crack in his door, looking at her as she tippytoed through his house. He saw her go into the bathroom and he heard water being spilled in the basin. And then he heard silence. Five minutes had elapsed when she emerged from the bathroom. She stumbled into the room and closed the door.

Jason continued to look and listen as the night wore on. Satisfied that she had gone to sleep, he lay quietly on his bed with pipe in mouth thinking about the girl's night move. He had a feeling it was not good. Yet he made up his mind not to confront her with this knowledge.

He was up at the crack of dawn and went about his chores as he was accustomed to doing. There wasn't much food in the house, so he decided to drive to town to buy some. Upon returning, he noticed it was drawing close to noon and the girl was still asleep. He went into the house and to the room where she slept. The door was slightly ajar, so he looked in. He noted that she had fallen asleep in her clothes and was snoring heavily. The suitcase was still open, but nothing seemed to be taken out of it. He gently pulled the door closed and continued about his business as he had decided not to disturb her rest. Content to believe that her illness was not serious and that it had passed, he let her rest. He still was mindful of the nocturnal activities of the young lady the past night, but he had no notion of what it was she could have been doing. He knew she had burned something because he smelled the odor, yet nothing in the house had been burned except for the matches he saw in the bathroom. He let it pass for the moment. He knew the girl didn't take a bath because she was still in the same clothes.

Eventually the girl awoke and came down to the kitchen.

"You hongry?" Jason asked.

"No, uh, I never eat when I first get up. What time is it anyway?" the girl inquired as she looked around the room for a clock.

"Well, the sun done started going down now, so I guess it's about five o'clock or so." Jason had been standing in the door looking out at the stretch of prairie and holding his corncob pipe in his mouth.

"Dag!! You could tell what time it is for real just by lookin at the sun? I had heard that people could do that, but I never really saw nobody do it for real. How you know dat??" Jason explained to her that he had been in the fields so long picking cotton and doing various jobs out in the open during his lifetime, that he had developed a knack for doing such a thing. The girl was genuinely impressed with his explanation and seated herself at the kitchen table to better listen. As he continued to talk, he further educated her on other facts such as the sun's position in the morning as oppossed to its position in the afternoon and evening. And what it meant. And how travelers had learned to use the sun as a directional aid like a compass.

"Wait a minute now, uh you say it rises in the east! East, right?"

"That's right! In the east. That's pretty good," Jason confirmed.

"And it sets down in the west!" she cheerfully added. "So dat's how they know they going the right way. Right?" Jason glanced approvingly at the girl and chose this time to make a transition in the conversation.

"Well, if they was going the right way, then they sure to be going God's way. Cause that's the only right way. You know much about that?" He turned to look at the girl's expression after posing that question. She was still perplexed from trying to comprehend the sundial and compass lessons.

"What? What you mean, God's way. I know some stuff from when I used to go to church, but that's been so long ago. What you mean?? If you mean do I believe in God and all, I don't know. He sure ain't been there for me, I know that for sure. Hey!! You probably didn't even know that I'm pregnant, did you?" She was rubbing her stomach and smiling as she said these words to Jason. Jason was stunned. He hadn't known this fact. He began to look at her more closely. She wasn't showing her pregnancy as Jason was accustomed to seeing pregnant women. His surprise now under control, he could speak with a little more calm.

"Now that there is some of God's best work. Yes suh, can't nothin' top that. How far gone is you?" He was genuinely concerned at this point.

"I'm about, uh, six months now." She seemed to have to think about it for a second. Jason stared at her for a moment and then asked "How old you gettin' to be anyways? And what's your name again?" The girl looked at him with pursed lips as if surprised he didn't remember.

"Evelyn, I told you. And I. . . ."

"Hold on now. That ain't what you told me back there. You said your name was Jessica. . . ."

"Oh, yeah, you right, um. I did say that, um I said that because I didn't know you. You know what I mean? But now I do . . so . . . I'm sorry. I know I lied."

"Unhuh!! And, how old are you, Evelyn?" Jason was feeling for truth.

"I'm twenty-eight." She had turned and put her hands on the table now as though preparing to be quizzed. "And where are you on your way to, twenty-eight-year-old Evelyn?" Jason asked, sarcastically.

"Well," she sucked her teeth, then looked up at the ceiling and brought her index finger to her chin. "If I had some more money . . . I was going on to California. That's where I was going at first." She looked at Jason after the mention of money as though expecting him to get the hint.

"So where are you going now??" Jason continued his quest for information.

"You heard me!! I said if I had some more 'money,' I was going to California. Now can you help me with that??" She had seemed to become a little more agitated and aggressive in tone than one would have expected. She now stared Jason square in the eye and had a questioning look on her face as if expecting a response right then and there. But Jason didn't respond, at least not as she might have expected.

"That still don't tell me where you going now." His expression had not changed. He continued to look at her with soft, yet piercing eyes, intent on an answer.

"Hey!! I told you. California!!" She pushed herself away from the table. "And if you gone be all helpful and shit, you can help me with some 'money.' Okay??" With that and an attitude that seemed to spring from nowhere, she headed for the stairs. "If not, Mr., you can just take me back to the bus stop, or bus station, whatever y'all call it down here and I'll take care of my damn self." Jason sat still as he heard her footsteps ascend the stairs and her room door slam. Silence followed.

He had decided it best to allow the situation to unfold itself. He was on the porch now. It had been at least an hour since Evelyn's unexpected tantrum. The silence was deafening. Not a sound was heard save the slight creak in the rocker as he rocked slowly back and forth. Then the howl of the coyote broke the deep quiet. Then another howl from a different part of the prairie. The bark of dogs added to the conversation. The dogs reminded him that there was a small Indian village not far off. He thought of smoke signals. The thought made him smile. He was still smiling as he turned to listen when he heard a sound in the house. She was in the bathroom and water was running in the bathtub. A bath was being prepared. He leaned back, rocked and clutched his corncob pike, satisfied that she was finally going to wash herself. Lord knew she needed to. Her hair was uncombed, dry, and full of little lint balls and knots. She was not smelling very pleasant, nor was the sight of her brown, ashen face very appealing. Jason was somewhat relieved by the fact that he didn't have to tell her to do it.

Other than the moonlight that shone directly on the porch, it was very dark. The doorway to the porch was dark. When she came down the stairs, she didn't immediately come out on the porch but rather lingered in the doorway. Jason felt her presence. Neither said anything for a short period.

"Uh, look, uh, I'm sorry I got so mad at you this afternoon. I just feel so lost sometimes. I don't like people asking me a whole lot of questions. I . . ." Jason felt the sincerity in her apology and interrupted her.

"Ohhh, that's okay. I guess we all get like that at one time or another. You gonna stand in that doorway all night?" She had indeed felt foolish for the outburst and he was comforting. Safe, even. She wasn't accustomed to men of Jason's caliber or concern and she just didn't know how to reciprocate. She at first planned to treat him like another trick. Get some money, use him for what she could, and be off to her next jaunt. But he was different. She felt his reverence, his security. She couldn't identify it, so she figured she'd try something new with him. She would tell him the truth about her journey, her past life, and how she had no one and nowhere to go.

"No. No. I'm coming out. I just was looking at the stars. They look so bright and there's so many of them. I never saw stars out in the sky like that before." She slowly sauntered out onto the porch and sat on the wooden swing that hung from the porch roof by ropes. It seated two. "It's so quiet out here. It's really peaceful. I guess that's how you get to be so cool, huh?? Sittin' out here in the quiet. Ain't you scared a coyote or something gone come up here one night??"

Jason hadn't looked at her until then. He turned to see she had transformed herself from the smelly, grimy tackhead he first met, into a decent-looking young lady with clean clothes and a glow on her face. Vaseline, he figured. She looked to be about the age she had said. He held his stare for a minute. Her hair was neat in a pony tail, still a little rough around the edges, he thought, but much better than it was.

"Well, I got to say, you scrub up nice."

Scrub up nice???? she thought. "What's that supposed to mean? Oh. Never mind, I know what you mean." She took a moment to smile and revel in the compliment, then she slid over in the swing so as to make room.

"Why don't you come over here and sit beside me. . . I got some things I want to tell you. Okay?" Jason didn't move immediately but mulled over the request in mind. Then decided that she was no threat. He got up slowly from his rocker and turned first to the door to the kitchen, which he had to pass to get to the swing.

"Mind if I get some cider first?"

"No. Go head." She continued to smile at him. He stopped midway through the door.

"You care for a glass?"

"Uh, yeah. Yeah, I want some." Jason returned with two glasses of apple cider and handed her one before sitting beside her. She was wearing a short pink skirt that hid the paunch of her pregnancy and she wore a sweater that buttoned up the front, but was not buttoned all the way up, therefore exposing her cleavage. Her thighs were also very much exposed in the moonlight. They were shining. Jason couldn't help but notice, although he tried not to. Vaseline, he thought.

"Ummm!" she said, as she sipped the cider. "This is really good. It's cold." She deliberately allowed the liquid to remain on her lips, allowing them to gleam, as a small amount dribbled down her chin and on to her chest where it drained into her cleavage. "OOOO!! It is cold! Feel it!" She was smearing the fluid on her chest and turning to Jason as she spoke. Jason looked. He was flushed. She was indeed a woman, he thought. He reached for his handkerchief, and it was apparent that he had gotten a little nervous. He started to wipe it, then he handed it to her.

"Uh, here," he said as he pushed it in the direction of her chest.

"No! Why don't you want to feel it with your hand??"

Jason could feel his hands trembling and his face flushing, but he tried to conceal it. He dropped the handkerchief in her lap and took a long drink from his glass.

"Now, what was it you had to tell me??" He had regained his composure and was attempting to put things back in perspective. Evelyn picked up the hanky and slowly began wiping juice from her chest.

"What's the matter?? Did I make you nervous??" Jason had no control over the erection that had begun to protrude in his pants and had tried to conceal it by crossing his legs, but not before Evelyn had spotted it. She immediately reached for it, but Jason firmly grabbed the encroaching hand and held it hard.

"GET THEE BEHIND ME, SATAN," he said in a low voice, then he shook her hand violently as he admonished her to stop. "Now just stop that. You just stop it." His tone was sharp. The message was clear. He was not facing her but looking off in the distance, but she could see the look of disgust on his face.

"Okay. I'm sorry. I just thought maybe you might be as horny as I am. That's all. You don't have to get so mad. I'm sorry." Her voice was restrained as she explained and gently pulled her hand from his tight grip. She had felt the nervousness in his hands, but she had seen the excitement in his clothes.

"You got to stop talking like that an' an' and acting like that. You, you gettin' ready to have a baby!! You can't go 'round doing stuff like that. Besides it ain't right in God's eyes."

Evelyn shifted her body away from his and sat back in the swing, arms folded on her chest. *I'm horny*, she thought. She had just done the last of the drugs that she had, and it was just a small amount. Just enough to make her a little less on edge and horny. *Well*, she thought. *Now what??*

"I know. You're right!! Well, then could you take me to town or wherever they got bars and stuff at for a while? I don't feel like just sittin' here and not doing nothin'." Her mind was back on dope again and she had the notion that, if she could get to town, she could easily find a trick, make some money, get some more dope, and satisfiy her sexual urge, all in one stop. "Huh?? Could you please??" she persisted.

"Thought you said you had something to tell me?? So why don't you want to tell me now," Jason reminded her.

"Oh, man. I'll tell you when we get back. Come on. Take me somewhere. Please." Evelyn was beginning to get determined at this point. Almost pushy.

"Do you know how far the nearest town is from here?? Thirty-five miles. That's how far. And besides I don't go into bars or into town for that matter. Decent people are at home this time of night anyway. There ain't nothin' but trouble out there at night."

Evelyn had heard it before and she wasn't listening now. She was oblivious to Jason's presence. She did hear the thirty-five miles part and that was a problem. Thirty-five miles. She wasn't about to walk it. No buses ran on this dirt road that led to his house.

"Well, could you give me some money to get a cab?? I could call a cab and they could come get me, take me, and bring me back. Right??" She thought she had solved her problem.

"Wrong! I ain't got no phone." Jason casually responded.

Damn, she thought. Now her mind was alive with ideas. She sat and she thought. Scheme after scheme, foiled by one thing or another. Her addiction was growing rapidly within her. Jason sat quietly, holding onto his corncob pipe.

The last little taste of her drug served to whet her appetite and make her begin to crave for more. She was feeling as if she needed it now.

"Hey!! Come on. Please!! Please!! I'll do anything you want me to do. Just come on. Take me to town." Jason noticed the change in her personality. She was almost pleading. He sensed something wrong.

"Now you just calm down there, young lady. Ain't no way you gettin' to town tonight les you walk. An' I doubt you want to do that." Evelyn peered into the night. It was dark. Very dark. She didn't calm down but continued to rant and rave and throw promises around, using every means she could think of to convince Jason to take her to town. When all of her initial attempts failed, she resorted to loud and abusive language that merely made Jason ignore her entirely and he retired to his room. He could hear her still talking as he sat on the edge of his bed. He knew there was more to this than he was familiar with. He always blamed actions he was not comfortable with on the devil. This situation was definitely influenced by the devil, he concluded. He prayed. Eventually she stopped the loud talking and he heard her in the house rummaging through his belongings. He had his keys and it wasn't much else she could take or use of any value, so he allowed her to continue uninterrupted. As he was on his knees praying, she knocked on the door. He stopped and looked up at the door as it was being pushed open. He could see her standing there. She was nude and she was breathing heavily.

GET THEE BEHIND ME, SATAN, IN THE NAME OF JESUS, I REBUKE YOU!" He was pointing at her from the floor where he continued to kneel as he successfully prevented her advancement. The nude girl stopped as though she had been pushed back. She backed out the door, not uttering one word, as she did so. Her eyes held glued to his. Her backward movement steady. The door closed. Jason continued praying. The girl slithered into her room where she begun to search for any type of residue she could get together to put into her hyperdermic needle. She scraped the bag and burned the spoon and managed to get just enough to make a little more than a water hit out of the heroin residue. She made it do. Then she lay on the bed and proceeded to masturbate violently and without restraint until she faded into sleep. Jason never went to sleep. He prayed throughout the night.

Morning found him on his knees where he had been all night. He left his room to find the girl had gone. Her bags were gone, the bed unmade, and the dresser drawers and closet opened. It was clear to Jason that they had been searched. He went downstairs and out the door. She was nowhere in sight. The door to the truck was open. He thought for a minute. He decided to look for her. He got in the truck and proceeded to drive toward the bus station where he first met the girl. He didn't drive very far before coming upon her sitting beside the road on her one piece of luggage. The wind was blowing and the sun was beaming down on her. The road was dusty as was her face and hair. Jason slowed down to a stop just as he pulled alongside of her.

"Where you goin', with no money? Nowhere to go . . ." he yelled out of the truck. The girl said nothing. Jason got out of the truck and stood before her.

"Just leave me alone. Okay? I can get around without you. Okay?"

The sun was going down as they headed for Jason's house. He had managed to convince her to return. She came, but reluctantly. No words were spoken as they got out of the truck and entered the house. He sat in the living room, she, in the kitchen. He soon heard a whimpering sound and got up to see her head lying face down on the table. She was crying. He thought about it for a moment, then went in and gently laid his hand on her back. She looked up into his face and then got up to embrace him. They held their embrace for several minutes.

"My mother told me something I never forgot. She said when you get to where you don't know where to turn, let go, let God. I never forgot that. I been to that point many times in my life and each time, I let go and let God. He hasn't failed me yet!! Maybe you might have reached that point. Why don't you sit down and let's talk? Let's talk about God and what He can do." She looked up into his face with tears streaming down her face. Her eyes seemed to be searching his as she slumped back down in the chair.

"I just don't know what to do. My life is so messed up. I'm by myself, pregnant, no money . . . and," she hesitated, "I'm a junkie. I'm a prostitute, a hoe. I just ain't no good. Mr., I ain't never met nobody like you before. You ain't like most men. You don't want nothing from me. I ain't gonna' do nothin' but bring you down. If I stay around you, I'll bring you down. I don't want to do that to you. You a better man than that. You don't need me. That's why I packed up and left. I just ain't the kind of woman you need. I was going to steal your radio and anything else I thought I could pawn. I can't be trusted. I just can't be trusted. I don't know what you talkin' bout with this God stuff. I ain't never really learned nothin' bout that stuff. . ."

He interrupted her at this point. "I know, I know. But no matter what you may have done in the past or how bad you have been, the blood of Jesus cleanseth us of all sin. See, there's a way out and a way up. See we . . ." he hesitated, thinking that maybe he had said enough. "That's why I'm here. See, in a way, God sent you to me, and me to you. He uses people to do his work for him, see. We all God's children and God takes care of His children. He has His own way of teaching us about Him. Sometimes He makes us do things we don't understand, but He knows. See, God only wants us to love Him and serve Him. When we do other than that, we runs into trouble. He has His reasons for puttin' us in the trouble we in."

"Well, why He got to make it hurt so bad if He love us??" she asked?

"Like I said, sometimes maybe we need to get to see the bottom, so's when we get to look up, we can see the top more clearer."

There he was talking in circles again, she thought. "What you mean by that?" she asked.

"Come on into the room here and let's get to know one another and God all at the same time." He pointed to the larger room adjacent to the kitchen. He walked and she followed him. Both sat on the sofa. "Now we got a lot of time. So why don't you just tell me about yourself. Where you from? What you runnin' from? Where you runnin' to??" She took a deep breath and looked at him. Her tear-stained cheeks posed almost in a smile. She was preparing herself to attempt to do something she hadn't done in a long time. Be honest with someone! She always wanted to be truthful and honest deep down inside her, but she just couldn't always do it. Something in her always seemed to get in the way.

She proceded to tell Jason her story. "Well, let's see, I don't know, uh, I guess I should start with Michael. Yeah, I guess Michael because he's the father of this baby I'm carrying. He dead now, umm-umm-umm, but I'll get to that later. I had a couple people that I guess you could call friends. Like Gregory, Maddelyn, Curtis, uh this guy named Kenny, and my best friend Yvette. Uh, lemme see, uh, we go back a long way, but specially me and Michael. I thought I knew them real good, but it's just so much I didn't know about them...."

Michael

Michael walked off the court, dripping with perspiration and breathing heavily. He wiped his face and neck with the loose parts of his jersey. It was soaked. He flopped down on the bench and put his elbows on his knees, his hands clasped tightly together, and his head bowed.

"Them boys is runnin the shit outta' us, man. Damn, that little sucker stickin' me? Ahm gone haf' to fuck him up if he keep hackin' me. You see that shit? He fouled me blatantly a few times and I let him slide, but thass it for him, no more." The guy sitting beside Michael on the bench slapped him lightly on the muscle of his arm.

"Man, don't even get into that," he said, never taking his eyes off the game, "he's just over playin' you 'cause he scared you'll put them moves on him, thass all."

"Yeah, well, I *am* gone put some moves on him if he do one more thing to me, and you can believe that." Michael had gathered his wind back now and was sitting up and looking over his shoulder into the bleachers.

"Ho!!" he hollered, clapped his hands together, and whirled around to gesture to a figure standing under the section "D" ramp entry sign. The figure raised his arm in the air and began to step quickly but carefully, row by row down the bleachers until he was one row in back of Mike. He sat down.

"What's happenin?" the visitor inquired.

They looked at each other's faces, then a smile grew wide on Michael's.

"You tell me?" Michael responded.

"We cool??" The visitor smiled back "We good to go!" They gave each other five, then Michael said, "Hold on about fifteen, twenty minutes and we bookin'."

"Aw, come on, Ice, we got to split now!" His voice was high pitched and squeaky at this point. "We ain't got a whole lot of time, man. I got bitches in the car an' we still got to break this shit down!"

"Awright, awright, man, damn, let me change up." He was still grinning as he searched up and down the court floor. "Yo, Flat! Flathead-in-the-back mothafucka! Go in for me!" he yelled to another player who was sitting on the floor at the far end to the court. "Gimme a minute, I'll meet you out front. Where you parked at?" he barked at the visitor.

"Right at Broad and Norris, almost on the corner, I'll be in the ride, and don't take all fuckin' day, man!"

The visitor headed back up the bleachers and out of the gym. Michael took a quick shower and was dressed and outside in ten minutes. He looked up the street towards Norris Street, spotted the red Mercury, and dashed to it, gym bag slung over his shoulder. He was trying to fix his mind on how he was going to act. Hoping the girls weren't going with them. "Probably Correy ole lady," he thought out loud. He liked to know what to expect so he could know how he was going to behave. That's just the way he was. As he approached the car, the door swung open. The woman in the front passenger's seat had been watching him in the side view mirror.

"Hi, Michael," the woman purred in a sultry voice. She leaned forward to allow him to push the seat up so he could squeeze into the rear passenger seat. His bag grazed her hair slightly as he maneuvered his way in.

"Damn, Michael, you ain't all that big!" she joked.

"S'cuse me, Lena, my fault."

The driver, also a woman, was laughing and looking over her shoulder at Michael as he settled in.

"Dag, Ice, I hope you don't treat all your women like that."

Michael feigned shyness as he looked at the driver.

"You know I didn't mean to hit that girl!" The visitor's name was Correy and he seemed to be getting impatient.

"Come on, Bev," Correy cut in, "Cut that shit out and drive this car baby before I do something to *you* on purpose." Then he turned to Michael, who was also known as Ice. "Ice, can you leave them alone for one minute? Damn!" Correy wasn't really irritated, but as he spoke, he was pointing to the floor of the car between his feet.

"Aw, shutup. We only...." Michael had just noticed the bags of heroin his friend was pointing to. "Yo how that happen?" He was suddenly serious and attentive. Both women now engaged in their own conversation about the song that was now playing on the eight-track tape in the car. Both men were doing the drugs.

"Bev hooked us up! Matter of fact you remember the last thing we did? It went off just like that only better. What's that boy's name? I can't remember. You know who um talkin' about. Kinda tall, light-skinned? Used to like Maddie and we got Maddie to bring him and his shit over to Greg's spot? A long time ago. Remember? Chink! His name's Chink. Well, same thing today. This shit's free. We don't owe nobody nothin'!"

Michael looked him in the face, grinned a wide super grin. "Damn, Correy! All this?" They slapped each other five in mutual approval of the transaction.

"Bev," Michael leaned up to the driver's ear and playfully says, "Bev, you need to stop that shit!" Everybody laughed and looked at one another.

"That ain't all, sweetie. Look at this up here." She was pointing to a leather bag sitting between her and Lena. "Eight thousand. I counted it myself."

"Gotdamn!!" Michael said in disbelief. "He gave that up too?"

"Not only that, homey," Correy chimed in "This pussy had Bev's pussy dead on his face while me and Lena was takin' his shit from under his bed. He was all tied up and shit and I said, 'cover that mothafucka's face up!' I meant for her to put something over his face but...."

"And that's just what I did!" Bev added, "I covered his face with my ass and every time he whimpered, I think I came!" They all laughed heartily over that one.

"Come on, y'all, let's split to my crib and do this thing right," Michael said, and he leaned over to the driver's ear again.... "*And* where I can do your thing right too, baby." Bev looked at him out of the corner of her eye, smiled, and pulled off headed towards the part of town known as Germantown.

They stopped at the State Store and picked up a fifth of gin and a fifth of Johnny Walker Red. And then to the deli for four quarts of Newaller's Ale. Michael opened up a bottle of ale and just as he was about to take a sip, another car pulled up beside theirs.

"Hey, baby, can I go wit you??" They all looked at the man in the GTO.

"That's that fuckin' Greg!" Michael was leaning over Lena's shoulder as he put his head out of the window to better yell out. "Hey, boy, don't be fuckin' wit my women!" Lena also was still trying to see the man as Correy attempted to stick his head out of the window and yelled. "What you mean 'your women'? He ain't got no women less I get 'em for him." Michael playfully pushed him back.

"Get back over there and guard my shit, boy, before I slap you!" The man in the other car laughed at their shananagans and replied, "Y'all crazy! Where y'all goin'? I been on y'all shit since y'all crossed Stenton Avenue, pull over in that gas station, girl," he directed to the driver of their car. Both cars veered for the sloped entrance to the gas station and stopped. Michael got out of the car, this time purposely pushing the seat harder than necessary on Lena, and brushing his elbow against her head. "Damn, Michael, I'm flat enough as it is, gimme a break. Ooo, shit. See? You made me spill my drink."

"Aw, shut up, ain't nobody doin' nothin' to you, girl." He left the door open and reached back to try to push Lena again playfully.

"You play too much, Michael, stop!" Michael laughed and walked over to the GTO Greg was driving.

"What's happenin', nigga? Where you on your way to?" Greg asked

"Noneya!" Mike quickly responded, indicating none of your business.

"Fuck you, Mike!" Greg continued, "Where y'all goin' to wit *them* bitches? You know Lena be on them streets sometimes. I seen her. And Bev be out there too. What yall tryin' to do? Get yall dicks sucked?" Greg laughed. Michael grimaced and made a waving motion with his hands in the girls direction.

"Naw, man, we got some business to take care of . . . - *then* we gone get out knobs polished?" They both laughed and gave each other five. Greg suddenly became serious.

"Look here, why don't you roll wit me up the street to my pop's crib for a minute. I got some rap for you. I'll drop you where you goin' after that. Okay?"

"Okay! Hold on," he said as he started towards the other car.

Michael ran over to the car and told Bev to go on ahead to his house informing them that he would meet them there in about ten minutes. They pulled off. Michael got into Greg's car.

"So what's been happenin', buddy?" Michael asked Greg.

"Nothin much, shootin' a little pool, playing a little chess, gettin a little pussy here and there, you know, just tryin' to make it. Oh, yeah, I did come up with an idea to make some ends and that's what I want to talk to you about." Michael appeared to be interested. Ends means money and money interests Michael.

"Oh, yeah? Like and what we got to do? You know I'm down with some ends." Greg glanced at Michael as though annoyed.

"If you hold on, I'll run it all down to you."

The car pulled out of the gas station and proceeded up Broad Street to Sixty-seventh, turning onto Bouvier Street, where Gregory's mother and father lived. He parked the car and they both got out. They had been talking and laughing all the while. Long time friends. Never had what amounted to any conflicts between them. They were like brothers. As they entered the house, Michael walked straight to the sofa and sat down. Gregory walked to the base of the stairs and hollered up. "Yo ma?" he was checking to see if anyone answered, "Had to check to make sure nobody was here, you know what I mean?" he said to Michael.

"Solid! But what about these ends?" Mike asked anxiously.

"Man, yous' a greedy mothafucka, wait a minute an' I'll tell you." Greg went to the kitchen to get them both a Budwieser and returned to where Michael was sitting. Michael had taken his .38 snubnose gun from under his shirt and laid it on the floor. Gregory was not pleased with this.

"What you doin' wit that shit, man? Put that shit up!" Greg didn't like guns and was annoyed at seeing the gun so readily exposed.

"Man, this thing be stickin' me all in my side and shit and besides, it ain't botherin' nobody. Ain't nobody here but me an' you. Besides, if anybody come in, I'll be done swooped it up before they get through the door." Gregory went immediately to the door and put the latch on.

"Damn, Ice, you and that fuckin' rod. You always have to carry that thing?"

"Yep," quipped Mike, "never leave home without it."

"Man, you stupid. That shit there gone get you in trouble, but fuck that, dig the move... I was at this party the other night, you dig, and I was talking to this African dude, solid, and he was telling me about this scam they be runnin'. They be doin' it with income tax checks, you dig? And he was tellin' me how they be gettin' paid ungodly." At that point, Gregory reached into his back pocket and pulled out a brown envelope folded in half. He unfolded it and produced an income tax check.

"Damn. Lemme see that?" Mike studied the check. "Damn, how long it take to do this? This jaunt is... hold up... this ain't got your name on it! How you gone bust it?" Greg stood up and snatched the check back.

"Give me that, damn! I ain't even told you the deal yet, see, what I'm tryin to...." A knock at the door distracted him. "Shhhh." Greg signaled Michael to be quiet as he tiptoed to the door. He peeped under the shade and saw Evelyn standing at the door. Michael tipped up behind him.

"Who is it?" he whispered.

"Shhh," Greg told him again.

Michael pulled him aside in a further attempt to look, but Greg still wouldn't allow him a straight look out of the little peephole.

"Stop it, man, we ain't supposed to be here, my mom and pop is supposed to be at work!" Another knock. Greg looked again to see the girl turn to walk away and down the steps. Michael had made his way to the window that faces the steps and peered through the curtains. Looking both ways up and down the street, he also saw Evelyn walking away from the house and she was looking back as if to make sure no one answered the door. Gregory immediately looked at Michael.

"I didn't know she was coming, man, I swear to God!"

Michael had suddenly become very angry. He was glaring at Greg. "You a fuckin lie, Greg!! What my girl doin' comin' to your mom's house in the afternoon for??" Gregory knew that Michael had a quick temper and he was trying hard to think of something to say that would make sense and calm him down.

"Wait a minute, Ice, don't go thinkin' dumb shit. Hold it." He had noticed that Michael was high from the outset, but he had no idea just how high he was or what it would take to reach him in this state at this moment. He started for Michael to attempt to touch him, but Michael bolted for the .38 lying on the floor, picked it up and pointed it at Gregory.

"Oh no, mothafucka! You ain't pullin' that jive shit wit me. Thass my girl, Greg! Thass my bitch! You know that!! You *know* she pregnant?" The word "pregnant" seemed to infuriate him even more. He looked at Greg with contempt, as though he were looking through him.

"Who the fuck you think you ... you think ahm stupid??"

"Wait a minute, Ice, I knew she was pregnant, but you know damn well I. . . . " Blam-Blam-Blam! Three shots rang out. Gregory reeled back and fell into the chair he was standing beside. He was shot. A look of shock on his face. His eyes looking blankly into space. His mouth moving but not saying anything. Michael suddenly began to act robotically, as if he too were in shock. He looked around the room, then he looked at Greg, then around to the sofa where he had been sitting. "Nothing!" he mumbled, "I ain't touched nothin." Remembering the beer, he reached down to pick it up. *Correy an' Bev an' them! They waitin on me,* he thought. *No prints, can't leave no prints,* he was muttering to himself as he frantically looked around the house. "I ain't touched nothin." He noticed the check lying on the floor, picked it up and pocketed it, and pulled out his handkerchief.

He was sweating profusely and his vision had become blurred by the constant drip of the excretion in his eyes. He wiped frantically as he looked about the room. He looked at Greg's now still body slumped over in the chair, then to the keys on the lamp table beside the chair where Greg had laid them. He picked up the keys with the handkerchief curled up in his hand and jammed them into his pocket. He also was careful to use the handkerchief to open the door. He cautiously looked around outside to make sure no one was around. "Nobody out! No neighbors lookin'! People on the other side of the street! They don't know shit noway, Michael assessed as he gathered his confidence, stepped all the way out the door, and onto the steps. He held the screen door open and waved his hand as if he were saying good-bye to someone inside. Then he let the screen door close, walked directly to Greg's car, and got in, using the handkerchief he had cleverly concealed in his hand, and drove off, very careful not to touch anything with his bare hands.

How long had he been lying there, bleeding, was his first thought. Greg tried to move. Pain was everywhere. He couldn't see. Something was blocking his view in one eye and the other was stuck closed. Blood, he quickly concluded. He feebly reached out to try to grab on to something, anything, the first thing he touched. He pulled on something. It was the pillow in the chair he was in. He pulled it, but it didn't offer him enough leverage to pull himself up. He reached further, the arm of the chair. He grabbed it and with all the strength he could muster, he tugged and pulled his otherwise limp body further into the chair. He felt numb below his neck but knew he was hurting. He knew he had been shot. Bad, but he had to keep moving, for the phone . . . for his life. He pulled. There was unbearable pain in his head. He had been shot in his head. He tried to grab where he thought the phone was. He felt something. A cord. He grabbed it and pulled. He heard the dull dink of the phone bell as he reeled the cord to him. He got the phone within reach and attempted to pick up the receiver, but his hands were slippery with blood and the receiver fell. He grappled with the cord with his hand. He noticed then there was pain in his hand. He had been shot there, too. He had no thumb and his forefinger was dangling. This appeared odd to him; he felt woozy but forced himself to get the receiver near his body. He pushed his body off the chair with his shoulder and tumbled to the heavily carpeted floor with the thud of a piece of furniture that had been dropped. He lay there for a second, then felt pain again in his head. The phone had hit him in the head as he fell. He reached over his body with his good hand, managed to find the base of the phone, and began fumbling for the buttons on the phone. He peered out through his blood-soaked eye and saw the digits he wanted-911. With his thumb he pressed 9-1... and the life ebbed from his body.

Michael had just turned the corner and was heading towards Spencer Street where he lived. He had been thinking, thinking a lot. He thought about how he had no idea that Greg and his main girl Evelyn had been together. He never suspected anything between them.

"That lame!!" he said aloud. He was being bombarded by thoughts. *How could I have been so dumb?* Then he thought, *fuck it, and fuck him too.* He shouldn't have done it. Even if she gave it to him, he shouldn't have done it. And her? How could she play me like that? She was a lame, too. How long had she been doing that shit anyway. "Fuckin hoe!!" he said aloud. She's a hoe! That's all it is to it, a fuckin' hoe. *She ain't nothin' but a prostitute noway*, he thought. Fuck her too! She ain't shit. He was almost blinded by his anger. Noticing that he was about a block from his house now, he decided to park the car right there on Ogontz Avenue and walk down to his house. He contrived that he would tell Correy and the others that Greg dropped him off there and went into some girl's house. It was believable. They had no reason to question him.

Greg knew a lot of women. He wondered how long it would take before Greg's body was discovered. He hoped they would find it fast so so he would have less chance of forgetting things and he would be able to act more naturally concerned. After all, nobody would suspect him of having anything to do with it anyway. It could have been anybody. Greg had gagged a lot of people and he'd be the last one to be suspected. They were tight, they were like brothers. He had no reason to kill him. No motive. All he had to do now was to be cool and act as though the last time he saw Gregory was when he let him out of the car right there at the top of the block. Yeah, this way he could go to the funeral and all that and really play it up. Oh, Evelyn? No problem, he thought, he would act like he didn't know anything about it. No problem. Everything was cool. He had reached his house now and was about to put the key in the door when it suddenly swung open.

"It's about time! Correy been trying to wait for you to get here before he do anything with this package." He looked past Bev to see that there was no one else around.

"Where he at? Where that other girl?"

"They up stairs now gettin' busy. They got tired of sittin' around." Mike had taken off his jacket and sat down near the bags of heroin but pulled out a bag of cocaine from his pocket. His mind not fully on Bev.

"Why they call you Ice anyway? You that cold?" Bev was sounding a little sultry now, a little arrogant. Mike looked up to see her posing in front of him. He had failed to notice her bow legs or the short tight skirt she was wearing or that her thighs were that big, or that her blouse was opened in the front so as to expose one of her breasts. He noticed now—and was almost gawking at her. He caught himself.

"No, baby, they call me Ice because I melt when I get around women like you. I'm too easy."

"Easy? What does that mean?" Bev asked sarcastically as she turned and begun to slowly walk towards the dining room. Michael had failed to notice the fullness of her perfectly rounded butt or the split in the skirt that was just about to expose her butt if she moved the wrong way. But he noticed now and began to feel a stirring in his groin.

"What you looking at me like that for?" Bev quipped. She had her hand on her hip now and her head was slightly tilted to the side, as she stared directly at Mike.

"Something wrong? You ain't answer my question! What does that mean—easy? Easy to get over on? Or easy to get?" A challenge. Mike thought. He was feeling a little more at ease with himself now. A little more himself now. He knew how to handle these type situations. She looked good, real good, and he sensed that she was all but telling him what she wanted to do. She kind of looked hot, like he had seen so many other women look when they're ready. And the way she was posturing, she was definitely ready. He was feeling real comfortable now. He knew this game and he liked it. And he played it well. He sat back in the chair and opened his legs wide and let his hands fall between them. His eyes had finally met hers now and he was looking with much self-assurance and hers were looking intently.

"Well, no," he said softly. "I meant it like 'easy like Sunday morning,' but if you come over here real close to me, you'll find out that I'm harder than you think." She came.

Gregory

All his life he had it good. Everything was easy for him. As a child, he learned to walk at the tender age of six months and he could get into any cabinet, drawer, or door that wasn't locked. He learned how to climb out of the playpen and get himself around the room by holding on to anything that would support his small frame and advance him to whereever he was attempting to get to. His parents were extremely proud of him. He was a good-looking baby. Long, black curly hair, thick eyelashes, and big round eyes set into a coffee-colored face. Fine features, in general, and a smile that would capture anyone's heart who fell prey to it. He learned quickly how effective his smile was, and he learned how and when to use it to get what he wanted. Most importantly, he learned it was easy to get what he wanted merely by smiling. That smile!!

His parents seemed to be partial to his younger sister, Maddelyn, he had concluded and he learned that at an early age as well. She always got her way. She was always the one they talked about and praised. He used to stop whatever it was he was playing with or doing and listen intently whenever he heard them speak of, refer to, or speak to her. He could never figure out how to get the attention she got. He was their first born child. He never quite understood how they could love her more than they loved him. He conceded that she was pretty and smart, but so was he, he figured. Why should that have been any reason for them to cater to her more than him? He felt that she always got away with things and that he always got caught. He always got the beating or punishment for his crimes in the house, but she always got scolded and let off the hook. When he got caught telling a lie, it seemed that they made such a big thing out of it, but when she got caught telling a lie, it was a different story. He got blamed for things she did. He was held responsible for things she did. He had to watch her. She cried all the time, but if he cried, he was called a "crybaby." She told their parents everything he did if she thought he would get in trouble for it. But when he told on her, he was called a "tattletale." It was okay for her to sit between them on the sofa and cuddle or be carried in their arms, especially "daddy's" arms. When he tried it, he got rebuffed.

He couldn't quite figure these things out. So he figured out a way to compensate for his losses. He began to rely on his cunning. He became adept at hiding his feelings about her. He wouldn't show his true feelings. He would flash his winning smile and act as if he enjoyed seeing her being held in their arms. When in truth it hurt. He learned how to talk and act like he actually meant what he was saying. When he actually despised the attention she was getting. When he wished it were him and not her in their arms. When he wished it were him, not her sitting cuddled between them on the sofa. He learned that if he wouldn't play with her afterwards, if he rebuffed her, she in turn would be more pliable. He would always find something else to do and tell her to get away. He knew this would hurt her feelings. He also knew Maddelyn loved him and looked up to him and enjoyed his company. He taught her how to be silly and funny. He showed her the best hiding places. He taught her how to sneak and be real quiet so they could listen when Mommy and Daddy were in their bedroom. He showed her how to get rid of food she didn't want to eat.

He taught her how to be sneaky, and he knew she liked that... and wanted to know more. And this made him feel better. He grew to enjoy this position. It didn't make up for his lack of attention from his parents, but it made him feel better. And for a moment, it put him in charge. The more he did this to her, the better he liked it. The better he got at using her. He noticed that when she truly wanted to be around him or play and learn more sneaky stuff with him, he could do any number of his little acts. He could act as if he didn't want to be bothered, or wasn't going to show her any more sneaky stuff, or didn't want to play what she wanted to play, but at the same time, he made sure to let her stick around, keep her nearby. He saw that he could make her feel indebted to him for allowing her to be in his company. He could get her to do things for him as well. He often used this ploy when he had to clean up his room or make up his bed or fold the clothes or do the dishes. He would act irritated or angry towards her and intentionally make her feel like she had done something to cause him to be this way. Once he had her feeling this way, he could easily manipulate her into helping him or doing it for him. Because he could flash that smile in approval of her action, making her think that "it's all better now" and "I like you again." And he got his way. And he was somewhat compensated for his losses.

He learned he was "conniving" because he heard his father use that word when referring to him. He liked that word. He learned that he could work his cunning similarly with his mother. He could get out of doing things around the house by acting sullen or hurt or flashing that smile. And once he got her to notice, he could easily manipulate her as well. He got out of going to school. She would let him off punishment when Pop wasn't around. He could get hugs. It was great. It didn't work so well with his father, he learned. Pop always seemed to be hard to penetrate. He didn't seem to fall for the great smile or the hurt little boy act. Or the witty little explanation. Pop always treated him the same no matter what. He could never quite figure him out. Pop was always trying to teach him something. Always trying to tell him something "for his own good." Always showing him what he was doing wrong. Always looking mad or something.

So he found it best to avoid Pop as often as possible. He felt a little better out of earshot from him. He learned how act and what to say and how to look in order to get away from Pop and keep out of earshot from him. When Pop was around, he knew sooner or later he was going to ask if anybody seen this or anybody knew where this was or "Boy, go get me this," or "Boy, go get me that." So he began to know what Pop was going to want. Sometimes he would hide the item so that only he knew just where to look for it. Sometimes he just knew where Pop laid it and he would get it and bring it to him with a big smile. It didn't seem to make Pop any happier, but it allowed him to be able to skip off in a direction away from him and be out of earshot for a little longer. He knew the longer he stayed in sight, the more chance he had of getting told to do something. Go to the store, dust the table legs, straighten up the cellar, cut the lawn, something. He learned how to talk to Pop, say what he thought Pop wanted to hear. He learned words he'd hear Pop use and he'd use them.

He was quick to learn. It was easy remembering words. All he had to do was think before he talked. Get it together in his head what he was trying to say, and then say it. He didn't always say the right things to Pop though. They never had what could be considered a conversation. Just a few words spoken between them. He would question something and either Pop answered or he didn't. But if

Pop said something, it was a different story. He "had" to respond. He tried to appear as though he weren't going to answer one time and he got put on punishment so fast he couldn't believe it. He was always on punishment for one thing or another, so he spent what seemed to him like most of his early childhood in the house or in his room. He figured this was pop's idea of keeping him away from the rest of the family. Put him on punishment. In his room, by himself. So Pop could have him out of their way. He could hear them talking and playing with Maddelyn downstairs though. He would just sit on his bed and listen to them having fun. While he was alone in his room, not permitted to leave. *Why??* he used to ask himself. He couldn't quite figure out the justice in punishment. Ah, but he found a way to avoid that for a little while, too. He learned to lie. He learned that if he lied and stuck to it, he could get away with a lot of things. Or if he blamed it on someone or something else, he could get off the hook. He practiced these methods well. He learned to combine that smile with that sullen, hurt look and glib talk and a lie. And he just got better and better at it. It got to the point where people just couldn't tell. And even if he got caught, he could talk his way out of it or lie again and get you to like him anyway in the end.

    By the age of thirteen, he was a pro. Proficient at everything he did. He was blessed with a good strong athletic body and he was learning to play all sports. Sports were easy. Easy to learn and easy to play. They were games and he played games very well. His instincts were sharp and he could anticipate his opponents' moves accurately and beat them. Not all the time, but most of the time. His agility was exceptional. He could spin and twist and move in ways that few could. He had the best skato in the neighborhood. He built it with the help of another boy who had help from his father. So his was built well. His had bottlecaps everywhere and it was faster than the others. He oiled the skate wheels that it rode on regularly.

His senses were acute and he had a keen sense about trusting his feelings. He was affable and well liked in school. Popular among the boys as well as the girls. He was gregarious so he had little difficulty with people and had accumulated a number of friends, one of them being Michael Watkins.

He and Michael were alike in a lot of ways. And he had come to like Michael a lot and hung out with him more than anyone else. Michael had a cool skato too, but he had to help him put it together. He showed him how to keep the wheels oiled and how to make it look sharp with the bottlecaps. They both always had their skate keys too. Never without them. And Michael was cool, smart, nice looking, and good at sports just as he was. But Mike had shown something that he didn't have. Something that he seemed to lack but would liked to have had. Michael could be cold and uncaring. Almost ruthless. He felt that he could never be that way, but he sort of wished he could. He couldn't believe the way Michael could just pick out somebody, walk up to them, and just take their lunch money from them, or make them give it to him. He saw that Michael could get a look in his eyes and a sneer on his face that was just plain scary. He soon got to be known as the "Iceman" or "Ice." Michael had people just giving him things because he told them to. Mike could be intimidating and he seemed almost fearless. Even though he knew he could get people to do things for him and give him things too, he was doing it in a different way and most of the time, he felt some sense of remorse or something. Not Michael. "Fuck em," he used to say.

But he knew that Michael couldn't do it his way either. Where he could get that lunch money from them and be smiling and talking all the while, Michael couldn't. Michael couldn't con them out of it, couldn't trick them, and couldn't charm them. He figured that sort of made them even. One thing he noticed, though, was that after he did his little thing to someone, he may have to avoid them for awhile afterwards, but when he finally saw them again, they at least still liked him. And he noticed that although people still acted like they liked Michael, he knew that they didn't. He sensed that they were afraid. He sort of admired that too about Michael. Although he, himself, never feared Michael. Michael treated him like a brother. Better, Michael respected and trusted him. He knew that and he held their relationship in high esteem. They got along well and they worked well together. They both liked to dress in khakis and knit shirts and they both wore high top comforts and Stetson hats. That was the lay.

By the time they were sixteen, they seemed to think alike and share similar points of view. If one came up with an idea, the other always liked it or at least went along with it and vice versa. It only depended on whose idea it was as to how it was carried out. It was his idea to get a short piece of metal and break into lockers. They got coats, jackets, money, and just about anything they wanted this way. But it would be Michael's idea to go up to the rich, white people's neighborhood, and beat up a white boy and take his coat and money. Or wait outside the bar and roll a drunk. That's the way Michael did things.

Then there was the girl thing. He knew the little girls liked him and he knew he didn't have to do much to get to go with anyone of them. But he didn't try to have sex with them all, although it seemed they always wanted to. He wasn't as nasty with them as they often wanted him to be. He had learned to respect girls, and it was hard for him to take advantage of them. He got in more trouble rejecting their advances or turning down their favors than he thought possible. He later found out that was because girls didn't like to be told no. And that this would anger them. But Michael took advantage of all he rejected. He seemed to have an enormous appetite for sex. Michael was the first black guy he knew that would openly admit that he ate pussy. Plus Michael told him that he should do it, too. But he could never bring himself to do that. He always knew that that was the same place they pissed from. Michael got to do it to a lot of girls, and he didn't care if they got mad or not. He would make them his girlfriends anyway afterwards. Whether they wanted to be or not. He just seemed to know how to appease them or something. Like he had some sort of spell over them. He just made them his girlfriend. That's what happened to Evelyn. But Greg knew that Michael liked Evelyn more than any of the other girls.

Evelyn was only fifteen at the time. She was cute, with an appealing complexion. Her face kind of reminded him of the butterscotch candies that they sold at the 5 and 10 cent store. She was thin and her hair was always in plats. She was quiet and shy, but she always seemed to be looking and smiling at him. She and Greg became good friends in time, and they would talk and share their concerns with each other. As a matter of fact, she was the first one he practiced having sex with. She was just that way. She was easy and they were good buddies. He felt that she would do anything for him. But then it seemed she would do anything for anybody. She was so timid and gullible. It was as if all you had to do was ask and she would do it. He respected that in her and tried not to use her all the time.

It was hard because she was too easy. He later found out that, just as he suspected, she was doing it with a lot of guys.

That's how he met Juice. It was through her. She was talking to him one day and she introduced them. His real name was Curtis D. Jouscar (pronounced Joosar), but everybody called him "Juice" for short. He was a hustler and a good dresser. He always had money and girls. They ended up becoming friends as well. It was Juice more or less who got him to see that Evelyn had a real weakness. He realized that she felt she needed to have sex with guys to have them as friends. And that she thought she had a "white liver." He was a little confused about this behavior in her because it was so different from a lot of the other girls he knew. He later found out that she also got things for doing it too. She would tell him how she got to go to the drive-in movies a lot. And she got to go the park, get taken out, and turned on, just by being nice to guys. So Greg accepted her behavior, but he never quite understood why she did the things she did. Even though she didn't seem happy about it, she felt that it got people to like her and pay attention to her. To say the least, she was well known by many a young boy. He tried not to take advantage of her weakness until he really needed some, but Michael, on the other hand, took full advantage of her weakness. Michael would make her do it all the time as well as other things that she didn't even want to do. He even made her do it to other guys. And she would always end up telling him about it. He didn't really like to hear it, but he knew Michael liked her and he knew how Michael treated girls. Especially Evelyn. He couldn't help her there.

Then there was Kenny. Everybody knew Kenny was a sissy. He always played with the girls. Especially Maddelyn. Kenny and Maddelyn acted like they were sister and brother, or really, more like just plain sisters. He didn't mind, though, because Kenny acted so much like a girl. But Michael couldn't stand Kenny. He always was laughing at him or making jokes about him. He used to make him go to the store for him or give him things. He treated Kenny bad. He made Kenny sit in a corner one time and Kenny just sat there and cried and cried. Maddelyn even laughed at that, but she at least got Michael to stop taunting him in her presence. So Kenny came to despise Michael as much as Michael despised him. Whenever Michael came on the scene, Kenny split. Sometimes Maddelyn would leave with him and sometimes she would make Michael leave before Kenny left. But Michael, of course liked Maddelyn and more often than not, the three of them would end up in the house together with Kenny, more often than not, being forced to leave. Kenny used to cry and threaten to do real bad things to Michael. Only if he could! Greg couldn't help him there. Maddelyn, on the other hand, knew how to handle Michael. She never gave him anything. Maddelyn was different. Maddelyn use to tell him to "watch out for that Michael." She would say that "he don't mean nothin' but no good to you and he ain't gone do nothin' but get you in trouble." She went out with Michael a few times, though. And sometimes she even acted as if she liked him. Michael would always say that she'd come around sooner or later. But then, Michael would talk about Maddelyn differently too.

Greg and Michael talked about everything. By the time they were grown men, they had done much together. They also had done things separately. Not that they had grown apart but more so that they both had learned to respect each other's individuality. Michael sort of branched off and got involved in drug dealing and pimping and was making a lot of money and doing a lot of shady things. Greg was barely sustaining himself by running small time cons here and there. Since he never finished college, he never quite attained what he had hoped to attain in life. He even resorted to robbery. He robbed a few gas stations and a few drug stores. Never used a real gun. He was just getting by when he happened upon a scheme that was beginning to bring him in a fairly consistent flow of money. He was excited. He had run the scheme with one of his old college buddies, but he was sure he could do better if he had someone like Michael involved. One day he went looking for Michael to tell him the exciting news. He just knew this was his "get rich" dream come true. He finally caught up with Michael as he was driving up Broad Street. He couldn't wait to surprise him. He knew that Michael hadn't been doing so good either with the drug thing. He couldn't wait to tell him. He had no idea just how fatal their meeting would be.

Maddelyn

Maddelyn Burks, founder and CEO of SURROGATE INC. Extraordinarily good looking, tall, and elegant. This particular morning she had arrived at the office earlier than usual. She wanted to make sure everything was in order. She was nervous, yet determined to make herself feel as if she had nothing to be nervous about. Her business was being reviewed by the federal government on this day. She got up from the desk and walked slowly past the large triangular conference table, noting that the silver ashtrays were in place and that they were shiny. The pitchers, filled with ice water and coffee, were shiny. The table was shiny, really shiny. She liked that. She pushed the large oak door open and walked into the office lobby. She was in kind of a daydreamy state. Glancing at her Seiko watch, she noticed it was 6:52 A.M. She sauntered over to the wide picture window that enveloped the lobby and peered out over the river to the other side. Camden! she thought. Dingy, air pollution hanging over it. It looked dull and uninteresting. She looked to the other side. Center City. She was on the fourteenth floor of the INA building and could see as far as the eye could see over the city. Not much better, she thought. Then she turned to move toward the elevator, which was on both sides of the lobby, pushed the down button, and reached for her cigarettes and lighter, which were in the pocket of her suit jacket. She lit the cigarette and poised herself to wait for the elevator to arrive. It was a cloudy dull day and reminded her of schooldays when she had to wear a raincoat and galoshes. She began to reflect. . . .

Even as a child, Maddelyn had taken a special joy in being with boys. It was something about them that was different. There was something about *her* that was different. And she knew it even then. She had girlfriends, but Kenny Bailey was one of her closest playmates. She could talk to Kenny about almost anything. She could talk about all the things she wanted to talk about with Kenny, even the girl stuff, like the dolls they played with, how to dress them, and how to comb and style their hair.

Michael, on the other hand, was one that she couldn't talk to about anything. It seemed that most everything she said around him was made to sound ridiculous and irrelevant to what he and the other boys were talking about. She didn't like him. Or at least didn't want to like him. She knew he paid a lot of attention to her in his own way. She knew he watched her. And she knew he treated her with respect.

She was content to know that she was considered to be pretty. At least by her father's standards and by some of her schoolmates' remarks about her cute little face and almond-shaped eyes. She always had clear, smooth, brown skin and a thick curly black head of hair that she liked to wear in a ponytail with bangs. At thirteen, she was pretty well developed and had been wearing a bra since she was ten. She was about 5'7" then and growing. She actually looked to be about seventeen or eighteen years old, and her mannerisms were equally as matured. That accounted for the fact that she had quite a bit of interaction with boys, and by then, she was fairly confident that she could do just about whatever she wanted with them. They were easy to manipulate. They all seemed to like her. They all seemed to want something from her. Even her father's friends seemed to like her. She was always getting quarters and dollars and comments from them whenever she saw them.

She was attractive. She also had a very uncanny sense of perception with people in general. It was as if she could control them by using her charisma and charm and get whatever she wanted. She was enthralled with this ability at first, but it just came so easy that she began to know exactly when to use it. When to turn it off. When to turn it on. When it wasn't necessary to use at all. That's when she called it "just being herself," when she didn't have to use it. She was always quick witted and smart. A fast learner, able to pick up on things merely by watching. She loved school and all the homework that went with it.

She had reminisced to one particularly dreary day when she had been doing her homework (and loving it). She recalled how her brother Gregory had come into her room and sat down on the bed. . . .

"Maddie," he had said to her, "do me a favor?"

Greg was two years older than she and he knew how to get what he wanted out of her. She had noticed he hadn't been too aggressive that day and he had acted as if he really didn't want to ask, with a somewhat pained look on his face and pleading eyes. She looked up from her studies.

"Uh, oh!" She remembered thinking, *What?* She remembered how he sort of scooted over closer to her on the bed.

"Aw, come on don't be that way." Then he smiled. "What I need you to do is real simple. All you got to do is *act* like you like this guy. You know what um sayin'? Just *act* like it, you know, like you think he's cute and shit and get him to come to this jam we havin' at MOTIONS in two weeks." At that point, she threw her hands in the air as though it were a stickup.

"Wait a minute, hold it hold it. What are you talking about? Who is this guy? Do I know him? And why can't you ask him yourself?" She remembered Greg's wide grin then.

"Noooooooooo, that's the whole thing, baby, you have got to *get* to know him. You know what um sayin? Look all we, I, want you—"

"Hold it," she had cut him short. "What's with this WE stuff?" She was no stranger to manipulation, she had angled her eyes at him accordingly. She knew the signs well and Greg was clearly flashing them now. "Look, Greg. I don't know what yall up to this time, but I ain't doin' nothing till I know what's going on, so if you want me to help you, you might as well just tell me." Greg was still smiling and he held his eyes tightly shut.

"Okay, okay, okay! Damn, you get so upset." He had fixed a serious look on his face now as he began his explanation.

"It's like, okay dig the move, it's this guy named, um, Nate, I think. See, I don't know him all that good, see, but Juice do, but Juice don't talk right and he don't want to ask this guy to do this thing for us, see? So—"

"Do what thing?" Maddelyn remembered making Greg tow the line. Greg, however, began acting like she were annoying him.

"Damn, I'm tryin to tell you now, damn, so anyway, listen, uh, me and Juice and Ronny and Ice is supposed to be doin this set at MOTIONS, Saturday after next, see, and this guy Nate's pop has a studio, right? So, and we need to mix up our tapes in his studio. But we broke, see, and it cost too much to even try—"

"Okay," Maddelyn broke in. "So what you thinking about is getting me to get Nate to get his father to get y'all into this studio that he's supposed to have—for free, right?"

Greg had sat straight up on the bed "Right!, That's all." Greg responded in a whispered exaggerated voice. "Right, that's all! He can get us in there for nothin'!" Greg had been staring intently into Maddelyn's face as she had remembered and had been waiting for a response. She peered over at him.

"What he look like?" She frowned at him.

"He don't look all that bad!" Greg quickly answered. "He do got a car though and some bucks! He probably okay! I do know that he supposed to be messin' around wit Renee though. You know Renee! Got them big lips and that big butt. She live on Norwood Street. But, see, she messin' around wit Skitter too, see. So this boy we talkin' about can't be doin' it right, you know what um sayin? Plus, you a lot better lookin than she is anyway."

"How old is he?" Maddelyn seemed a little more interested after listening to him plead his case.

"I don't know, about sixteen or seventeen, somethin like that. He don't go to school no more, I know that much!"

Maddelyn turned to the window. "I don't think—

Greg cut her short. "Awright, listen, why don't you let me and Juice show you him and you can make up your mind then, how about that? That sound okay to you?" Greg was headed for the door, but Maddelyn grabbed him by the shoulder.

"Wait a minute, not so fast. Why can't yall just ask him for yall self?" Greg stopped, turned back to meet Maddelyn's stare.

"Cause. You don't understand!! None of us like him, you know what um sayin?"—

The elevator doors parted and Maddelyn stepped between them and on to the plush carpet of the elevator floor. She still seemed to be in a daze and was trying hard to bring herself out of her reminiscence of her younger days but at the same time, still faintly remembering the scene with her brother Gregory. It seemed so long ago. She had just turned thirteen at the time. She smiled to herself and thought, "grown." She used to refer to herself as being grown when she was thirteen. How could she have ever thought she was grown at the tender, naive age of thirteen? Or twelve for that matter.

The elevator let her off at the lobby floor of the office building and as she approached the door, the security guard opened the door for her and spoke to her. She barely responded, she had noticed that "Benny," her Mercedes—she liked naming things of hers after men—was parked a little crooked. Benny was sharp! Silver gray, classy, shiny. She liked it. She opened the door using her 5 code key to the alarm, leaned in a little to put her briefcase on the passengers seat, then her handbag. Then she slipped into the seat behind the wheel. The smell of leather! She liked it. She wiggled around a little to find that comfort spot, adjusted the rear view mirror, straightened her sunglasses and looked at the inscription on the dash "CLASS." Benny was a gift to her from Juice for her brilliant seductive qualities that led to his success. It was one of her prize possessions. She loved Benny and took as good care of him as any man could. Kept him clean, shiny and running good. Yeah, she liked that. Backing out of the parking space and reaching for her Aretha Franklin tape, she kept her eyes in the rear view mirror, put the gear shift in drive, and pulled off.

"What's that address?" she mumbled to herself. "Dauphin Street, okay, I'll have to hit the drive, hum, let me turn here. I always miss this short cut. Glen Echo Road runs right into Wissahickon Drive. Go head, girl!" she said out loud about Aretha Franklin singing on the tape that had just begun playing. She proceeded to drive. She was singing with it now. It was her favorite tape, "Respect." She turned the music up, she knew all the lyrics to every song. She was in her world.

The Benz pulled up beside a parked Chevy as she leaned over to get a better look at the address of the house she was in front of. *Hope she don't give me no grief!* Maddelyn thought as she backed the car into a parking spot.

Marcella Williams, twenty-three, no job. Perfect candidate, she thought about her prospective client. She gathered her briefcase and purse and exited the car, allowing her eyes to scan the immediate surroundings. "Neighborhood ain't bad. No niggas on the corners anyway," she muttered. The lawns fairly kept up. Rowhouses, but in good-looking condition. She walked between her car and the car parked in front of it, careful not to touch either fender and stepped onto the sidewalk and up the first four steps. As she stepped off the landing to go to the next set of steps that led to an inclosed porch, the door opened.

"Ms. Burks?" Maddelyn stopped and smiled as she looked up into the young girl's face.

"Maddie!" she replied, "and you must be Marcella!"

"Marcie!" the young girl quipped back. They appeared to naturally get along at this point, and both seemed to feel comfortable with each other.

Maddelyn was invited to sit in a chair that was almost opposite the one Marcie sat in, each adapting to their respective roles very cordially. The "Interviewer," pen and pad in hand, authoritative, and precise as the interview got underway. The "Interviewee," sitting with undivided attention, listening intently, attempting to have all the right answers and asking few questions. "Well, Marcie, I think you'll do just fine. The couple I'm planning to have you work for have been married two and a half years, and will do just about anything for a child. They'd considered adopting, but the adoption process was too lengthy and grueling, that's why they opted surrogacy. They are willing to be flexible with terms and payment, which I'm sure you're most concerned with. Oh, and they *are* receptive to post-surrogation visitation, which is an extremely important aspect of this business. Now I want you to understand that everything we've discussed is contingent upon what is actually negotiated and written within the terms of the contract. I will leave you a sample copy of the contract we use and you can have an attorney look it over with you."

"Excuse me, Maddie, let me ask you this?" Marcie's eyes danced around the room before settling on the floor then to Maddelyn's face.

"Sure, what?" Maddelyn focused on her intently.

"How much do the, uh, what do you call it, uh." She decided to rephrase her question, "Um, what do people usually get paid for doing this?" She put her hands together in front of her and leaned her elbows on her knees. Maddelyn sat back, crossed her legs as if to take a moment to ponder the question.

After a moment. "Hum. I'll tell you, Marcie, it varies, it really does. It depends on several factors. How much the donor family has to invest *and* is willing to invest. Um, how badly they want the child. How much the carrier is willing to accept. See," she broke off her explanation, "I've intermediated in $5,000 contracts as well as $25,000 contracts, so it depends, really." Maddelyn was satisfied with her answer and knew by the look on Marcie's face that she had accepted it as well. She ended the interview and set up a time for both parties to meet, and she left explaining that she had a meeting to attend.

Upon arriving at her office, she was met at the door by the doorman with an urgent message for her to call her parents immediately. She also had a message to call Kenny. *What could be so urgent? What could have possibly happened?* she thought. She took the elevator to the fourteenth floor and to her office where she went directly to the phone and dialed her mother's number. Six rings, no answer. She hung up. *Where could they be?* she wondered. The phone rang just at that moment. It was Kenny and he sounded very upset. She could tell because he didn't say what he usually said when he began talking, which would have been a cheerful "Chello, Dahling." Instead, he began with, "Oh, Maddie, I feel so sorry for you." Maddelyn had no idea why he was saying this to her.

"What?? What are you talking about, Kenny?? What's wrong?" She felt herself becoming agitated and confused now.

"Maddie? Oh, my God, you don't know? Oh, my God? You haven't talked to your mother or father? Oh, my God!! Oh, Jesus! Maddie, I didn't know. I thought . . . uh your father just called and told me a minute ago." His voice began to break up now. A lump had formed in his throat and he had become silent.

"Kenny? Kenny, what's the matter? Get a hold of yourself and tell me now. You're upsetting me." She was getting frustrated and sensing something very wrong.

"Greg's—been—killed!" Kenny was speaking in broken words. Maddie's body turned cold as the words penetrated her ears. She felt wobbly as if her legs could no longer hold her up. Her thoughts became jumbled. She was visibly shaken.

"Wha—what do you mean, killed?" The words seemed to come from some place other than her mouth.

They seemed to float out of her mouth. She wasn't aware that she was talking even.

"You mean my brother Greg?" She was numb. "Where is he? I mean is he dead? What???"

Kenny broke in. "Just stay there. Where are you? At your office?"

"Yes, I'm here, that's where you called me at!" She was talking as if she were in a stupor and slightly annoyed.

"Oh, yeah right, I'm sorry, I'm not thinking right. You just stay there. I'll be right there." He hung up. She continued to hold the receiver in her hand, which was shaking uncontrollably. She couldn't get her thoughts together to think, so she just sat and stared blankly out the window, phone still in her hand.

Kenny

His 5'9", 150-pound frame always allowed him to dress well and look good in what he wore. He had curly hair and has always worn it long. Not bad looking by his standards. He kept his small waistline and cute looks from his teen years and was extremely vain and attentive to himself and his appearance. His interests at this point in his life were modeling, money, and men which comprised his 3M's Inc., a modeling company. He'd been very successful as a result of his tenacity and innate ability to perceive what women liked in designs and the models that display them. He got paid well.

On this particular day, Kenny was preparing to make a trip to New York with his purchasing agent. He glanced at the clock: 12:32 P.M. The telephone rang. "Who the hell is that? Don't these people know I got to get outta here? Shoooot." He was overexaggerating his anger as he walked hurriedly towards the phone and picked it up, "Chellooo?" he answered in a sing-song voice.

"Hello! Kenny? This is Greg's father." Kenny recognized the voice.

"Oh. Hi there, Mr. Burks. How have you been?" Then, he detected a strange silence from the other end. "You all right?" he asked pensively. There was no response, just what sounded like low heavy breathing. "Hello! Mr. Burks, you okay?" He was concerned and listening very closely.

"Ken," the voice was quivering and mixed with sniffling, "Greg's been killed." The voice then burst into uncontrollable crying and sobbing. Kenny's mind went blank.

Chills came in waves up and down his entire body. He felt as though he couldn't catch his breath.

"Greg? Killed? What? You mean our Greg? Who? Who?" A lump formed in his throat, and he himself could no longer restrain the tears that had welled up in his eyes. He slumped down in the chair he was standing beside, the phone, no longer at his ear, but he was still holding it. After about a minute, he regained enough of his composure to try to confront this hellish nightmare he had been thrown into. He wiped the tears from his mouth and eyes and attempted to talk.

"Mr. Burks? You still there? I'm so sorry, Jesus! When—"Once again he could not contain the rush of emotion, and he went into another lengthy crying spell. He appeared to be in the worst state of despair that anyone could be in at this moment. He was almost convulsing, he was crying so hard. His complexion had turned a deep reddish hue. One of his assistants had heard his outburst and had come to console him, but Kenny could not respond to her attention. She slipped the phone from his hand and slowly put the receiver to her ear.

"Hello, this is Mr. Bailey's assistant, uh, Mr. Bailey is very upset and he can't talk any more."

"Hello? I understand," the voice on the other end responded. "Would you please tell him to come to Gregory's house as soon as possible. It's very important. Thank you."

"I'll be sure to tell him," she assured him. She hung the phone up and continued to try to console Kenny.

Kenny had loved Greg like a brother and more. He had been Maddelyn's closest friend since childhood. He and Greg and Maddie grew up together. He credited himself with teaching Maddie about styling hair. Where she would merely comb the doll's hair straight down, it would be he who would suggest that she curl up the ends or put a little flip here or let it fall to one side. He took pride in knowing that because he noticed that Maddelyn respected him more for it. She seemed more willing to trust him than anybody else. And she would do things for him at the drop of a hat. Like the time he wanted to get to know a certain guy. He sought Maddelyn's help.

Kenny never had any trouble accepting the fact that he was gay, and Maddie always accepted him unconditionally. So he had no problem asking her to go out with this guy who liked her just so she could have him bring his friend, whom, Kenny was infatuated head over heels with and the four of them could go out together. She did this with no problem. She did it several times. He soon knew that he could use Maddie as a means to get to know the men he wanted to get with. He would use her. And she knew she was being used. And she didn't mind. As a matter of fact, it got to the point where he depended on Maddie's skills and natural ability to attract the attentions of men to get men for him. Although he had no trouble accepting his feminine ways, he knew the general male public didn't. And he often had to try to conceal the fact that he was a queen until he felt comfortable enough to know that the company he was in would be accepting. This bothered him because he wanted so much to be blatantly openly and boldly feminine. He knew that women had nothing on him. He was pretty and had a better shape than most of them. And most of all he had the ass that he felt was the envy of all women. He had experienced enough men to know that they too had an eye for that ass of his. Only he knew that they had to be discreet in letting it be known. But he knew once behind closed doors, they enjoyed what he could do for them. Knowing these things gave him the confidence to become more and more bold with his sexual preference through time.

Kenny idolized Greg. That was another reason he spent so much time with Maddelyn. So he could be close to Greg. Greg knew he liked men, but after being around him so much, he too accepted Kenny for the person he was. Kenny always had a secret crush on Greg. And he would throw slurs about his girlfriends and would constantly test Greg's manhood by saying remarks like "You can never say you won't try it, and I know you want to." But Greg was too secure in his manhood to be affected by Kenny's bogus attempts. Gregory could never be intimidated by Kenny, or anybody else for that matter. And Kenny knew that, but it gave him practice, so he could use those same words on other, less secure men. Kenny was adept at intimidation. It was his best tool as well as his best weapon.

Once Maddie got the unsuspecting, unknowing extra male around, Kenny would always mysteriously appear on the set and work his way into the group. He and Maddie knew what was going on, but the others had no idea. It always worked, and more times than not, he ended up getting what he went after. Maddie knew about all of them. And Greg knew of a few as well. This gave all three of them somewhat of an edge on people they knew, but didn't know they knew what they did about Kenny, and his clandestine activities. They had a bond. Maddie and Greg had been key elements in Kenny's homosexual development. He truly loved them both. Michael, on the other hand, was a thorn in his side—one of life's mistakes, as far as Kenny was concerned. Michael treated him like a girl and he hated it. He knew Michael was doing nothing but tormenting him and ridiculing him. And he would always do it in front of people. Oh, how he abhorred that man. . . .

Kenny finally got himself together enough to at least accept the horrible news. He was worn from the emotional outburst, but he forced himself to reach apathetically for the phone to call Maddie. He figured at least he and Maddie could comfort each other. He dialed Maddie's office number. But he dialed wrong and had to redial. This time the phone rang.

Juice

ASCOTT Inc. occupied the penthouse suite of the INA Building, one of the tallest buildings in Philadelphia. It was impressive, with blue-tinted windows and a menagerie of office suites. It towered over the center of the city. Curtis D. Jouscar was President of ASCOTT Inc. and Chairperson of the Board of Directors. He was the decision maker. The man in charge.

This fact was becoming blindingly clear to the two well-dressed men poised in front of Jouscar's desk. The taller of the two men was talking.

"Yeah, Mr. Jouscar, but he swears he don't know that much about the project, only that it's waiting for your approval." Jouscar was listening but didn't seem to be convinced. He took his hand out of his pocket and positioned his thumb and index finger on his chin, his index finger making a sweeping motion over the dent in the middle. Both men looked at each other as though they were thinking the same thing, that they didn't do a very thorough job and were about to be lambasted for it.

"Thanks, fellas. That's about what I expected," Jouscar said after an agonizing minute of contemplating, "I'll get back to you by Wednesday. I think I will have made my decision by then and I just may want you to take that ride across the bridge with me." As he rose to get up, he pointed a finger at the shorter of the two men. "Oh, Dennis, did you get that thing I asked you for?"

"No, um, uh, probly not til tonight 'cause that's when his new package comes in and what he's holdin' now ain't that good." Dennis knew what he was talking about.

"Oh, yeah?" Jouscar asked. "About what time?"

"About 10, 10:30. You want me to call him now? And check it out?"

"Uh, no, not from here. Why don't you run past there and find out for sure, then, give me a call at my spot when you know something, okay?" Jouscar reached into the inside pocket of his suit jacket as he was speaking, and produced a brown envelope. He handed it to the taller man, whose name was Vance. Vance took the envelope, looked inside, saw some fifty dollar bills and a couple of hundreds, and looked up at Jouscar.

"Damn, Curt, this a lot of scratch!!" Jouscar walked past them both to the door and as he reached for the knob, he directed his eyes at both men.

"We straight??" Vance picked his hat up from the chair, a smile fixed on his ebony, round face.

"Yes suh, buddy, anytime, Curt, anytime!" Both men started out the door, Vance reached to shake Jouscar's extended hand. The two exchanged looks at each other. Jouscar was expressionless. Vance stepped out the door first, obviously pleased with the transaction. Dennis followed taking Jouscar's hand, which was notably larger than his.

"Bout ten, right?" he confirmed with Jouscar.

"Right! And, uh, make sure he knows it's for me!!"

"Oh, you know it, I'm gone do that and thanks." The two headed for the elevator.

Jouscar closed the door and walked to his desk, not bothering to straighten out the two chairs in front of it. He was suddenly mindful of the time. "What time is it?" he thought aloud. He walked toward the phone and looked at it, then to the clock, which was built into the hi-fi system just beyond. The hands were positioned at 12:50. *Almost one o'clock*, he thought. He picked the phone up and dialed.

The soft professional voice of a woman answered on the second ring.

"Surrogate Inc. Ms. Burks's office, this is Deanna. How may I help you?" the voice inquired.

"Hello, Dee? This is Curt. Is, uh, Maddie around?" Jouscar lowered himself to sit on the edge of his desk to get more comfortable.

"Oh! Mr. Jouscar! Hi, uh, no, Ms Burks had to leave for the day. Would you care to leave a message? I'll see to it that she gets it as soon as she gets in touch with me." He could hear soft music in the background.

"Uh, no, Dee, that's okay. I'll catch up with her later. Thanks anyway." There was a brief pause. "How are *you* doing these days?" She noticed his tone had changed. Softer, not so businesslike. She leaned her elbow on the desk and moved her chair a little closer under the desk.

"I'm doing okay," she purred. Her sultry voice heightened the softened mood.

"You ever take that real estate course you were trying to get into?" Jouscar relaxed himself even more and pulled his pants leg up to check his alligator boots out as he was talking.

"Oh, you know what? I'm doing it now." She was surprised that he remembered. "It's not that hard either, except for the math parts. I'm not all that good in math." She giggled, "But yeah, I only got, let's see, two more weeks before I can take my first test."

The phone rang on another line; she looked to see whose line it was. Ms. Jamison's, she noted, wondering why she was not picking it up. "Excuse me, Mr. Jouscar, would you care to hold while I answer another line?" She was trying to peep into Ms. Jamison's cubicle to see why no one was answering that line.

"Uh, no, Dee. That's all right. You go get the phone and let me know if I can help you with that course if I can. I'm not bad in math. Okay? And don't forget to tell Maddie I called? See you, bye, bye." He hung up. She turned her full attention to Ms. Jamison's office, which was behind her. By now the light on the phone had gone steady, indicating she had picked up. "Damn, I hate that shit," Deanna, muttered as she replaced the receiver back in the base of the phone. Every time she had an opportunity to speak to him, something happened.

Jouscar was still sitting on the edge of the desk, looking pensively at his phone. She sure sounds sweet, he thought, as an image of Deanna formed in his head. He envisioned her standing in the door of Maddie's office. She had on those stockings with the little butterflies on the back and a yellow mini skirt that revealed just about all of her long shapely legs and full thighs. Her hair was cut short on the sides and in the back, perfect shape-up. Perfect shape. Rock-hard body. He smiled to himself as if assured that one day he'd have her. He sensed that she liked him by the way she flirted with him. Her eyes were telling, plus he knew she liked tall men as she often commented on that point. There was a knock at the door. He looked up as his secretary opened it just enough to peep her head in.

"Mr. Jouscar? Sorry to bother you, but Mr. Grant's here. Would you like me to show him in or what?" Jouscar pulled himself out of his daydream and moved away from the edge of the desk to sit behind it.

"Give me a minute, Cheryl. I'll buzz you on the intercom, okay?" Cheryl confirmed with a nod of her head and closed the door. Jouscar sat down and swirled around in his highback leather chair to face the microfiche machine. He searched for the name GRANT. The data on GRANT ENTERPRISES appeared on the screen.

GRANT ENTERPRISES was a fairly new organization and had profited nicely as a result of following ASCOTT'S leads and consultation as ASCOTT INC. had already become a leader in the real estate field with a fifteen year track record. GRANT ENTERPRISE'S profits in the first year had tripled in the second year and they were continuing to prove themselves to be successful black entrepreneurs in a predominantly white-dominated business. There had been a significant increase in stocks being purchased in the corporation and each year stock prices went up. Its assets were growing in proportion to its profits.

Harold Grant was President of GRANT ENTERPRISES, and he was largely responsible for the corporation's rapid growth. He was becoming more experienced and knowledgeable about the workings of the real estate game and had gained credibility from the East Coast to the West Coast and more recently was become recognized internationally. GRANT ENTERPRISES had been affiliated with ASCOTT INC. five years now and had never experienced a loss with any of its investments, but this latest one seemed a little shaky and Grant felt uneasy about it. The proposal had called for a 10 million dollar investment in a condo/development project on one of the Bahamian Islands. Grant just didn't have that kind of capital on hand at this time but knew he could procure it with a little time. He needed to know more about ASCOTT'S position now. Vance and Dennis worked for an ASCOTT INC. subsidiary, ASCOTT MANAGEMENT COMPANY, and had been assigned to visit GRANT ENTERPRISES that morning to check their readiness to invest, but Grant had insisted on speaking to Jouscar personally, hence, the reason for his visit.

"Come on in, Harry," he said, never looking back. "Make yourself a drink if you want." Harold proceeded to the small bar within the office and fixed a VO and ginger ale mix. He stood at the bar and tasted it while looking around. Finally, Curtis turned around to face him.

"Uh, sorry for the wait, Harry. How are you? How's things looking?" Harold walked toward the chair facing the desk and sat down.

"Oh, not too bad, considering they could be worse." Curtis responded with a smile.

"Well, that's good then. Hey, did you take my advice and hire you some more women?"

Harold smiled at this question. "Got two more and you should see 'em. Man, this one chick is—" Jouscar cut him off with a hand gesture.

"Okay, man, I believe you, but now how about our deal in the Tropics? What's up with that?" Harold put his glass on the desk.

"Hey, hold on, use a coaster, man." Curtis handed it to him.

"Oh! Sorry." He set his glass down on the coaster and sat back to look directly at Curtis. "Well, to tell you the truth, Curt, I'm not sure that I'm ready for that at this point. I been hearing things. And I think we should look into this a little further before we continue into this venture."

"Oh? Like what?" Jouscar said, "Tell me what you been hearing, 'cause I been hearing things too, Harry, and I don't particularly like what I been hearing either." At that moment, the intercom light came on and Jouscar excused himself to respond. "Yes, Cheryl, what is it?"

"Sorry to bother you, Mr. Jouscar, but I have an urgent call from Ms. Burks. Will you take it in there or how should I handle it?"

"Send it back, Cheryl. I'll take it. Excuse me, Harry."

"Well, hi there, Ms. Burks," he opened with.

"Curt?" she said. He immediately sensed distress in her voice. "Curt, I got to see you now, Greg's been shot."

Michael

Michael was sitting in his metallic blue Pontiac Lemans outside the gym waiting to meet his partner, Correy, so that they could continue distributing their wares. He was thinking that he still had a lot of time until he was to meet with Vance in Camden and that he wouldn't have to rush. It had been two days since the Greg thing and so far so good. The music was blasting and the convertible top was down when—"Hey, nigga, give it up!" startled him so bad he ducked down in the seat and went for his .38 snubnose, which he kept under his seat, bumping his head on the steering wheel as he reached. When he finally turned to try to respond, he saw the face of Russell, a guy he knew.

"Shit, Russ, Gotdamn, you scared the shit outta me. Boy, don't be doin' shit like that, man, I coulda bust yo ass, you see I got my shit on you. Damn." He really had been surprised and was noticeably shaken, but by now had tried to make it seem harmless.

"Whoa, Ice!" Russell was laughing very hard at the scene and could not stop to try to look at the gun or anything else. "Whew. I ain't never seen a nigga do that shit before. You almost knocked yoself out." He was laughing hysterically now, tears coming from his eyes and his breath was getting hard to catch. "Whew, I swear, man, I didn't mean to blow your cool but—" again he burst into a fit of laughter at the thought of what just transpired. "Whoa, whew, I'm sorry, man, but you just was moving so fuckin' fast you bust your fuckin' head open. Damn, man, I know that had to hurt." He continued to laugh in between his explanation. "I'm sorry, Ice, but, shit, you supposed to be the 'Iceman,' looks like your shit meltin' in the seat." Even Michael cracked a wide smile on that one.

"Awright, mothafucka, yeah, you got me." He slid the snubnose back under the seat and twisted the Jeff he was wearing around so that the bill now faced the back of his head. He had a habit of doing that when he wore his Jeff. "Now, chump, what you up to?"

"Aw, not too much, Ice. I'm kinda fucked up over Greg though. You heard about him?" Mike's face turned to look squarely into Russell's face, appearing to be extra attentive. "Naw, man, I ain't heard. What?"

"Aw, man, Ice, you ain't heard? Damn, man, Greg was killed night before last I think. The way I heard it was somebody rolled in on him at his mom's crib. Don't nobody know nothin' about it though, who did it or why or nothin'. Man, that shit's fucked up, you know?" Michael appeared to be very upset. He snatched the Jeff off of his head and was sitting up in the seat and looked straight ahead as if he couldn't believe what he heard.

"What? You talking bout Greg Burks? Maddie's brother? My boy Greg? Get the fuck outta hear. You sure?" His face was showing anger, his lips terse and his eyes squinted, fists balled up as if he were going to hit something. "I was just wit Greg the other night and me and him had some business we was talking about doin'. Damn!! You talk to anybody else? No, I mean who told you about this shit?"

"I heard it in the bar. And I seen somebody, I can't remember who it was. I think it was that faggot. You know him. He grew up wit yall. You know him, though. That's all they told me. But you know what? He did say you probably might know somethin' about it 'cause you was with him that night."

"How the fuck would he know where I was? And why the fuck would he bring my name into this shit? This is the first time I'm hearing about it." Michael was obviously surprised and angry.

"I don't know, man, but das who I got it from. You know though, Greg was into a lot of shit," Russell said, "That mothafucka was runnin' more scams than a little bit. And had all the hoes doing anything he wanted em to do. Shit. Coulda been one of them bitches he was fuckin' wit. You know? Man, I remember when Greg first turned me on to the empty envelope trick at these new George machines. You member that?? But see, he was slick, he would get one of his bitches to stand in line behind some jerk and have them peep over they shoulder and get that secret code. And see, Greg would roll up on 'em and either pick their pocket or steal they pocketbook or just plain mug them mothafuckas and take they card and then have the broad go back to the machine and slip the empty envelope in and they would clean up the account. Man, that shit was too easy, but it always worked for him. Man, that guy knew how to get them ends. You know what though? Sometimes shit like that back up on you, you know what I mean? Oh, yeah, an' I remember when he was runnin' that Reverend Burks letter scam. Man, that shit probably still workin' now. And he dead. This mothafucka was sending out form letters to people, I don't know how the hell he got they names and shit, but he was telling 'em he would be praying for 'em and all they had to do was send some money and he had a PO box and all, and he said that mothafucka was always full. That boy was something else. Wasn't he?"

Mike had been listening, but not really. He was realizing that people were starting to talk. He was thinking about seeing Kenny now because, how could he have implicated him?? He wasn't even around. Who could he have talked to. Bev? Correy? That other girl who was there? Who? Nobody knew!! He had something to do now. Get with Kenny.

"Uh, yeah, Russ, that was my nigga. I knew about all his shit, and then some. I still can't believe you tellin' me this. Look, I got to split. I got to find out some shit about this."

"Awright, Ice. I got to split too. I'm fittin' to hook up wit this girl that work in that hoagie shop right over there. So let me know something, okay?" He moved away from the car as Michael began to pull away from the curb. Michael was very focused, yet a little confused. He headed for Kenny's place of business. He decided to stop at the bar first and drop off a package to Phil, who was one of his workers. And Phil greeted him with yet another surprise.

"Ice? Hey! What's happening, man? Hey, what's this shit I hear about Greg?" he said all in one breath. "Kenny said you knew somethin' about it. What happened?" Mike was stunned. Thrown for a loop. His first response was anger.

"Man, you the second person that told me some shit like that. Where that little bitch at?"

"Hey, man, I just thought you might have heard something, thass all! What the fuck you at my throat for?" Phil had not expected this hostility.

"Hey, Rose," Mike called to the bar maid, trying to calm himself down now that he saw he was the center of attention "Gimme a tall Taylors and a Bud."

"Hi, Ice. Hi you doin?" she recalled back. "You want ice in it, right?" she responded while casually attempting to overlook his outburst.

"Yeah, baby, you know, but not a lot." He turned his attention back to Phil who was now looking at the juke box. "You know what? Let me tell you somethin', man. See, Kenny grew up with us in Germantown. Me and Greg and Juice and all us up this way. You just now gettin' to know a lot more people since you moved up here. But, anyway, Kenny always been part bitch. He always had that bitch blood and, see, he always been Maddie's close friend. You know Maddie? Right?"

"Yeah, Greg's sister. I know her." Phil never looked up from the jukebox.

"Right, well, Kenny always liked Greg you know? On the sly. But Kenny never liked me. Cause I didn't play his little bitch shit and I useta treat him just like the bitch he was. Make him do things for me and shit. He didn't like it. Anyway, I found out that him and Maddie used to go to these fly clubs and shit, and Kenny would psyche Maddie into gettin' these guys to talk to them so that he could get men to talk to him too. Sometime he even dressed up like a bitch."

"Wait a minute, what you mean? He used to dress up like a girl and go out with Maddie? Wow. That's deep."

"Deep? That shit's fucked up, man. Dig it. Kenny was gettin' his ass kicked regularly when these guys would find out that he had a dick big as theirs. That shit's crazy. But I used to laugh at his ass every time I seen him with a black eye or his lip busted and he knew that I knew what had happened to him, but I never told nobody either. I just liked fuckin' wit him. But anyway, thass why Kenny don't like me to today. He thought I was puttin' his business in the street and he thought I was tellin' Greg to watch out for his slick bitch shit, but Greg wasn't never about that noway and so he didn't give a fuck what Kenny thought about him! And neither did I. See, so now, I think he trying to start somethin' but see, Greg was my boy, my roadie."

The barmaid interrupted the conversation to position the drinks in front of Michael. "That's two-dollar, Ice. And

I heard about Greg. That's a shame. I know y'all was tight. Let me know when the funeral and stuff is, okay?"

"Yeah, thanks, Rose, but I'm just finding out about it myself and I'm trying to find out what the deal is here wit Kenny. He goin round tellin' people I got somethin' to do wit that shit. Here you go." He handed her a twenty-dollar bill, but as he pulled his money out of his pocket, he also pulled out the check that he had recovered from the floor of Gregory's parents house the day of the shooting. It slipped to the floor unnoticed along with a telephone number written on a piece of paper. Michael was so intent on keeping his composure going right and appropriate that he knew he had dropped something, but when he briefly looked at the floor, he saw nothing and didn't think about it again.

"I'll bring your change right back, Ice. I have to see if they have any in the back. We ain't did no business today."

"That's okay, sweetheart, you keep the change. You been good to me plenty times. All them girls you turned me on to. Shit, don't worry about it." Michael was feeling a little looser now. He knew that he and Rose would be together later that evening.

"So, um, yeah, Phil, Greg was my ace-boon-coon, from way back and I think Kenny tryin' to spread shit on me 'cause he don't like me. I'll fuck his little faggot ass up if I find out he done said one more thing about me."

"Hold it, Ice. I see what you sayin', but I think Kenny only meant to say that you bein' on the streets and all you mighta picked something up. That's what I thought he was sayin' anyway. I didn't know all that stuff you just told me." He was peering at Michael peculiarly now.

"Yeah, well, I know him better than you do, and I think he's up to something." Michael picked up his wine, drank it straight down, and put a napkin around his beer so he could carry it out less conspicuously. "Hey, look, I got to book, but get back to me on that other thing that I just gave you by about eleven, all right?" He glanced at Rose. "I'll probably be over at Rose's. You know where she live, don't you? Right there on Beechwood Street?"

"Yeah, you know I know where she live. I been there enough times. Awright, Ice, be cool!" Michael exited the bar in a haste. He was cool, smooth, but very intent, almost determined. He had something to do now for real! Find Kenny!!!

What Michael didn't know was that Phil was a very good friend of Gregory's also. He had pulled many stunts with Gregory in the past and he too was very distraught over his death. Very distraught because he was now left thoughtless and clueless as to how to continue the venture he and Gregory had begun. But since Phil lived in Pulaskitown, Gregory's association with him was confined mostly to the high-rise Projects and their immediate surroundings. What Michael knew was that Phil knew Gregory, but he never suspected they had been tight in college the one and only year they both attended Community College—or that Maddelyn had once been Phil's "side-thing" at one time. But what Michael didn't know was that Gregory also had talked to Phil about the tax refund scam he had planned to employ—because Michael never gave Gregory a chance to finish. And what Michael also did not know was that Rose had just spoken to Phil about her conversation with Kenny and Maddelyn the night before. And what Michael couldn't figure out was how Kenny had run into Russell. What did Kenny think he was doing by suggesting that he knew something about the murder?

He reached in his pocket, brought out his cocaine package and his gold coke spoon, and snorted some more. It was time for a hit.

Maddelyn

Kenny and Maddelyn had met about a half hour after Kenny's call. They both had a good cry over Greg's death and now were very much into trying to console each other. "Whoever did this to him, girl, I swear, they will be taken care of. You know what I mean, shoot, Greg ain't never did nothin' to nobody that he had to be killed, shot like a animal for. I know he gagged people and shit, but everybody knew that about him and besides he wouldn't have been with nobody if he didn't think he could trust them! You know what I mean? Shoooot!!"

"Yeah, Kenny, I know, I know, but you right, I don't think Greg was with somebody he didn't know either. Like you said, he knew that person. Whoever it was, he knew 'em, I'm sure of that!"

"So what are you two trying to do now? Solve the mystery?" chimed in Mr. Burks.

"Yeah, right, Daddy, somebody has to do it! You can't rely on the police to do it. You know damn well they ain't gone try but so hard. Greg wasn't nothin' but another nigga to them and they don't mind us killin' us. But, Daddy, look, Greg was not a gangster, you know? He was nickel slick and all that but not a real bad guy. He hated guns! I just don't know, but like me and Kenny have been thinking, whoever shot him knew him and he knew them or else they wouldn't have been here in the house! First of all."

"Maddie, I don't doubt that for a minute, honey. Me and your mother both said that when we first found out. But who? Who the hell would do this to him?? I just don't know. It don't make no sense."

"Mr. Burks, you know what?" said Kenny. "I think it was somebody that was real close to him. 'Cause you know why? 'Cause from what the police, Maddie, and yall said? Whoever it was didn't break in, see!! No. They had to come in with Greg!! And, they didn't leave right away, which leads me to believe they was in here talking for awhile a-a-a-and Greg might have pulled out some money or might have owed him some money or something and maybe got him mad and they got to the point where ... oh, I don't know, shoot, I don't know, but anyway, Greg ended up dead."

"Wait a minute," said Maddelyn. "Remember when Greg was sayin' that he had just discovered a way to get rich off the government and that he would tell us about it as soon as he got all the details? Well, I remember he mentioned this guy's name, Phil, who was supposed to be in on it with him. I used to mess around with him a long time ago, and I think maybe he may be able to answer a few questions."

"Ooh, ooh, Maddie! Phil?? I think I know who you talkin 'bout, you mean that real dark-skinned guy that just got out of jail? I know him and his fine self. He used to hang over Pulaskitown? I don't know him all that good, but I do know Rose who is working the bar down at Twenty-First and Church Lane, and I know he hangs in there a lot. You know what? You know what I'm gone do? I'm gonna get right to her and ask her if she would ask around and especially if that guy Phil comes in to see if he can find out something. Shoot, 'cause you know if him and Greg was about to do somethin sneaky, then they apparently had been in touch. Yeah, girl, I think you might of hit on to somethin' there with that one. Well, look, Maddie, Mr. and Mrs. Burks, I'm gonna get ready and leave now. I got choir rehearsal and stuff to do and it's gettin' late. I'm glad we got together and talked and, oh yeah, yall got most of the funeral arrangements together. Right? If I can do anything else to help, anything at all, just let me know, 'cause I will be more than happy to do it. Yall be strong and don't worry. We gone find out who did this, cause shoot, Greg did not deserve to die like that."

"Okay, Kenny, look, thanks." Maddie and Kenny hugged and exchanged good-byes. He hugged the parents as well and left. Then he came back to the door. Maddelyn didn't even have a chance to take a step away from it. She opened the door.

"Maddie, come out here, I want you to come with me."

"Where? Where you goin', Kenny?"

"Just come on, girl. I got a hunch I know somethin' and I bet you I'm right too."

"Wait a minute. Let me get my shoes on and what am I supposed to say to my mom? Oh, never mind, wait a minute."

"I'll be in the car. I'm right in front of Mr. Brooks's house. Hurry up, girl, for real, it's gettin' late and I got people to see and things—"

"Oh, shut up, Kenny. I'll be right out."

Maddelyn and Kenny got in his car and proceeded to the bar at Twenty-First and Churchlane. "Micky's Playhouse" was the name.

Goldie was the owner and Gregory used to go with Goldie's daughter Rayray and everybody around the neighborhood knew Gregory. And knew what Gregory was like and everybody accepted Gregory as he was. They liked him. Especially those in the bar. The regulars, they knew him well. Kenny knew that. And Kenny knew that was one of the best places to get started finding out information. He and Rose always got along well. He knew that he had turned Rose on to a few men that she wanted to get with and they seemed to communicate on a level that only they could relate to when they wanted to. And now he wanted to. He and Maddie arrived at the bar around 12:40 P.M. Not a lot of people in there. No music, nobody arguing, nobody on the pinball machine. Relatively dead on a Thursday.

"Hi, Rose. What you still doin' open? Ain't nothin' happenin' in this joint. Why ain't you closed up by now?" Kenny said jokingly as he was looking around the empty bar, "Darn. It's dead in here. Here, Maddie, you sit down here, shoot, ain't nobody even in this place," he remarked as he looked around at the empty stools.

"What you want, honey?" he asked Maddelyn.

"Oh, Kenny, I don't want anything to drink. I thought you were going to show me something or something. What did you bring me down here for? You know I don't—"

"Oh, shut up, girl, I forgot you don't like slummin'. Just sit down then and wait. I'll tell you. Rose?" He called to the barmaid who was still sitting at the other end of the bar talking to another young lady.

"Oh, I'm sorry, Kenny." She looked in their direction, seeming genuinely concerned that she had not recognized their presence. "What? What yall want? I'm sorry. I'm so busy runnin' my mouth I forgot all about yall. I didn't even ask yall what yall wanted. But yall was talkin' an' shit, so I . . . never mind. Okay! Can I get you something, dahling?" she said in an exaggerated voice.

"Yeah, dammit, me and my girlfrien' been sittin' here for ten minutes waitin' for yo ass . . . no, let me stop, I'm only kiddin'. Rose, hi you doin'?" He paused for a response.

"Not bad Kenny. What's new?"

And Kenny began. "Oh, you know Greg was killed, right? And you know Maddie, don't you? Greg's sister?"

"Wait a minute, Kenny!" Rose exclaimed "What? Greg? When? What? How did that happen??? Oh, Lord. What?? Noooo!! I ain't heard nothin like that. Oh, my Lord. Oh. Maddie. Yeah, I know, Maddie." She looked at Maddelyn now who was sitting next to Kenny.

"Hi, Rose. Yeah, Kenny, I knew Rose from when Greg used to go with her. She used to come to the house, I mean Greg used to sneak her in and tell me not to say anything. You remember that?" Maddie asked Rose.

"Shit yeah, but you used to seem so much older," Rose answered back, "I didn't even know if I should even say anything to you or not. I used to think you was stuck-up or older or somethin' at first, but after you started helpin' us get past those creaky floors, then I knew you was alright." They both laughed, then Madelyn added to the story.

"There you go. Those floors were creaky as hell. You know what? Not only did I help yall get past those creaky floors late at night or early in the morning, whichever it was, but Greg helped me out a few times too." They all began laughing and talking about Greg and the "good-ole-times."

It was close to closing time, two o'clock. And the girl who had been sitting at the other end of the bar had finally exposed the fact that she was sloppy drunk now and had begun to stagger towards the door that seemed to move each time she attempted to go out of it.

"See you, Gwen. You be careful, now, honey, Oops. You alright??" Rose was showing mock concern for the inebriated young woman as she bounced off the door frame. "That bitch is fucked up! Look. That bitch can't even find the door, she fallin' all over the place, look, Oh, shit, Gwen, you alright? Look!" She continued to goad Kenny and Maddelyn to watch. "That maafucka can't even find the gotdamn door. Gwen? Gwen? Kenny, will you please help her ass out?" Kenny moved to aid the young drunk.

"Gwen, darlin', you alright?" he said to her.

"Um awright, um awright, thanks, hon um cool. I just fucked up on that last step um cool." She made it past the door this time and out. They all began laughing uncontrollably at her final exit, but they continued looking at the door not knowing what to expect.

"Now," Kenny straightened up, "Rose, before you close, I want you to do me a big favor, okay? Me and my girlfriend here been talkin', and we think that this guy Phil, you know Phil, that real black fine guy," he threw his head back to show extreme pleasure "that come in here all the time? I think he just got outta jail! Well, anyway, he was gettin' ready to do somethin' with Greg, you know, pull some kinda con or something, but, anyway, I want you to do me a favor and see if you can find out uh ... how big his dick is?" They were caught off guard by his comment, but after a second they realized he was joking and they laughed. "No. I'm only kiddin'. For real though. I want you to see, to kinda look out, and see if maybe, he knows anything about Greg's death. Anything! You know what I mean?" Maddelyn didn't feel that Kenny was being explicit enough for Rose to understand what was being asked of her.

"Rose?" Maddelyn chimed in. "Look. We think that somebody close to Greg killed him because of a lead we have and we know that Phil and Greg were planning to try one of their little schemes and—"

"That's what I said, Maddie." Kenny was looking at Maddie as though he couldn't believe what she was doing and he didn't feel it was necessary.

"Oh, shut up, Kenny, ain't nobody sayin you didn't say that," said Rose, "Maddie knows what she's talkin about too." Rose came to Maddelyn's aid in the discussion and looked at Kenny while she lambasted him and then back to Maddie. "Excuse me, Maddie, but I hear what you sayin' and I'll definitely keep my ears open and see if I can find out somethin'. You know Greg was awright wit me, he wasn't worth a shit, but I loved him and, uh, I just can't believe it. Damn!! Greg dead!! When yall find out somethin', yall let me know too!!" The conversation went on about Greg's death and how everybody was suspect, but they finally parted after getting a good understanding about what was to transpire.

"And look, Rose. You make sure that Phil knows what we talkin' about, 'cause I don't put nothin' past him either, but if things are like you say, then let Phil know to play it like on a low key tip and tell him to feel people out, you know tell him to say shit and watch and see how people act you know, see how they respond."

"Okay, okay, Kenny. I know how to act. You ain't the only one that pick up on shit." She looked at Maddie and laughed. Maddie laughed too.

"No. She right, Kenny. I could tell she knew what you were talking about and you didn't have to treat her like she was dumb."

"Oh, no. I didn't mean t—." Both women cut him short and they left.

Evelyn

It seems Evelyn had always been around. Although she didn't move there until she was fifteen, she was a staple in the heart of this neighborhood. Even though she didn't grow up in that neighborhood. She knew everybody, everybody knew her. Especially the men. She had always catered to the men as though she were obligated to them. As though she owed the male population a debt that she must pay and keep on paying. Like it was her duty to please. She'd been a heroin addict and she'd been a prostitute, and she'd been a pain in the ass to everyone who had known her and tried to help her. She'd been a user and she'd been used, well. Drugs had pervaded her life. Tricking had become a way of life for her. She did it for the money so she could buy drugs and booze. She turned tricks for herself when she was not tricking for Michael and giving him all the money. She liked sex anyway. Someone told her that she had sex so much because she had a white liver. She believed them.

At this stage of her life, she was trying to find herself, for real. She knew that she was on a mission to find herself for real this time. She'd been found before and she'd been lost before, but this time she was bound to stay found. Evelyn had been trying to find herself for a long time and now she knew she had to do it. Ever since she ran away from home, twelve years ago, to get away from her abusive father, she had been grappling with her self-image as a woman. In a way, she had a lot of pride about herself, always had. And she'd always had very high standards about life and how it was to be lived. She knew that she had a level of moral dignity that rivaled few. She just didn't practice it. She knew that she was confused though. She dropped her pride frequently and she lowered her level of moral dignity at will. And she didn't like that about herself. She knew that she needed help. Right now she was overwhelmed with something that was tormenting her. She couldn't put it out of her mind that she had probably been witness to a crime. A crime she knew that she had to do something about.

This particular night she was torn between getting high or doing the right thing. Usually when she had that choice, she got high and ended up doing the same thing. Having a bad night and a worse day the next day. And not giving a damn until it registered to her brain. Strangely, tonight, she was drawn in another direction. She'd been looking for someone to talk to. Talk to someone. She made herself stay on that track, even though something within her told her to go pull a trick and make some money and get that high, she forced herself to stay put and find somebody to talk to. Somebody who would help her do the right thing.

"Vet!! Good, Vet! I'll call her," she thought aloud to herself. And she did. The phone rang twice and she wanted to hang it up, three times and Vet answered on the third ring.

"Hello?" answered Vet. Evelyn didn't say anything. "Hello? Who's there?"

Evelyn started to hang up, but her mouth started moving. "Vet?" she finally answered back.

"Hello? Who is this?" queried Yvette.

"Vet? This is Evelyn. I'm sorry to bother you but I, uh, I thought maybe you might be home and, well, I thought I could talk to you." She could no longer control how she felt. She burst out crying and hung up the phone.

"Now why the hell did I do that?" she asked herself. "See, girl. You don't want no help." She slowly stopped her sobbing, began to reach for her sweater, and head for the door. Yvette was left holding the receiver and was totally displaced by the episode. But she knew Evelyn and she knew Evelyn needed her.

"Lord. What was that all about?" She was perplexed. "What is that girl's number?" she lamented as she searched for her address book. "Oh!" she remembered. And she frantically dialed the number. Three rings. Four, five, finally the silence was broken. "Hello?" the quivering voice answered.

"Evelyn? Evelyn? What's the matter? Don't hang up!! What is wrong? This is Yvette! You called me and hung up on me. I am so—don't hang up, I'm so worried."

"Vet, oh, Vet, I'm glad you called me back 'cause if you didn't— "She was no longer sniffling and sobbing, but there was remorse in her voice. "Cause if you didn't, I know just what I would have done."

"Evelyn! Calm down, baby. I'm glad I called back too. Are you all right? Is everything okay now?"

"Yeah, yeah. It's okay but I just need to talk to somebody. I got a problem. Well, I got a lot of problems. But I got a big one this time and I just don't know how to handle it or what to do." Yvette was listening intently now, trying to get a sense of where this was going. She knew from past experiences that Evelyn was adept at conning her. Out of money or sympathy or whatever. And she knew now that sometimes she was too quick to go with the con only to realize that she'd been had once again. This time she was skeptical. Determined that she was not going to be caught up so quick this time.

"What is it this time, Evelyn?" she asked, as if annoyed but still really ready to sympathize and help if this call proved true.

"Well, you know I'm pregnant, right?"

"By Michael right?" Yvette responded, "Well, you did tell me that you thought you were pregnant a while ago, but you weren't sure then. And I guess now you are. Is that it? Is that's what's bothering you?"

"No. No, listen it's a lot worse than that. Uh, well anyway, a couple days ago me and Michael had a argument and he said he wasn't gonna take care of the baby unless I worked the streets again for him. I'm tired of that shit, Vet. You know. I been doing that shit for a long time, Vet, and I'm just plain tired. Well, anyway. the next day, I borrowed this guy's ole raggedy car and I was goin' down the street where Greg's parents live and I saw his car parked out front. So I thought he might be in there and I could maybe talk to him to try to get him to talk to Michael for me. You know?? You know, me and Greg always been like brother and sister. You know? He give me money and stuff, but it ain't like he tryin' to get something for it or nothin' he just cool wit me like that. We can talk. And I help him out sometime when I can too. Well, anyway, I went up to the door and knocked, but nobody came, so I left and went back to the car and the damn car wouldn't start. So I just sat there, you know, tryin' to wait and see if it would start back up after a minute.

"So anyway, I had just looked up in the rearview mirror, thinking maybe Greg had come back or something 'cause I didn't think he could have gone very far with his car parked out there and so I looked up and saw Michael getting into Greg's car and he was by hisself. So I ducked down to make double sure that he didn't see me, you know? 'Cause I didn't know what he would do. He act so crazy sometime. So anyway, I waited till he left and made sure he was gone for real and then I went back up to the house and knocked again. And still nobody answered. I knocked for a while, then gave up and when I got back to the car this time, it started up and so I pulled off. Well, anyway, I had went past the bar yesterday and somebody had came in and was saying that they had heard that Greg had got killed. I saw faggett Kenny in there too, come to think of it. This fucked me up!! You know? And I stopped to listen, but they didn't say no more about it, but, and I got goose pimples. I mean I got scared and I thought, *Damn, I just was lookin' for him!!* You know? Then I thought, *When I was sitting there waitin' for the car to start? I had heard three, like, pops. You know? They had sounded like firecrackers, but I didn't pay it no mind then. But now I'm thinking. They was gun shots!!* Oh, shit, I'm thinkin' something really foul happened to Greg while I was there and..." she paused. "Guess who else was there?"

Yvette was stunned at this revelation. "Michael!!!" she accurately guessed. "Ooooo, Evelyn, are you sure? I mean, are you sure you heard gunshots?? Oooooh, but wait a minute, Evelyn, how do you know for sure that the story you heard about Greg is true? You know?? How can you be certain that it was the same Greg you are talking about?? I mean, there is more than one Gregory in the world, you know!! Let me ask you this. Have you tried to get back in touch with him since?" Yvette tried to be objective before jumping to conclusions and especially before getting caught up in one of Evelyn's wild imaginings. Because she knew Evelyn could get paranoid and real stupid when she wanted to. She had a way of distorting the truth. She made up stuff, invented her own little stories. "You should check out the story first before you go assuming it's true. Don't you think so? Huh??"

Evelyn was quite now, then she spoke softly. "Yeah. Yeah, I guess you're right, but if it's true then—"

"Wait a minute now, Evelyn," Yvette cut in. "Why don't you and I go talk to Maddie or Kenny or somebody or even better, let's go to Greg's parents' house. I know where they live. On Bouvier Street. Right? We can go over there ourselves and check it out first, and then we both will know for sure. Because I don't want to get myself all worked up over something like somebody getting killed and then it turn out to be a stupid mistake or something. What time is it?" She looked at her own watch and continued. "Look, it's early yet, why don't you come pick me up and we could go now?" thinking that Evelyn still had access to a car.

"But I don't have the car no more. I gave it back already. Besides, it don't half work good noway."

"Okay, then I'll get Snuff and he can take us both over. Okay? Oh, by the way did you know him and Terry had their baby?" Evelyn was only half listening now. Her assurance at what she thought she may have known was now getting weaker and not seeming as important.

"Oh, yeah? What did they have?" she halfheartedly answered back, not really wanting to know.

"A girl. and they named her Adrian Shantell, but they all call her Dray. I seen her too and she is adorable. Oh, child, she is precious. Got the prettiest eyes and such a beautiful smile. She is one of the prettiest babies you have ever seen. I think she looks more like Terry, but everybody else thinks she favors him; you have got to see her. Oh, yeah, and they just moved into this cute little apartment up there in Mount Airy. Yeah, child, way up there where them white people used to live. But I hear more and more of us is moving up there now, you know how them white people do, soon as a few of us get a little money and want something better than ghetto life and we decide to move where they are, they up and move somewhere else. Well, let me call him and see if he's there. If he's there I know he not doing anything but sitting around or talking to Junior and his other friends and Terry's probably cooking dinner or cleaning up or something, you know how she is. But I'll call you back and let you know when we'll be by there for you. Okay?"

"Okay," Evelyn said. "I'll be here. Okay bye."

After Evelyn hung up, she got a strange feeling. She began to feel as though she wanted to get away and not find out what happened at all. She felt that she didn't even want to know. This was too serious. Maybe she wouldn't be able to handle the truth. She now had to decide if she was going to be here when Yvette called back. After very little thought she decided, no, she wouldn't. She decided to leave. Now. Where to?? She decided that she could go to West Philadelphia to her playsister's house and stay there for a while. She felt very uneasy as she headed out of the door. No change of clothes, nothing but her pocketbook. She headed for the subway at Broad and Olney. She could walk there, as it was right around the corner and besides, she needed to walk and think this thing over again. Things were moving just a little too fast for her. She decided she needed to slow down a little now. As she picked up her pocketbook, she went for her wallet and began checking to see how much money she had just in case she may want to get a little something to take with her to West Philly. After very little thought, she decided that, yes, it would be better if she did that, go get something to slow her down. Things were moving too fast. God knows she needed to slow down.

Kenny

Kenny was in the process of parking his car. He had just left Maddelyn's after dropping her off and talking for another forty-five minutes about what they felt about life and death and their fears and coming to grips with death and how they both didn't fear it.

Kenny never heard the sound of the gun. But for a fleeting moment, he heard glass shatter and he felt a most excruciating pain and some strange, sharp particles of something in his mouth, then, this awful burning sensation in his tongue. His first thought was to continue parking the car, but this new intense sensation was overwhelming him at the same time. He was becoming disoriented and very, very confused as to what was happening. *The car is not acting right!!* his mind told him. His eyesight was becoming distorted, and he was beginning to lose sight of what was in front of him. The car veered out of control and into an on coming car as he attempted to pull out for a better backup. It happened just as he had decided to pull the car out of the parking spot again to get closer to the curb.

The first bullet tore into his lower left jawbone, shattering it. It destroyed his wisdom teeth on that side of his mouth as it continued through to lodge into his gum on the right side of his mouth . . . severing his tongue on the way. The second bullet just caught the tip of his nose and took it off. Kenny lost consciousness and had flopped onto the steering wheel with his tongue dangling out of his mouth, hanging only by a shred of skin and bleeding profusely.

That was how the man who was driving the car that Kenny's car was now plowed into, found him. The man was amazed at the amount of damage he thought had been done by this accident. He could not believe it.

"How the hell did that window get shattered like that?" he wondered aloud. Then he noticed the small holes in the shattered window. Upon closer inspection he saw that the holes appeared to be caused by bullets. He panicked, looked around and quickly got back into his car, and backed away from Kenny's car. He kept on backing down to the little street that intersects with Sixteenth Street, made a U-turn, and disappeared into the night. In the meantime, Kenny began to regain consciousness.

His vision slowly coming back, he focused on his feet, the brake pedal and the floor of the car. He realized he was still in a car and now was peering through something and looking at the floor of the car. This struck him as funny for a fleeting moment but just as quick the pain in his face informed him that this was no laughing matter. He lifted his head up off the steering wheel. He now saw that this, the steering wheel, was what he had been peering through. He had to pull his head out from between the bars that make up the steering wheel and as he did so, he felt something wet lightly slap him on the side of his cheek. He instinctively reached to grab it and at the same time, to spit out these foreign particles from his mouth. He grabbed the wet thing and pulled it. It made a slight resistance but came off in his hand.

What the fuck? he thought. He was dumbfound at what he saw he was holding. He couldn't quite make out what it was, but he knew it was part of him. *Enough of this.* he thought. He was thinking more clearly, but he was in shock and was beginning to move as if by compulsion. He was thinking, but it was dislocated and scrambled. He transferred the thing in his right hand to his left hand and shifted the gear into drive. The car was pulling but not going anywhere because the fender was caught onto the car that was parked in front of him from when he was trying to park.

"What??" he said. He knew he checked out everything, but had to look again. He saw what was preventing his forward motion and backed up. He could see the lights from the hospital just over the hill. He put the car in gear and headed for them. The car swerved out and back onto the street as he fought the feeling to panic. He continued to make himself drive despite the ungodly pain he felt and the blood that he had been trying to ignore all the while.

"Damn, what the heck happened? I didn't even do nothin." He was disoriented but trying to bring himself out of it. He got to the gates of the hospital and something in his mind told him it was okay to let go and he lost consciousness again.

The car continued to roll through the gates, onto the grass, and into one of the columns of the hospital front entrance. The guard had been standing outside, smoking a cigarette, and had watched the careening car head towards him. He had run into the building and was calling for help. Help arrived almost immediately after the car crashed.

Kenny was removed from the car, onto a stretcher, and into the emergency room. As he was being prepped for surgery, one of the interns noticed his hand.

"What's that in his hand?" he asked as they entered the receiving room. Another of the interns groped and peeled it from his hand.

"Damn, I don't know! It looks like a piece of his tongue. As he was explaining his finding, he was looking at the swollen, bloody mass that now was substituting for

Kenny's face. He pulled open the horribly swollen bottom lip, only to discover his guess was right.

"It's his tongue!!" He looked around as if it was unbelievable, "He must've bit it off when he had the accident. Shit. His teeth are all broken up in his mouth." He began to try to recover the larger particles as he was thinking that they could very well cut up his insides and further complicate matters. This was his first head trauma and he was frantically trying to put together his medical school training, unable to take his eyes off the piece of tongue in his hand.

"Tilt his head to the side," said a voice, "and use your fingers to clear the airway. We don't want to obstruct his breathing, and Nurse?" Another intern had arrived and took charge and was speaking to the nurse closest to Kenny's head. "Check his vital signs and keep a close check on them because we don't want him to go further into shock. He's already in shock trauma and probably had no idea he was driving. And, Doctor, this injury is not the result of an accident! This man's been shot."

Juice

Vance and Dennis had informed Jouscar that they had made the connection and were on their way to take Jouscar his package. They had made the run across the bridge without Jouscar and had met Michael themselves. Michael was Jouscar's cocaine supplier, and they had a predisposed meeting place in Camden for conducting their business. Jouscar had instructed Vance and Dennis to handle the transaction themselves because he was busy. Busy enjoying his favorite pastime. Sex.

He called himself the "indoor sportsman," and he reveled in his capacity to maintain a constant flow of competition. Tonight he was with Ellena. Ellena Woodson, one of his clients who was trying to better her investments with ASCOTT INC. She only saw Jouscar when she thought it would benefit her. All of her men were successful in one way or another.

"Curt? I thought you said we was going to get high? You ain't brought nothin out yet but your dick, and now that's soft and I ain't about to start on it again." She taunted playfully. Jouscar knew that he still wanted to have more sex, although they just finished a short session.

"Baby! Baby! Relax!!" he consoled her as he reached for her inner thigh with his hand.

"Just wait a few more minutes. My boys should be here any minute. Besides! Why you so worried about that shit? Here." He lowered his head to her thigh and she fell back onto the pillow where she had just propped herself up on her elbows.

"Oh, Curt, damn, I was lookin for—" his mouth began moving and his tongue was moving, both slowly. Slowly toward what he knew to be her pleasure spot. She relaxed her body and allowed herself to fall into that same stupor she always fell into when she knew she was about to be done. Curt felt the relaxation in her thighs and peered up from his position to see her closing her eyes and placing her arm over her forehead. He noticed that her lips had curled now to form that expression that always let him know that she was like pudding now. Ready to be shaped and molded and consumed in sex. He shifted his body so that he was now between her thighs. He used his hands to gently push them apart to make room for his upper torso. He gingerly lifted the left thigh up and onto his shoulder and traced his tongue along the inner portion. She let loose a moan and reached for his head to pull it closer to that pleasure spot, but he resisted.

"Hey, what you trying to do, smother me?" He looked up at her from her lower regions.

"Oh, Curt, don't play with me." She had gotten into a feeling of passion that had now overcome her and she was not wanting to be gamed. Curt sensed this in the tone of her now coarse and sultry voice. He turned his head again to her pleasure source and moved his fingers to the lips of her vagina and his tongue to her clitoris. She responded violently, as if she had no control of her actions. Her legs moved to enclose his head so tight that he had to push with force to continue his performance. He grabbed her buttocks and pulled it flush to his mouth. She was moving now to her own sexual melody and had found the tune that made her sing out. Jouscar heard the music and continued to do what he had been doing to make her croon. He enjoyed this song and tried to make it last, but she couldn't stand it and her juices flowed as she insanely and forcefully had to push his head away.

"Oh, shit! Stop! Oh, shit. Put it in, put it in!!" she demanded. Curt was erect and wanton also, but knew how to keep the moment. He continued to try to lick and suck and kiss her as he had been doing but she adamantly warded him off. He smiled to himself as he began to position his body so that he was squarely between her supple thighs while making his way to put his you know what into you know where. He let his stiffness linger between the lips of her you know what just at the point of insertion. She was burning and didn't let this happen very long. She reached down with a motion that allowed her to grip his back with one hand and grip his penis with the other. Pulling, pushing, straining, the whole time until she had his penis pointed where she wanted it, and it was making its way deep within her.

"OOOOO, OOOOO," she was loud and uncaring. "Oh, shit! You feel so good." But this loud talking was no turn-on to Jouscar. He put his hand over her mouth only to have her quickly begin to suck on his fingers. He began to stroke her methodically at first. His hands placed evenly on either side of her slender body so as to evenly distribute the weight of his 6'5" muscular body. Caught up in the passion, he could now ignore her moans and loud utterances. He found that spot within her that "he" wanted and went for it. She allowed him his freedom. He reached climax and began to hear himself uttering just as loudly as she was and now she was trying to cover his mouth with her hand. He panted and gasped and pushed himself up to look into her eyes. They both began to laugh. He collapsed onto her body.

"No, No!! You got to get off me." They both were still laughing and gasping for breath. He tried to roll over but couldn't because he was spent, exhausted and laughing. She gathered her strength and pushed with all her might and had him off of her body. His hand, though, traveled back to her vaginal region and began to move along her clitoris.

"Oh, no, you don't. OOOOOH, Oh, no, you gone stop this foolishness." It was all she could do to push herself away from his still pulsating body looking at his still erect penis spilling semen onto his leg and onto the sheet.

"Look!! Look what you doin'?? Why you still coming? Look!! You making the sheet and everything wet !! Get up. Move!! Never mind, you just lay there and—look at the sheet!! Why you got to mess the sheet up every time you do it?? Get over, move." She wriggled herself to the edge of the bed and tried to stand up.

"Whoooo!! Damn!! My knees is knockin!! I can't even stand up straight." She flopped back onto the bed, giggling. Jouscar flipped over laughing hysterically.

"Oh, shit!! Oh, my god. I done buckled your knees." He was taunting her now because he knew she didn't always like to make it known when he had pleased her, when he had satisfied her. She realized what was taking place now.

"Oh, shut up! You ain't did shit. Don't try to think you did something, nigga!! I just was still a little tired from workin' yo ass and makin' you lose track of what you was—"

"Hold it, hold it!" Jouscar suddenly sat up and focused as if he was straining to hear.

"Shhhhh!" He heard what he thought he heard, the doorbell. "Hold it! Go wash your ass and get dressed." He commandingly directed her. She was still naked and poised on the side of the bed, but obeyed instantly, reaching for the robe on the chair in front of her.

"Who is it?" she inquired. Jouscar just glanced at her as he slipped his shorts over his still partially erect penis. He looked back at her again.

"You see this shit?" He was pointing at the protrusion in his shorts, "You ain't finished with me yet, baby! How the hell am I supposed to walk with this shit like this??" They both laughed. He continued towards the door. The protrusion subsided. He peered through the peep hole. "Who is it?" he demanded, but he clearly saw it was Vance with Dennis standing behind him, Vance looking directly into the peephole and Dennis holding the outer door and looking behind him.

"It's Vance, man. Me and Dennis. Open the door!" Jouscar glanced at his underwear, noticed a wet spot, and covered it with his hand. Opening the door to allow them to enter, he directed both men to have a seat, insuring them that he would be back as he headed toward the bathroom, hand cupped firmly on his groin area. He opened the now closed bedroom door, and had his finger pressed to his lips, indicating that he wanted the young lady, who had now covered herself, to be silent.

"It's the blow!! Shhhhh. You wait here. I got to take care of this business. Don't even bother to get dressed." He flashed his smile that he thought was his best and slipped on his pants that were lying on the floor at the foot of the bed. Ellena smiled and motioned that she understood and waved him off. He turned and opened the door, closing it behind him.

"What we got, fellas?" His eyes shifted back and forth from one to the other of the two men in the room.

Vance, the taller of the two, spoke up. "Hey um, uh, Mr. Jouscar. We sorry to interrupt you. We didn't mean to break up nothin—" Jouscar waved a hand and acknowledged the intended apology like a man who knows the drill.

"Naw, Naw." He squinted at him. "Yall ain't breakin' up nothin'!"

He changed his voice diction to what he considered to be acceptable to the men he was talking to. Jouscar knew that these men were familiar with the streets and he was comfortable talking with them on what he considered to be "their level." He had always adapted to this style when talking to Vance and Dennis and anybody else he had stereotyped as "hoodlums."

"Man, don't worry bout that shit. What yall got for me??" Vance had always thought that Jouscar looked down on him and had always played him accordingly. He knew that Jouscar thought he was "the shit." But it didn't really bother him. He knew that Jouscar paid them well. And it wasn't as if they was kissing his ass.

"Can we pull it out here??" Vance inquired respectively.

"Yeah, yeah. Let's see what we got here. How much yall get?" Before they could answer, "How the fuck much did yall spend?" He threw a serious look at them both.

"This here a ounce," Vance answered quickly. "Ice had said you wanted a Z right? So we gave him eight-hundred." Vance looked at Dennis and Dennis spoke up.

"Ice said he had already talked to you about the money," Dennis added and looked straight at Jouscar."

"That maafucka told me he ain't have that much," Jouscar retorted, as if displeased. Vance shifted in his seat as if readying for a conflict.

"Well, he said you would understand. He knew you wanted a good bit. Is it a problem?"

Jouscar looked at the sizable amount of the product in the plastic bag and looked up at the two men.

"No. No. Everything's cool. I'll get wit Ice later. What I owe yall??" Vance quickly looked at Dennis and back to Jouscar.

"Nothin, Mr. Jouscar!! Maybe a ball of that blow. That would be okay by us. Right, Den?"

Dennis smiled and responded. "Shit, yeah. That's cool!! We can work wit dat!! But, um, Mr. Jouscar? Um, one thing we noticed bout Ice. He was upset about something when we saw him over in Camden at the motel. He acted like he was high, or fucked up or somethin'. He wasn't actin' right. He didn't count the money right, an' shit and, he was sweatin' an shit and I don't know, he just wasn't cool. You know?? Me and Van both noticed it and we spoke on it. He tried to tell us that he had just took care of some business. But he was acting nervous an—"

"Me and Den think you should check him out," Vance butted in.

"Naw, Curt. What happened was, he lunched, and he dropped a whole Z on the floor and didn't even know it. He was so busy fuckin' wit that gotdamn gun he always carry and fiddllin' wit it puttin' in his pocket den puttin' it in his belt and shit, man. Dennis hipped me to the fact that it was laying on the floor and the bitch had rolled under the coffee table. And when I dug it, I told Dennis to pick that motherfucka up and put it in his pocket. Me and Dennis think he might of just stuck somebody up for it. We don't know, he just was acting weird."

Jouscar was very much involved in what he was being told now and was directing all his attention to the two men he had been talking to. He no longer was conscious of the status that he felt between them.

"Hold it. You mean Ice dropped a whole ounce? And didn't know it? And yall left and he still didn't know he did that shit?" Everybody was looking at one another. Jouscar was flabbergasted.

"Thass right! We got it right here." Dennis produced a plastic bag wrapped in a rubber band and exposed a good quantity of a white substance, purportedly to be cocaine. "Look," Vance assumed a serious look on his face and poised himself to stare directly into Jouscar's face. "I don't know what's goin' down, but me and my man here, think Ice done did somethin shady wit dis shit. You know? But, um, look we respect you enough to let you know that we think you should watch your back with that crazy mothafucka, cause, um , somethin definetly wrong! Das what we talkin about!!" Jouscar felt out of control. He was lost. He didn't know what to say.

Vance rose first, followed by Dennis; they both strolled towards the door, Vance opened it and motioned Dennis to go ahead of him; he looked back at Jouscar who had merely begun watching the movements of the two as they made their way for the door, and said, knowingly, sarcastically, "Better watch yo ass, man. Somethin up wit dat guy?" Vance closed the door and the two men walked to the sidewalk and poised in front of the car to talk.

Jouscar popped up and peered out of the blinds to see this and quickly closed them back. He didn't know what to make of the situation; he did know that he felt betrayed, somehow. He felt dumb, out of control. He sat back down on the couch and tried to replay what happened. He felt like he had lost control. As he sat in his confusion, he heard Ellena calling to him.

"Curt?" he heard the sexy voice calling to him, but his mind had been blown. He couldn't assimilate the sex thing now.

He angrily hollered back, "Wait a minute, girl!! Don't be fuckin' with me now. I'll be in there in a few. Just shut the fuck up." Curt's mind was blown. He had a lot to piece together.

In the meantime, Ellena had dressed herself anyway despite Jouscar's directive to stay put and was walking out of the room toward Jouscar as he sat in a stupor.

"Hey, uh, look, honey, I got to split, but can I just take a little of this stuff and be on my way?" She unwrapped the package and spilled quite a bit of it in a bag that she had in her hand. Jouscar was not paying her any attention.

"Oh, and don't forget to draw up those papers for me. I really would like to get started on that deal that you promised me. Okay?" She had been moving and talking the entire time and had now worked her way to the door and was primping in the mirror as she turned to say goodnight.

Jouscar looked up. "Wait a minute. Where you going? I thought you wanted to do something?" He was too late. She was out the door now. Pleased with the night's take and consciously ignoring him.

His thoughts turned to the plastic bag sitting open before him and where Michael may have gotten it from.

Yvette

Her brother was home and agreed to drive her and Evelyn to Maddelyn's parents' house where they could confirm or dispel the truth about Gregory's death, as the case may be.

"Now, don't take all day, boy. I know how you are. A half hour gone by and you still haven't left! Now come on!! Yvette was still on the phone with Snuff, who's real name is Glenn, Glenn Jr." He did arrive in about fifteen or twenty minutes and found Yvette at the door of her apartment. She lived directly on the corner of Upsal Street and could see the cars pull up from either Upsal Street or Thouron Avenue. She quickly turned off the lights and the hi-fi, locked the door to her apartment and was down the steps to meet him.

"Dag, Vet. How long you been standing there waitin??" he quipped sarcastically. He knew that Yvette was prompt and organized and often teased her because she was so structured.

"HO," he laughed, "I just called your house and your answering machine said, 'THE WAGES OF SIN ARE DEATH, BUT THE GIFT OF GOD, IS ETERNAL LIFE. GOD HAS A WONDERFUL PLAN FOR YOU.'" He couldn't remember the rest but he continued, "Why your machine got to be so deep?"

"Oh, shut up, stupid! First of all I can see you or anybody else for that matter, coming, because I can see out of both sides of my apartment windows. And second of all, *you, above all, should know what I'm saying*. You heard it enough when we were growing up. Now just let's come on," she continued as she pushed him ahead of her.

"Where we goin'??" he asked. "I don't even know where we goin'." He really didn't know.

"We are going to Clearfield Street. To Evelyn's house. You know where that is? Don't you?" Yvette glared back. "Over there by the Esquire Movie Theater. And I know you know where that is."

"Oh, yeah, yeah. I definitely know where that is. Why didn't you just say that? Shoooot. I used to stinkfinger all my babes in there, I got babes all around that neighborhood. Matter-of-fact, I got this little honey that live right on Clearfield, but she down a little further from Evelyn though."

"You are so nasty," she disgustedly let him know.

As they continued towards their destination, Yvette revealed to her brother what Evelyn had revealed to her.

"So what she trying to say? That she think Ice offed him?? No way!! Them two is thick as thieves, Vet! If he dead, that is. Naw, wait a minute, they tight like this." He gestured by crossing his middle finger over his index finger and continued to assert his feelings. "That's bullcrap."

"Oh, you don't know no more than nobody else, so just shut up." Yvette intervened, "God has a way of bringing the truth to the light, so don't you try to think you can outthink him. We'll know soon enough." Snuff had to agree.

"Yeah, you right, you right. Hold it, ain't that her crib right there where all that trash and stuff is?" He pointed to a really crummy house on the left side of the street. "Oh no, that's right," he corrected himself, "She live on this side." He swerved to park on the other side of the street in front of Evelyn's house. Yvette was looking up and down and on either side of the house. She was not sure.

"You sure this is it, Snuff?" She knew to double check her brother.

"Yeah, Vet! I'm sure." He couldn't stand the fact that she did this to him. "Just go on up the porch and ring the bell—that probably don't even work!" he said with a smirk. He joked a lot. He's was a joker. She knew it and glared at him out of her peripheral. "Better yet," he continued, "just put your hand through the broken glass in the door and just turn the knob and—"

"Oh, shut up! You are *so* stupid. I swear." She again looked at him with mock disgust but did indeed notice the shambles the house was in. Old flyers and newspapers, milk bottles, milk crates, dirt and tin cans cluttered up the porch area she was approaching. Most of the windows were broken or cracked or not in at all. Sheets or covers or something were hanging in the bedroom windows intended to prevent people from seeing in. The front door was barely hanging on the hinges. No screen door and—there was no bell. Yvette stepped up on to the porch and just as she was about to take another step towards the door, something scrambled up from the mess and dashed past her feet. She screamed out and instinctively threw her hands up to grab either side of her face as she attempted to shrink away while frantically looking around her feet and everywhere else her little eyes could find to look.

Well, Snuff was just breaking up laughing at this scene. It was more than just funny to him, when he saw his sister taken out of her structured, organized composure. It was hilarious. He loved it. He couldn't stop laughing. The scene played over in his visual mind and kept him laughing and rocking side to side, front to back, clapping his hands. She regained her composure, relaxed her hands, and untensed her petite body when she realized that it was merely a cat. She glared at the cat who was now also glaring up at her from the pavement. Then she succumbed to her vulnerability and looked at Snuff, who was still laughing quite hard.

She turned her body to look full at him, hands on hips. The moonlight was strong and was reflecting very softly off her golden skin. It made her appear to glow. She was radiant, as it was, but the moonlight exaggerated her brown skinned beauty. She herself began to laugh, then. Now that she'd come to grips with reality.

"Oh, shut up, stop it, Snuff. It wasn't all that funny." But she really did think it was funny. She knew that her structure broke and her organized demeanor got scattered revealing what she knew he already knew. That she was sensitive, yet strong and able to express emotion without a problem. That she could be vulnerable sometimes and not so self-righteous as she may seem to be.

She took her attention off the experience and Snuff, and proceeded cautiously this time, to the door. She knocked, waited a few seconds, peered in through the broken glass. No answer. Again, she knocked and waited and peered. Again, no answer. She pushed the door in a little to allow her upper body to lean in and holler.

"Hello???" She could see into the dimly lit living room. "Evelyn?? It's me, Yvette. You here?" She got the idea. Evelyn's not there. She began to feel uneasy though, backed out of the house, turned to Snuff, who now was looking hard at her and the door.

"Hey, Snuff! You sure this is where she lives?" He reassured her once again that it was the right house. "Okay. Well, she's not here then. Where could she be?? She knows I was coming. Come on, Snuff, take me around the block and let's see if we see her in the street. I know her, see, I know what she's trying to do now."

She was puzzled, but almost sure she knew where to find her. She directed the driver to go down Eighteenth Street and head towards Boyer Street. They both were looking as they rode. Snuff spotted her walking briskly towards the bar, which was two blocks away yet. He headed towards her and came to a stop in the middle of the street at the same spot in the block where she was.

"Hey, girl!!" he playfully yelled at her. She stopped and looked very alarmed at the car.

"Oh!! Darn, Glenn. You scared me." She was startled and was standing very still looking at the person in the car. She recognized the brown Nova. She was holding her hand to her heart and smiling as she spoke. At this point Yvette popped out of the car.

"And just where do you think you're going young lady?? Huh? You get your little narrow butt in this car now." Yvette was adamant, and not to be denied.

"Oh, Yvette!!" She failed to notice Yvette in the car initially. "I was just gonna—"

"I don't care," Yvette maintained control, "You just come on and get right on in here. You hear me?" Evelyn reluctantly got into the car still feebly trying to explain it all away.

"Now come on, Snuff, take us to Bouvier Street, to where Maddie and Greg's parents live."

She was relieved that they caught Evelyn and satisfied that she didn't get a chance to do what she does best. Get high.

They arrived at the house on Bouvier Street. All exited the car and headed up the steps. Snuff was teasing Evelyn like a child who just got in trouble. Maddie came to the door on the first ring.

"Oh, Yvette, Evelyn!! Good to see you both. Hi, Glenn! How you been?? Please, come on in!" They did. They exchanged greetings as they entered the house and were directed to be seated on the sectional sofa that surrounded one entire half of the living room. Maddie divulged the sad news about her brother but was surprised to find out that they had now known for sure. They all were disheartened and sad now that they had confirmed what they feared was true. All expressed remorse and were speaking in stunned tones as they each attempted to give their most heartfelt words of consolation and concern. The phone rang and Maddie looked at it and extended her hand to gesture them to wait. "Excuse me, y'all while I get this phone, it's been ringing off the hook cause the funeral is day after tomorrow." She picked up the phone in the kitchen. The guests continued to marvel at the reality they had been thrown into. Maddie returned after only minutes.

"I'm sorry, yall, but you know who that was?? Curtis!! Yall know him, right?" They nodded their heads and muttered indicating that they did. "Well, he's on his way over. I told him I'd be right here. Oh, can I get y'all something to drink or something??" she offered her guests. The girls declined, but Snuff requested a beer.

"Sure I'll take a Bud if you got one."

"Oh, sure, Glenn, I'll be right back with it." She left to retrieve the beer. Yvette again glared at him and he stuck his tongue out at her and grinned. She returned with the Budweiser opened and hands it to Snuff who took it, but did not immediately drink any as he just held it in both hands between his legs.

"Maddie?" Yvette started in. "Uh, Evelyn first told me of the news, but she wasn't sure. Uh, she also told me something very disturbing. Now I don't know, but, well, I think what she has to say could be of some importance to you." Maddelyn planted herself where she was standing, wondering what it could be.

"What?" she asked searchingly.

"Go head, Evelyn. Tell her what you told me." Yvette directed to Evelyn. Evelyn was looking as though she didn't know what was being asked of her.

"What? You mean about when I came here that day? Oh?" She knew!!

Evelyn began to relate her story. Maddelyn was sitting down at this point, listening closely and very much intrigued. She knew Evelyn's history but she listened anyway. As she neared the end of her story, Jouscar arrived and was invited to listen in. Evelyn started all over from the beginning for his benefit. When she finally finished, they were all silent and in thought at first. Then they began to express possible scenarios either linking Michael to the murder or exonerating him of any wrongdoings.

"You know what, though? Michael has been here and talked to my mom and pop!!" said Maddelyn. "I wasn't here but they told me he came by and he assured them that he would be at the funeral. So, I just don't know!" Jouscar now added more to the inquisition.

"I don't know. I don't think he could possibly be the one because, if you think about it, he couldn't be that cold to kill him and still come to the funeral! They was running buddies. I think they were too tight for him to do something like that. You know? Like, only Italians do that kind of stuff!! Come to somebody's funeral after they kill 'em. You know? Anyway I'm supposed to meet him later tonight and I'll check him out then."

Maddelyn suggested it was wrong to point the finger based on so little evidence and especially since Evelyn's credibility was poor. The others neither agreed nor disagreed but at this point, they all were fairly sure they knew something. Something that had raised a little more than their eyebrows. Something that was quickly forming into a dark shadow, a shadow of a doubt about Michael Watkins.

Michael

Michael had picked up Rose that night. It was the same night that he spoke with Phil. He and Rose were driving to her house according to plan. She had closed the bar and was finished working. They were talking as they usually do, about sex, and what was going to happen when they reach her house. She and Michael shared a common understanding about the sex act.

"You think you gone wear me out? Watch. I'm gone have your ass coming and asleep in ten minutes," Rose confidently assured him.

"Yeah, yeah, we'll see," Michael snidely retorted.

They reached the house and as they entered, Michael attempted to seat himself. She stopped him, turned the light on, and smiled in his face.

"No, baby. There'll be none of that." She then leaned forward to grasp the arm of the sofa, which was right as you come in the door, with one hand and with the other she untied the draw string of her sweat pants and in a sweeping motion, pulled them down to mid thigh. She returned the hand to support her weight as she leaned her head in between her hands and wiggled her very much luscious, light-skinned butt as if to ask, "You don't know???" He knew. In an experienced move, he was exposed and pointed towards her exposed bottom. She acknowledged his rigidity.

"OOOH, put it in the first hole you come to!" she requested. She was impatient. He found the one with hair around it. As he worked to maneuver himself into position, she helped him. Once into place, he began to stroke her methodically, then he moved both hands to the small of her back. He liked to watch. She liked to watch too, apparently because she now had her head and neck twisted in such a way as to see what was going on behind her. Hands folded in front of her. He tapped her lightly on her right, buttock.

"You move!" he sexually demanded. She began to wriggle and grind and move in ways that would have been pleasurable no matter who was doing it. He came in a matter of ten minutes and she heard his telling moans but continued working her body against his. Even though he reached orgasm, he remained hard because of her constant movement and her experience in knowing how to keep it like that. She reached around her body, balanced only by her forehead pressed on the arm of the sofa, grabbed his hips, and pulled him into her as far as she could. He was rather large and it brought some pain to her as he climaxed, but she continued to move and grind and wriggle until she herself reached that much sought after plateau. They both wanted to collapse, but didn't. They remained as they were, with him planted deeply within her, panting and breathing hard, both of them. He finally, slowly withdrew his tool and straightened up. She pulled her panties and pants up and sat on the arm of the sofa. She looked at him as he put his penis away and adjusted his clothes.

"So, where you goin' now? Over to your other woman's house?" She was playing, but not entirely.

"None of your business," he responded. They looked into each other's faces. This sex act had been completed. They were finished with each other and they knew it.

"Well, give me some money before you go, punk." She headed toward the kitchen as she spoke these words. He heard her, reached into his pocket to retrieve a crisp $100 dollar bill, and threw it on the sofa.

"There you go. Later!!" He reached for the doorknob and opened the door. She turned in time to see him throw the money on the couch.

"Don't be throwin' money at me like I'm some kind of hoe, Ice . . . an when ahm gon see you again??" Her tone was hard, but still in her own way, kind of soft. He looked back from the door, which was about to be closed as he left.

"When I do!" He was gone, leaving her to stare at the door. She was tired and decided to take a bath and go to bed.

He traveled towards Evelyn's house. Top down. Temptations singing on the radio, he turned up Sprague Street and then down Wister. *Yeah, let me go see my baby*, he thought. He had been wanting to talk to her anyway. It didn't matter what time he went to her house, she'd always open the door. Then he thought of Phil. "Damn, I was supposed to see him tonight." he remembered. He decided that he would just have to see him later. He suddenly became aware that he didn't wash after sex, as he had a fleeting smell of it in the air. *Got to wash soon as I get there*, he thought.

He arrived but she was not there, so he went across the street to a speakeasy that he frequented. He positioned himself by the window so that he could watch for her appearance. She didn't appear until about 5:30 in the morning. He had been there an hour and a half. He was about ready to leave anyway. The people in the speakeasy were snorting up all the cocaine he offered them, and they were about to get on his nerves. He got up and timed his moves so that he came to the door just as she opened hers.

"Yo! Hold up!!" he hollered to her. She immediately recognized the voice and as usual, started to get very nervous. Her heart began to beat unusually fast and her legs almost wanted to give out from under her. She took a deep breath and turned around to see him almost upon her now.

"Michael?" She attempted to try to seem calm, yet surprised. "What you doin'? You been over to Bennie's?? Who's in there?" She was better now. Once she accepted the fact that there was nothing she could do about it, he was there now, and whatever happens, happens. She got better, more relaxed, the hell with it.

"Fuck that. Where you been?" he asked as he grabbed her. "I been here since three o'clock waitin for yo ass." Get on in the house, girl. Shit." She knew where this was going. She continued into the house, stepping over things as she walked. He was behind her, kicking things out of his way and lamenting on her poor housekeeping. "Where you been, I asked you?"

"I been with Maddie over to her mother's house. I been finding out about Gregory's funeral. You goin'? You know it's day after tomorrow."

Michael glanced at her. "Yeah, I'm goin," he said angrily as if annoyed at the question. "What the fuck you think?? Yeah, I been over to the house, too. I know where it is and what time it is. All that shit."

Michael cleared a space on the sofa so he could sit down. He looked at Evelyn who had gotten a drink of water from the refrigerator and was holding the glass to her lips as she looked at him. Not sure what to expect next or what to say. He looked her over. She was slender with legs that seemed to not have any thigh portion. Just legs straight up. But she had a very nicely rounded butt, small breasts, and a cute, though scarred face. *She's seen better days. She has been called a "tack" a time or two in her life.* Her clothes were not dirty but dingy and well worn. Her hair was pulled together in a short ponytail. It looked dry and dull.

"Come here." Michael motioned to her to come nearer to him. She did. Glass still up to her lips. Uncertainty still in her mind. "What you been doing with yourself? You ain't been takin' care of this house!! I can see that." He was searching, picking, trying to get her to talk. "I heard something the other day. Somebody said they saw you and Greg go into his mother's house not too long before he died. That true? He was bearing down on her with his killing stare now. "Huh? Answer me. Is it true? Huh?" She stopped and took the glass from her lips and tried to formulate an answer. *What is he saying this for??* She wondered. *What is he trying to say?* She knew that Michael was always prying as to her activities, but Greg?? He knew they were just good friends.

"No. No, Michael, I ain't been nowhere with no Greg," she exclaimed, attempting to maintain her hard-core, roughneck style, but it was hard to do with Michael because he was more hard-core. The original thug. He did that style to death and she couldn't really compete.

"What? What you say? You ain't been over there? See, you lyin'. Cause I seen you myself one day, bitch. Now what was you and Greg doing? Huh? Was he fuckin' you? Huh? Was he? How I know thass my baby? Huh?" Evelyn was through with this scene. She'd seen it before and it always ended up with her getting raped and beat up. *Not today*, she thought. She glared at Michael as she walked past him to the door. He, watching her.

"Why don't you just stop that, Michael? You know me and Greg was just like brother and sister. You know better than to say something like that." She sat the glass down and shifted her clothes around on her body in an effort to regain her composure. "Wait here a minute. I'm goin' over to Bennie's to get us a pitcher and some beer." Michael started to raise himself from the chair to get up. "Sit down,

I'll be right back," she assured him. He relaxed himself and sat back down still with an angry look pasted onto his face.

She opened the door and stepped to the porch, looked back through the broken glass to make sure Michael hadn't gotten up, tipped to the pavement and ran as fast as she could. Up the street, around the corner, down the next street to one of her girlfriends house on Park Avenue. She knocked until she was let in.

"Pat. I'm sorry to bother you so early in the morning, but Ice talkin all crazy and I ain't about to let him get started on me. Can I use your phone? I got to call somebody." The still half asleep girl could see she was out of breath and desperate. She agreed to let her in.

"I'll be upstairs," she said and headed upstairs. Evelyn reached for the phone and dialed Yvette. Yvette picked up and Evelyn immediately began to share with her what Michael said.

"Vet, that nigga's crazy. You shoulda seen the way he was acting. And the things he be accusin' me of doin'. But one thing I do know, ain't no way he coulda seent me at Greg's mother's no other time, Vet. You know? 'Cause I ain't been there. Plus he tryin' to accuse me of doin' it with Greg. And questionin' if it's Greg's baby. He crazy. I know for sure it was him. Vet. I know. The more I think about it, the more surer I am." Yvette just took it all in. Her senses told her that Evelyn knew what she was talking about.

"Okay, look, don't go back there. Okay? See if you can stay there where you are until maybe nine or ten and I'll be there and pick you up. I have to go to work first. But I can leave and come get you and we can talk, okay? Don't leave!! Don't go and leave me. You hear." Yvette knew how flighty Evelyn could be.

"I ain't goin' nowhere. I'll be right here, girl, I ain't even tryin' to run into that man on the street. So, about ten you'll be here, right?" She noted the clock on the wall read six-ten. "Okay. I'll be right here." They said good-byes and she hung up. She went to the window and peeped through the blinds, making sure Michael hadn't followed her. She was pretty sure he hadn't, so she sat down to try to relax.

She was thinking now that she was almost sure she heard gunshots, not firecrackers, just moments before she saw Michael get into Greg's car that day. And come to think of it, he was looking mighty suspicious. And why did he have to take Greg's car? And why wasn't Greg never seen? And why was it found on Ogontz Avenue two days later? She reflected back to the gunshots. BLAM, BLAM, BLAM. She heard the shots clearly now. In her head. They were definitely gunshots. She had begun to put the times together from when she and Maddelyn and Yvette and Snuff and Jouscar had talked. She knew that between the time she heard the shots ring out and saw Michael leave, and take Greg's car that he—wait a minute, she thought, he had something in his hand, a rag or something. That's right!! He could have been making sure he didn't leave any fingerprints. That's what he must have been doing. Damn, that motherfucker thinks he's so smart. *I got him now*, she thought. She was sure of what she knew now and made up her mind that he was the one who killed Greg. She couldn't wait to talk to Yvette. She just had this overpowering feeling.

Michael, in the meantime, had caught on that she wasn't coming back after about a half hour and a quick check at Bennie's. He was pissed but felt a little better about getting that off his chest. The thing about her and Gregory. He knew he could continue to torment her with that now. *Fuck her*, he thought, he had just had a good shot of Rose anyway. *Fuck her. I'll catch that bitch in the afternoon around the way,* he thought. He got in his car and drove off. He was tired now. He was done.

Maddelyn

The funeral was to take place the next day. The general atmosphere in the Burks residence was hectic and confusing. Lots of people coming and going. Some frantically checking to make sure that all the arrangements had been made. Others checking to confirm that everything would take place as planned and in the proper order, making sure everything had been taken care of. Preparing cards and other formal paperwork associated with the burial ceremony. The phone rang, as it had been doing the whole day, and Maddie's aunt from Baltimore got it.

"Hello?" the aunt answered.

"Hello? Ms. Burks?" the voice inquired.

"No, honey, this ain't Ms. Burks. Who you want? The sister or the mother?"

"Oh, I'm sorry, let me speak to Maddie please."

"Yeah, hold on, I'll get her for you." She turned to pass the word to others who were standing and moving about to tell Maddelyn to pick up. Maddelyn was in the basement preparing for the guests who would return to the house after the funeral service. She heard the message and hollered up the steps.

"Okay. I got it!" she relayed back as she picked up the phone. "Hello?" she said as she continued to look at the table and place settings, still visually rearranging the vases and whatnot as she spoke.

"Hi, Maddie? This is Rose. You know. 'Ole creaky floors'?"

"Oh, hi, Rose. How you doin'?" She wondered how Rose got her mother's number.

"Oh, I'm not sure, Maddie. It's just all of a sudden too much is going on here. First I hear about Greg, now guess what?" Maddelyn gave her undivided attention to Rose.

"What?"

"Somebody done shot Kenny now and he all laid up in the Einstein Hospital. He's in intensive care right now, but they say he's all right."

Maddelyn broke in. "Wait a minute, you got to be kidding, me? Kenny?? Shot?? Oh, my Lord!! When did this happen?? Who did it? Do they know? He's all right, though, right?" Maddelyn was astounded.

"Yeah, he's okay, but I think it happened early yesterday morning."

"Maddelyn interrupted again.

"You mean after we was just at the bar with you!! It had to be, 'cause me and him sat talkin' till about three or four in the morning and then he went on home. So it had to be after he left me. He's at Einstein? Right?"

"Yeah. I been up there already and that's where I got your mom's number from so I could tell yall. Um, he can't talk, but he can write what it is he wants to say. So you go on up there, he really wants to see you." Maddie could not believe what she just heard. She thought things couldn't get any worse.

"Oh, Lord. Uh, Rose, What do you mean he can't talk?? Where was he shot?" Maddelyn didn't quite know what questions to ask. She just started asking questions.

"Hold on, Maddie. I really didn't get to see him, but I talked to the doctor. I figured this would be a bad time to tell you. . . . I feel so sorry for you all this at one time. I tell you what, why don't you let me come over and I'll take you up? I know you probably tired and whatnot."

Maddelyn considered, momentarily. "Uh, yeah, Rose." Maddelyn was fighting back some emotion that was beginning to build. "Yeah, yeah, I'd appreciate that. But, uh, could you give me about an hour? I could be ready in about an hour. Okay?"

"Okay. So what time is it now, let's see, almost two. So about three? I'll see you around three. You all right, honey?" Rose induced concern into her voice.

"Yeah, Rose, I'll be all right. It's just that—oh, I'll be okay. So you'll be over about three o'clock? I'll be ready then. Okay? See you then." They hung up and Maddelyn methodically returned to her place settings but thought to call Jouscar. She dialed his number, but his answering machine picked up. She left the message to meet her at the hospital. She hung up and remembered that she hadn't told him where. She figured that he would find her and she would look out for him. She stopped to gather her thoughts. *What is going on here?? Geezus!! Who is doing this?? And why?? Why in heaven's name are they doing it??* She began busying herself again as people began to ask her about her phone call.

At about 2:50, a voice called to her from upstairs requesting her presence at the front door. She looked out from the basement window. It was Rose, double-parked in front of the house in the street. She strained to see Phil getting into the back seat. *Where did he come from,* she thought. Then she yelled out to tell them she'd be right out. She took off her apron, headed upstairs, and outside to the car. She got in and all was explained about how Phil wanted to go, too. The entire length of the ride all were consumed in discussing Greg's mysterious death and Kenny's mysterious shooting as Phil suddenly remembered something.

"Oh. And you know something else, Rose? Member that day me and Ice was in the bar and we was talkin? He dropped this, and didn't even know it." He produced a folded brown envelope with an income tax check in it along with a piece of paper with a telephone number and name on it. "I didn't even see it either, at first, then I dropped a cigarette on the floor and when I leaned down to pick it up, that's when I saw it."

"So what's that? Let me see?" Maddelyn reached for the object and he handed it to her.

"Here!! I don't know, but I swear I think this is one of the ones that we couldn't get the guy at the check-cashing place to bust. I ain't sure, but, see, this name kinda looks familiar. That's why I'm going up to get wit Kenny to let him know that he might a been more on track wit the Ice thing than he know." Maddelyn took the check and perused it.

"Well, I wouldn't know anything about that, but, what were you and Greg doing with them? I mean how did yall get them in the first place?" She was puzzled, but really wanted to know.

"Aw, shit. Oops, s'cuse me, I'm sorry, I didn't mean to cuss, but, man, Greg came up with the whole thing. I can't tell yall everything, but me and him was working 'em. We bust three or four of 'em already and was about to get some more when this here happened." Rose peered over at the check as she was driving.

"You mean Mike had it, right?" She glanced at Phil.

"Yeah, I told you that day in the bar. Member?"

"Yeah! But what was he doing with it?" queried Rose.

"See, that's what I don't know either."

They reached the hospital entrance and approached the guard at the information desk. They were informed that there could only be one visitor at a time, but Maddelyn was adamant that she, and at least, Rose go together. The guard wasn't hard to persuade as he had noticed that both women were gorgeous and built like the girls on Soul Train. So he allowed them both to pass with passes. Phil was told to wait until at least one of them came out. They were directed to the ICU. As they approached the door of the room, an intern was coming out.

"Excuse me, Doctor," Maddelyn stopped him. "How is he?"

The intern looked both women up and down then asked, "Uh, are you family?"

"Yes. I'm his sister and she's his cousin!! Is he okay?" Maddelyn quickly got off that subject.

"Well. He'll live. We know that much. His wounds have been sutured and dressed. He lost several teeth and his tongue had been severed, but...." Maddelyn put her hand up to her mouth in disbelief. Rose stepped back and tried to look through the little window to the room.

"What? Where was he shot? In his mouth? Oh, my God!" She was dumbstruck. *People just don't get shot in the mouth*, she thought. How stupid. "His tongue is out?" She could not imagine this at all.

"No, no, let me explain." The intern saw they weren't informed. "I thought you knew, I'm sorry. It appears that he was shot once in the jaw. The bullet appears to have entered on the left side of his lower jawbone. As it entered, it traveled through the gum, shattering his back and wisdom teeth and continued through, severing his tongue on the way. Now, it finally lodged itself in the gum on the right side of his mouth, displacing a few teeth, but none were broken on that side. The second bullet came within an inch of taking his nose off, but fortunately, he only lost the tip of his nose. And that can be reconstructed. His face is badly swollen and he is unable to talk at all. His tongue has been sutured back and should heal to 100 percent."

Maddelyn was appalled and stunned but continued to listen with the intensity of someone trying not to miss one iota of a detail. Her imagination had formed a picture of

Kenny that was not unlike some deformed monster. She was actually afraid of what she would see, both hands at her mouth, her shoulders hunched, and her eyes bulging.

"Stop!! Please, stop. Oh, my God!! Oh, my." She made several of those tongue sucking noises. Rose just stood there with her arms folded at her chest. Her lovely chest, as the intern had noticed frequently.

"Well, as I said, his recovery will be lengthy, but he should be talking in about one or two weeks. And reconstruction on his nose will begin after the tongue has healed and the gum swelling has gone down. Now, don't keep him too long, okay?" He touched Maddelyn on her arm and turned to head down the corridor and into another room.

Maddelyn and Rose entered the room where they were met by a note pad being held up by Kenny and written in big letters—I HEARD BOTH OF YOUR BIG MOUTHS ALL THE WAY DOWN THE HALL—They noted that his humor was intact, but it didn't seem to mesh with the moment. Kenney's eyes dropped and his head turned to the side as it lay on the pillow. Notepad dropped to his lap. He had seen the look of astonishment and disgust on their faces. Maddelyn's worst fears didn't compare with the reality of what she was looking at. His face was twice its normal size and did not appear to belong to him. His ears had become engulfed in the swollen mass of meat that was his cheeks. His lips were, well, they were very big. Rose thought of laughing at first, but that thought had been overcome when she looked at him longer. Maddelyn walked to him, face contorted, picked up his hand and spoke to him softly.

"Kenny!! Oh, my sweet little Kenny." Then the crying came. Rose moved closer to comfort her as well as to stare harder at Kenny.

Just about then, Phil came in. He stopped, looked, and said, "I snuck past the guard. Shhhh." His face began to contort too as he got a look at Kenny's face. "Oh. That guy Curtis is out there. He told me to tell you, Maddie, to come on out." Maddelyn looked up.

"Oh, thanks, Phil. I'll be right back, Ken." She departed to go retrieve Jouscar. Upon seeing her enter the waiting room, he rose to meet her.

"Maddie! Hi! What's going on??" He seemed genuinely concerned, "What happened??"

"We don't know!! Nobody can tell us nothing and Kenny, tch, poor Kenny can't even talk. He's laid up on the bed with a writing pad in his hand."

"What happened to him, though? I mean where was he shot?"

"Curtis. You won't believe this. He was shot in his mouth and his tongue was shot off too. Have you ever?"

"What? In his mouth?" Jouscar was truly stunned. "Did he do it hisself?"

"No," Maddelyn decreed. "Now why would he shoot himself in the mouth, Curtis?? Huh?"

"No. No, you know what I thought was that he put the gun in his mouth and tried to commit suicide or something. That's what I was thinking."

"No, it wasn't like that at all. He was shot by somebody. We don't know why or who or nothing. Look, why don't you see if you can't sneak in because they're not going to give you a pass. Only two people at a time are allowed in the room, and it's three of us in there as it is. Phil just snuck in. I don't know how he did it, but I'm going to go back in and you wait a couple of minutes and then sneak down to the ICU, that's where they have him now." Juice watched her as she walked away. Always checking out the body movements. He smiled as he watched her hips move rythmically as she walked and then he turned to walk the other way as part of his scheme to sneak past the guard.

The Plan

Yvette had picked up Evelyn from her girlfriend's house and had taken her to her job where she worked as a counselor for runaway children. They had been talking quite a bit about Evelyn's experience with Michael the previous evening, and her unchanging suspicions. Evelyn also told Yvette something that made her even more prone to believing what she was saying had some validity. She told Yvette that for some reason or other she had happened to look at a page in the Bible that was sitting open on the table of the friends' house she had stayed in. She told Yvette that the page she happened to read from was in Romans 1:21 and she didn't know what the word "REPROBATE" meant. But she said that as she read on, and began to gather the meaning of REPROBATION and the horror of a REPROBATE MIND, she could attribute just about every word to Michael and how he was. She told Yvette that she thought if there ever was a person who was like what she had read about, it was Michael. She thought the passage just about described him to a T. And it was scary. Yvette was familiar with the passage. She thought it was ironic that Evelyn would have come to such a conclusion. She wondered about that. But more and more she was beginning to be convinced that Evelyn was key in determining Michael's innocence or guilt, especially since she was the first eye witness to know anything at all about Gregory's death.

They had come to the conclusion that they would again contact Maddelyn and let her in on the activities of Evelyn and Michael and what had just transpired that evening to see if she thought it was of any significance. They had tried to reach Maddelyn, but she was at the hospital, of course, so they had to wait.

Unbeknownst to them, Maddelyn, Jouscar, Rose, Phil, and Kenny had also begun to fit pieces together. Gathering facts, such as: Michael carried a .38 snubnose. That's what both Kenny and Gregory were shot with. Michael had Gregory's check that Phil had found after he dropped it in the bar. Why? Evelyn definitely saw him take Gregory's car. Why wasn't Gregory with him?? These were some of the questions the group had come up with. Kenny still hadn't heard from Russell, whom he had run into prior to his unfortunate incident. They figured his account may help them form a basis of opinion. Kenny had expressed his concern that Michael may be able to find out something about Greg's death and had asked Russell if he would check him out and see if he knew anything or not. So since Russell hadn't come to them, Rose and Phil were elected to find Russell and see what he had to say. Phil was trying to verify where he lived.

"He lives on Spencer Street. Right? Right across from Spencer's drug store. And I think there's another store on the other side of the street too. I think it's called Mazer's. Yeah, I think I know where he live at," said Phil. "He got all them good-lookin sisters with them big butts." He was not looking at the pad Kenny was holding up and had written "YALL MAKE SURE TO GET WITH HIM AND LET ME KNOW WHAT HE SAYS." They assured him that they would. Satisfied that they had just about exausted the subject, they decided it was time to depart and let Kenny rest.

The funeral was to take place the next day, and they were all to watch and make sure they saw Michael's face. After the funeral they were to each in turn talk to Michael and feel him out. Sense anything that they could. Check out his every response. They planned to look him deep in his eyes and dig within the very reaches of his soul. They were close enough with him that they felt this would be effective because they had concluded that he had no reason to suspect that they suspected him of anything. So they figured that he would have no reason to act suspicious. They also decided it would be even better if Evelyn spoke with him too. They were not yet aware of Evelyn and Yvette's most recent encounters and therefore didn't figure on getting what they got from her when they finally did see her.

The day of the funeral arrived. There were more than forty cars in the procession line. They were lined up in front of the church and extended around the corner and then some. The hearse was silver gray with a black top. And the family had rented two white limousines for them to ride in. They were parked in front of the other cars. The sun was shining and it was surprisingly warm for that time of year. It was a good day for a funeral.

Everybody who knew Greg was in attendance. His viewing crowd was tremendously large and the funeral service crowd was even larger. At the beginning of the service, though, an unfortunate and disturbing thing happened. Maddelyn's mother had a slight heart attack and had to be taken to the hospital. She managed to recover all right, but she missed the entire service. That in itself was enough to further darken the atmosphere and made for additional despair for the family. Especially for Maddelyn, who had by now become desensitized by the series of events that had taken place within the last week. She was merely going through the motions. Whatever. As she put it, it was "in the hands of the Lord." She was out of it. She labeled her actions as "just being strong." And this was what kept her going, kept her sitting there on the front row, shaking hands with the well wishers. Kept her talking to all those who wished to express their regret and give their condolences. Kept her from not showing any emotion when Michael hugged her and expressed his. She didn't feel him. But yet she really couldn't tell if he was putting on or not. And, furthermore, she knew she wasn't finished with him.

The services were long and many tears had been shed throughout, but it had come to an end. The casket had been closed and people were beginning to leave.

Jouscar had pinpointed Michael and had made his way to him as the services ended.

"Hey, man!!" he said sympathetically. "How you makin' out?? I know Greg was your boy, and all. I know how you must feel. It's fucked up that this here thing happened not too long after you had seen him?? Man, I know it got to hurt." He paused as they walked outside. "I still can't believe it myself that somebody took him out!!" He was looking at Michael with what would only be construed as love and heartfelt concern. He pulled Michael to him to hug him. They embraced. No tears from either. Afterward, Michael responded.

"You know, Curt? I can't even feel everything yet, man. You know? It's like it ain't hit me yet that he's gone. You know? I mean, like you said I had just seen him. And me and him had been talkin' about some business that he was just about to let me in on. Right? And thass the last time I talked to him. You know? I just want to find out who did it. Thass what I want to know." Michael pretended to be angry at this point.

They both were standing partially in front of the steps and people were pushing and excusing themselves in an effort to get around them. Jouscar was looking at him as he was acting out his anger. Michael was decked out in a black Edwardian suit. Maroon necktie, gray Stetson hat with his best Avenue block in it. He was sharp. His cocoa brown, hightop Stacies were shining brilliantly, at the tips only. He was clean as the Board of Health. Jouscar couldn't help but notice his fashionable attire because he was somewhat a clothes horse himself.

"Hey, man. We in these people's way. Let's step over here and talk," he suggested as they began to move. "Uh, say, man, you got them comforts looking pretty sporty. They look better than they was when they was new!!" They both peered down at the shoes Michael was wearing. They were bad!! By any cornerboy's standards, and the high shine of the tip portion of the shoe would invoke a response from any cornerboy who saw them. This comment had Michael beaming and posturing arrogantly as cornerboys do when they know what they're wearing is on the money . . . and somebody says something about it.

"Yeah, well, you know!" This particular phrase had become chiché for the times. "Yeah, well, you know." Michael smiled back at Jouscar. "That's a nice Velour you sportin', too," he reciprocated. "Where did you cop from? Down South Street?" Jouscar took off the hat he was wearing and handed it to Michael. Michael took the Velour hat and began to inspect it, taking care not to disturb the curve of the brim or the crease in the block. While he checked out the hat, Jouscar pop quizzed him.

"Uh, say, Ice. Let me ask you something? What 'did' happen with you and Greg that day? I don't know, but, maybe what yall was talking about might have had something to do with why they 'iced' him. You know what I'm sayin'?" Michael positioned himself squarely in front of Jouscar who was now leaning against a car, legs crossed at the ankle and arms folded in front of him. He studied Michael's face and listened well.

"Yeah. I had thought about that myself. See," Michael began. And he proceded to tell Jouscar every detail, including the dropped check he had pocketed and lost. Every detail, save one, one crucial and exacting detail. That he shot Gregory and killed him because he thought Gregory was having an affair with Evelyn and he felt Greg betrayed him. Michael told Jouscar the truth about his and Greg's encounter, except he lied about he and Greg leaving the house together, he and Greg both getting into Greg's car together, and Greg dropping him off on Ogontz Avenue. Michael felt very at ease imparting this information to Jouscar. He was content that he did everything right. He showed emotion where it was appropriate, he spoke convincingly, and he saw that Jouscar seemed convinced. He was pleased with his performance.

"So that's what happened, huh? That's how they found Greg's ride up on Ogontz Avenue? That cockhound was over to Queetsy's house!! That's where he was. I should have known it was some broad involved." Laquita's nickname was Queetsy. And she did live on Ogontz Avenue, but little did either know that she had moved two days before Gregory's death. Lacking this knowledge, Michael continued. "Yeah, man, she came to the door and I saw her too. She ain't have on nothin hardly. He said he was cool and so I split. Shit. I went and got me some trim too. But, uh, that's the last time I see him. Goin' into Queetsy's house. I swear-ta-God!!"

While Jouscar was talking to Michael, Maddelyn was occupied with family, doing what family does at the funeral. Yvette, Evelyn, Snuff, Terry and a few others were gathered outside the church also and were huddled in their own conversation. Evelyn, of course had spotted Michael earlier, also, and had kept her eye on him since. He didn't seem to have noticed her though. Rose, Phil, and a few others had chosen to gather into still another pocket of people outside the church casually talking, but they were cognizant of what was taking place with Jouscar and Michael. They knew that Jouscar was going to get with them later and give them a report. So they tried to appear as though they weren't paying any attention to them the whole time they were there. Jouscar finally left Michael, as Michael became occupied with someone else. A woman of course.

Jouscar joined the others. He imparted his findings to them. As he finished talking, Rose let him know that there was something wrong with his story. Because she was one of the few people who knew that Queetsy was out of town then. Rose was pretty sure she was right but had to wait to contact Queetsy to prove it. She never did. She never got a chance to. But after vowing to do it, she looked over in Evelyn's direction and motioned for her to come to where they were. She came over and Rose graciously greeted and embraced her.

"Hi, baby. You look so nice. That's a pretty dress you have on!" It wasn't really. "What yall talkin' bout over there??" she asked. Evelyn thought about it for a second before she answered, "Nothin'. We just talkin' about the funeral and all, that's all." Rose changed her tone when she heard this.

"Look, I got to talk to you, girl. We been doing some checkin' around and we think you should know what we talking about!!" By now Yvette had sauntered over also and was lending an ear. "Hi, Vet. How you doin'?" said Rose. "Everybody wants to know." Yvette responded but was more concerned with why they called Evelyn. Everybody seemed to know everybody. She thought. Rose spoke separate of the others.

"Oh, I'm doing okay. And you?" Rose looked at Yvette and said she was okay, sensing why Yvette came over in the first place. She told her that they want to let Evelyn in on a little secret that they had been sharing. She knew Yvette would be interested also. They talked. They exchanged information. They all seemed to be on the same track. Rose and her group were surprised to find out that Evelyn had much more to say about the secret than they did. And Yvette and the others in her group were equally as surprised to learn of Kenny's misfortune, which they had not known about prior to this conversation. Things began to click. Rose came up with a plan.

"Evelyn. Since yall just went through that thing," referring to the most recent spat she had with Michael, "why don't you kind of act like you want to make up with him and get him to come over to your house after we leave from over at Maddelyn's mom's tonight.?? You know!! Kind of lure him there. You know what I'm saying, honey? You know how we girls do? Act like you want to make up with him. Apologize to him and make him think he gone get some if he be nice and come. You know how to do it!" They all smiled at that suggestion. As they did indeed, get her message. Yvette blushed. "And after you get him over there, we'll pop in too. Sort of a surprise visit. You know what I'm trying to say? We'll sort of take him by surprise and we can grill his little butt right there." They began chatting among themselves. Deliberating over Rose's proposal. Eventually the plan was 100 percent accepted by all.

The Lure

Jouscar made it his business to stop at Russell's house on his way home to change his clothes. He knew Phil was supposed to do it, but he was in the neighborhood. He found Russell on the porch talking with his girlfriend and one of his sisters. Jouscar immediately recognized the pretty face that was staring at him as he approached.

"Well, if I'd a known you were going to be here, I'd have come a little sooner."

The pretty girl smiled and replied, "Oh, Juice. You so full of it. Hi you doin'?" she asked shyly.

"Oh, I been all right. Much better since I seen you though." Forever the charmer.

"Where you comin' from all dressed up?" the young girl inquired. "You been up to the funeral? How was it? It was sad, wasn't it?"

Russell cut the young girl's questioning off. "Hey, cut-buddy. What's happenin'? You lookin' mighty sporty there. You just comin' back from the jaunt?" Jouscar was about to respond, but Russell kept talking. "I was up there to the viewing earlier myself, but I couldn't stay for the whole service." Jouscar was listening to him talk but was focused on the young lady who had approached him. He noticed this and turned his attention back to Russell.

"Yeah, I stayed the whole time, man. You know how me and Greg was." Russell walked towards him and shook his hand as he spoke. He invited him to take a seat on the glider. Jouscar took his eyes off the pretty girl again and seated himself.

"He looked good? Didn't he? Man, I know this shit fucked everybody up. I didn't want to see all the crying and stuff at the funeral, you know? I can't stand that part of it."

"Yeah, it was pretty sad. I know what you mean, but guess what else happened." Jouscar continued. "And this happened before the funeral even started. Greg's mom had a heart attack. Now the family has that to worry about." They all winced and commented when Jouscar told them this. "But look, Russ, um, I stopped by to check something out with you."

"Yeah? What?" Russell looked intrigued. But he was smiling. Russell was always smiling. He was a jolly guy. "Uh, yeah, let's go down here," he said as he glanced over at his sister and girlfriend. The sister caught the hint.

"Oh, I'll leave. Yall ain't got to go nowhere. Yall always got some private stuff to talk about." She went into the house. Russell didn't say anything to her but Jouscar did.

"But make sure you come back out when we finish, 'cause I got something to say to you too." He watched her as she entered the house. Russell smiled and alerted Jouscar that he'd better watch himself because pretty girl's boyfriend was probably on his way around. Jouscar caught on and continued with the business he came for.

"You hear Kenny got shot?"

Russell hadn't. "Kenny? You mean faggot Kenny? Damn!! I just saw him not too long ago. Who shot him?"

"That's just it. Nobody knows. But I was just up to see him at Einstein's. He in intensive care. He got shot in his mouth, cut his tongue off, messed up all his teeth. Plus he got shot in his nose. Damn near lost that too. He's in bad shape. He can't talk but he can write. Ain't that messed up?" Russell appeared astonished at this news. Even though shootings were commonplace, in that neighborhood, it was not often that you hear of two shootings in such a short time span and know both victims well. So this news was a bit unusual.

"But," Jouscar continued, "he said he had talked to you earlier and asked you to do something for him. Did you get a chance to do it?"

Russell remembered immediately. "Oh, yeah. Ice. What's happenin' wit him?" Russell looked at Jouscar inquisitively. "Yall think he shot Kenny?"

"We don't know! But what you think about Ice? I mean when you asked him to listen out for something on Greg. How did he act?"

Russell answered quickly. "Man. That guy was so jumpy. He pulled his .38 out on me when I came up to his car. I know I scared him, but he acted really scared. You know?"

Jouscar looked Russell in the eyes. "You think his conscience was botherin' him?"

"I don't know about that, Juice, but he was awful jumpy like he thought somebody was after him or something. You mean they still ain't found out who killed Greg either?"

"Nope, but I think we might know something tonight. Look, Russ, I got to run. But thanks for that tip, hear? I'll check you out later." He stood up and walked to Russell to shake his hand and left. Russell stood to walk him to the first landing of the steps as he continued to express concern for both tragedies.

Evelyn had approached Michael before she left the funeral and before the crowd dispersed and was successful in doing what was suggested she do. Much to her displeasure. She had requested that he come to her house about nine o'clock that same night, saying that she wanted to apologize for what she did the other night, the night she ran to her girlfriend's house and left him sitting in hers. And she told him that she wanted to make it up to him. He, feeling as though he was back in charge of things again, assumed the pose of a conquerer at this request. It was as if he had expected her to apologize all along anyway. He assured her he'd be there. His confidence had peaked. He strolled like a peacock after that. She was sickened by his actions.

The funeral crowd dispersed. The interment crowd went the way of the burial grounds. The well-wishers and attendees went their way. The hangers-on went to the house to await the arrival of the final crowd for the party and drinking and eating to get underway. Evelyn was taken to her house by Yvette and dropped off and reminded that they would be over by eight-thirty so that they could be there before Michael came. The funeral service was over by four o'clock, and that was plenty of time for everybody to regroup and get ready for this encounter. Jouscar had some business to attend to but was sure he'd be finished by at least nine or so. Maddelyn had not even yet been told of the plan. Rose and Phil decided to go to the bar where they normally hung. Snuff and Terry went home to entertain themselves until talk time.

The Kill

Michael arrived at Evelyn's house at eight-ten. Evelyn had been sitting, thinking, smoking and sipping on flat beer when she decided to take a quick bath. She had just taken off all her clothes and was leaning over the bathtub testing the water temperature when she heard a noise. *That sounds like the front door*, she thought. She didn't even bother to grab a towel to cover herself but started for the door to check out the noise.

"Who is it?" she called. She started for the entrance to the hall that led to the living room, she was met by Michael who had stealthily crept through the living room only to meet her coming to the door. She was startled and caught very much off guard at the moment, but Michael had already grabbed her and was pulling her towards him, roughly.

"Yeah! That's right, it's me. Surprised? What? You thought we was gonna talk? Huh??? Stupid mothafucka! Come here, bitch!" Evelyn could not even begin to gather her thoughts. She was being manhandled and was helpless and confused. She was thrown onto the floor of the hall and never had the presence of mind to struggle or fight back. She was just allowing him to dominate her. She was all of a sudden being pushed, rolled more likely up against the baseboard of the wall with his foot. His shoe was hard against her naked skin. This was just too vivid for her. She was in shock and humiliated. She found herself staring at the chipped-off paint on the wooden baseboard, her face was just that close to it, waiting for what was coming next. It came. He pushed her face into the baseboard and held it there. "You thought I forgot the other night, didn't you??? You left me sitting here and never came back??? Bitch, I'm gonna stomp the bone out your back!"

Evelyn responded to his voice and turned to try to look up at him, but he wouldn't let her head move. When he finally released it, she turned to look up just in time to catch the toe of his shoe on the side of her head. Her head rebounded off the baseboard, but it bounced back to allow her to see him. She looked up at him with pleading eyes, trying to bring her feet up under her, grabbing for her breasts to try to cover them with her hand.

"The baby!! Michael, please! The baby!!" she pleaded.

"Fuck you and that baby!" Michael resounded angrily back. "I don't care nothin' bout that baby. I don't even know who's it is. Huh?? How I know it ain't Greg's? Huh? How the fuck I know it ain't his?" She winced with each "huh." "I know yall was fuckin'. I care about that. Know how I know?? I seen yall. That's right! I seen yall a few times. You think I'm stupid? Huh??? You might as well tell me now, bitch. The nigga dead now an' it don't much matter! Do it?" Michael stood spread-legged over her naked, quivering, body. Domineering, threatening, belligerent. And she was submissive and cowering, but she took advantage of a moment of silence that fell between them. When no pain was being inflicted on her body, she somehow drew strength from within her. She hardened her stare. It was a direct stare now, looking squarely into the burning eyes of her oppressor.

"You killed Greg, didn't you? Didn't you?? I saw you, Michael!!! I know you did it!" She said this pointedly, assuredly, and without doubt. Her glare was piercing. Michael responded to this transformation by straightening up to look at her. He was stunned but quickly reasserted himself. He reached down, grabbed her by her hair, and leaned down as he tightened his grip on her hair. He pulled her face to meet his. Closely, eye to eye.

"You ain't seen shit, bitch, but I saw you!" He smacked her hard against her right cheek. She took it. No tears. No flinch. No sign that it hurt. She just maintained the direct, piercing stare into his eyes. She was no longer fearful of Michael or of what he could do to her. Something deep within her rose and removed the fear. She was void of feeling, and thought, yet clear about what she was doing.

"I saw you, Michael. I saw you come out of Greg's mother's house right after I heard those gunshots. I saw you take Greg's car and drive off in it. I saw that rag you had tied around your hand too!" She continued to assert her assurance of what she had all along suspected. Her body now being supported by her elbows and her legs had unfolded and were crossed at the knee. She looked almost comfortable. Confident. Arrogant, even. "What you gon do now, Michael? Kill me and the baby? Well, go head!!! Go head, Michael!!! Pull out your little fuckin' gun and shoot us!!! I don't even care, 'cause you know what, Michael? I know you killed Greg! Couldn't a been nobody else but you. I see that now."

Michael had straightened up and was looking down on her in pure disbelief and astonishment. She had never talked to him in that manner before. He spoke but his voice was weak, less intimidating.

"Listen, bitch. Let me tell you something." He began to look for something but didn't know what. The wall was the nearest support for his extended arm, so he leaned his arm against it.

"You or nobody else could prove that shit!" He looked down on her with questioning eyes, searching for something that could not be found in Evelyn's eyes, but he searched. "I don't care what you think you saw. You didn't see me pull no trigger!!" He stepped aside, pushing himself off the wall but continuing to search for a sign of weakening in Evelyn at this last ditch attempt to vindicate himself. Evelyn moved to stand up. With glare in place, cold as ice, she boldly stood straight up. This was worse than a slap in the face to Michael. He couldn't bear it. He turned to take a step away from her, but she pulled his arm hard enough to get his attention again.

"Maybe not," Evelyn pulled herself to him, "but I heard gunshots and I know gunshots when I hear them, Michael. And I know I heard gunshots come from Greg's mother's house and I know I saw you take his car not long after that." Evelyn saw the can opener that had fallen on the floor a couple of days ago when she was drunk. It was the kind of opener that one would open a can of juice with. The one with the pointed bent head. She lunged and picked it up in one quick move and as Michael realized what was about to take place, it was too late. She had gouged his right eye with it and had pushed him off her. As he grabbed for the injured eye, she managed to get the can opener between his arms and pull it across his throat, causing blood to gush from it as though it were a can that had just been opened and was being squeezed from the middle. Michael fell back. She tried to continue her attack as he attempted to cringe and protect himself, but this time she was restrained by a hand. She never even noticed that her guests had arrived. She was breathing heavily but was still focused, still glaring at Michael as he let go of life and flopped to the floor. Flatlined. Lifeless. Dead.

Snuff had restrained her final attempts but was amazed at what he was looking at. He pulled Evelyn gently backward from the still body. Evelyn looked at the faces of Phil, Rose, Yvette, and Snuff. They did not look at her. They looked at Michael. They had unconsciously formed a semicircle around him in an effort to avoid the rapidly spreading pool of blood, which was flowing from his wound. Unknowingly, they were somewhat symbolizing the ritual performed by animals after a kill. It was ironic. The silence of that moment could be heard for miles. No one stirred, nor blinked. Evelyn wrenched herself easily from the young man's grip, walked to her favorite chair, and sat down in it. She put both of her arms on the arms of the chair and crossed her legs as if she were finished. She looked contentedly at the scene before her. She lit a cigarette and blew the smoke toward the ceiling.

Phil was the first one to speak after what seemed like an eternity of silence.

"I ain't seen nothin!" he proclaimed. Everybody looked at him as though he had two heads. Evelyn was about to take a puff from her cigarette when he said this and she looked up at him and laughed. That laughter in the midst of this murder was surely inappropriate, but it broke the ice. All eyes looked to her. Then Rose spoke.

"Me neither. I ain't seen nothin'." Evelyn laughed even harder at this response. Michael just lay there. Yvette and Snuff were totally confounded by these comments but said nothing.

Evelyn's nakedness was stark and somewhat distracting in view of what was taking place, but no one mentioned it. Evelyn sat there in chair, cross-legged. Smoking. Laughing. Naked. Jouscar walked in in the midst of it all and went immediately to the semicircle to gawk at the body. Phil started for the body.

"Hey, don't touch him, man!" Snuff cried out. "What you doin??"

Phil looked up at him and said, "Hey man, we ain't seen nothin,' you dig?? We got to get dis here body outta here!"

At that moment Yvette stopped them. "No! No! This is not right. This woman has killed this man and we all witnessed it. It happened and there is no way we can just make it go away." Silence filled the room once again. Evelyn ceased to laugh when she heard the solemn voice of her friend. All eyes were upon her.

"There is no way that my conscience would allow me to ignore that. There is no way that we can allow this to happen in front of us and say it didn't. God, people! What are you thinking about?? God is our biggest witness. She did this before Him as well. And there is surely no way He can overlook it. I-I-I-I'm going to the police. And I suggest you follow me." She was decisive in ending.

"No, Vet. Not the police. You can't do that ! She'll go to jail sure as shit," Phil interjected.

"Well, I'm going!!" Yvette was not to be deterred.

Evelyn spoke. "I ain't goin' to no jail. Yall can do what you want, but I ain't goin' to no jail. I'm gettin' outta Dodge." She got up as she spoke. She had a look of determination on her face that indicated she also was not to be deterred, walking towards the bedroom; the others look on.

"The plot thickens!" Phil said as he reached for his hat. They look at him as though he had two heads. Rose started toward the bedroom after Evelyn.

"Where you gone go?" she inquired.

"I don't know but I know I'm gettin' outta Philly. I'm gone get on a bus and me and my baby gonna ride!!" She walked directly to her closet and began to rifle through her clothes, searching for a clean dress. Evelyn appeared to have an abundance of confidence all of a sudden. She was acting more self-assured than they had ever seen her. The already stunned onlookers were even more at a loss for words at this drastic change in her persona. She was cocky.

"Look!" Evelyn said as she pulled a tattered dress over her head. "I have been living my life for everybody else up to now and now that I don't have him on my back, I am going to change my life. I'm gone do for me! And I ain't about to go to no jail for that piece of shit in there. You hear me? I ain't doin' no more time for that bastard! They gone hafta catch me. I mean that." She was moving in a way that let Rose know she was not playing. Rose methodically began to help her pack.

"I don't blame you. Shit. You right. Take your chances, girl. You can go down South or somewhere and they will never find you. You got anybody down there?" Evelyn felt the support from Rose and relaxed a little.

"No!" she said flatly. "But I can make it. I been on my own since I was fifteen years old and I can take care of myself." She began to collect a few things she wanted to take with her as she prepared to go on the lam. She noticed the poem hanging on the wall over her bed near Rose.

"Oh, Rose, grab that for me, please?" Rose looked around at the room, noting the pale green color of the walls and how dirty the paint looked. She settled her eyes on a torn ragged piece of paper hung by two thumbtacks.

"Oh, you mean this poem here?"

"Yes. I keep that with me wherever I go. It reminds of how I used to be. Used to be?" she repeated. "That's a laugh. I still am like that."

"Wow," Rose exclaimed as she leaned over the headboard and took the poem down. She noticed how long it was. She was impressed. "You wrote this?" she asked, very much surprised.

"Yeah." She sounded pleased that Rose took an interest in it.

"Do you mind if I read it while you pack?"

"No. Go head."

"When did you write this?"

"Me? Oh, I wrote that a long time ago when I was in a detox unit. We was going to AA meetings and shit and the first step is to admit to yourself that you was powerless over your addiction and that your life had become unmanageable. Mine has always been unmanageable anyway, but I just wrote it. Go head, read it if you want."

Rose began to read the poem. It was entitled "POWERLESS."

"I drink, that's right and shoot up too
Don't worry about me, baby, you take care of you"
I talked like that as a means of protest
Never liked the idea of being POWERLESS

That booze, that dope. It feels so good
Keeps me acting like I think I should
Party hardy, didn't miss a stroke
Stayed out all night. Shot up big coke.

I had it made, I stayed fucked up
You never seen me with an empty cup.
Kept a feeling that I was always reeling
Telling lies and double dealing
Fucking anybody I want, didn't give it a rest
Never knew it but I was just POWERLESS.

No doubt about it I just knew I was right
Couldn't tell me shit, I had good hindsight
Did want I pleased, pleased who I did
My father was the only one from who I hid
Hated doing it for him I must confess
It never dawned on me.
Was it because of him? that I was POWERLESS.

Control!! That's it!! I'd do it right
I wouldn't drink in the day, I'd just drink at night
No low-class stuff, I'd drink the best
If I'd only knew it I was simply POWERLESS.

I thought I had it, two weeks went by
Only screwed up twice and that's no lie
No pills, no speed, no sweet cocaine
Just shot heroin alone
I figured this way I could save some of my brain
I though I could do it, Thought I'd passed the test
Little did I know, I was POWERLESS.

Went on like this but not for long
Couldn't understand what was going wrong
Drinking wine again, shootin' dope and shit
Too many men to take care of, I got to split
Not once did I think it, let alone suggest
That me, the nurturer, was POWERLESS.

Going home tomorrow I've worked hard in here
And I know it's going to be harder out there
To reach that point where I can say Yes!!!!
I can finally admit I know I'm POWERLESS.

"Wow, Evelyn, this poem is deep. I didn't know you could write. For real. This is really good." Rose was truly astonished at this discovery. It was as if she had forgotten about the dead body lying in a pool of blood in the next room and had begun to see Evelyn in a different light.

"Oh, I write things every once in a while. But my life has been such a mess lately though, I ain't wrote nothin in a long while." Rose handed her the poem as she looked her in the face, still very much impressed. Evelyn looked at it also, then rolled it up like a scroll and put it in the suitcase she had open on the bed.

"Are you sure you want to do this, Evelyn?" It was Yvette's voice. She had been standing in the doorway unnoticed by either.

"Yet. Look! I know you're right about what you sayin' and all, but I'm not about to have my baby in jail. I hope you can understand that. I know that God will punish me for what I did, but I just have to deal with that. You can go to the police or whatever. I don't care. I-I-I just don't care."

After a few unsuccessful moments of trying to persuade Evelyn to turn herself in, she proved to be undaunted. Evelyn left. Evelyn left the group standing in her house. She left a corpse lying in a pool of thickening blood. She left a history of despair and unhappiness. She boarded a bus to anywhere.

Kenny Speaks

Maddclyn had just awakened and for some reason or other, she had Kenny on her mind. She lay there with this vision of him as she had last seen him. She could still see the cute little Kenny she always knew anyway, even through the swollen pulpy mass of flesh she had looked at. She was thinking about why this happened to him. Who? It seemed such a shame to happen to someone like him. He wasn't all about hurting anyone. Why? She pushed the covers off her body and shifted her feet to the floor, fumbled under the bed for her slippers and slipped them over her feet. It was cold. *What was the heat on?* she wondered. She went to the thermometer, pushed the lever up to 75°, and continued on to the bathroom, checking the time as she passed the clock: 7:38 she noted. The television was still on from last night, and the news was in the process of being broadcast. She was in the bathroom when the announcement came over the air of Michael's death. She never saw the picture of Evelyn that was flashed in the background of the reporter giving the details of the murder.

But Kenny did. He was up bright and early that morning as he had been each morning he had been in the hospital. He immediately called Maddelyn. Her mother had answered the phone in a half-wake state. She was still groggy from her medicine-induced sleep and wasn't fully aware of the excitement in Kenny's voice, although it was extremely difficult to discern what he was saying anyway. She couldn't make it out and was satisfied to hang up, feeling that someone merely didn't know what they were doing. So she just hung up the phone and sank back into oblivion. Maddelyn thought she had heard the phone.

"Who was that, Mom?" she called to her sleeping mother. "Mom?" Still no response from her mother. She continued her morning bathroom rituals, but still wondered about the phone call. As she exited the bathroom and started down the hall to her room, the phone rang again. She stopped before she got any closer to her room and realized she was closer to the phone in her mother's room, so she turned and quickly stepped to the door and to the night table just inside where the phone was. She hurriedly picked up the receiver.

"Hello?" she answered.

"Haraugh? Maaghy?" It was Kenny again. He was trying to talk, but it was very hard to understand what he was saying. Maddelyn knew it was him as she barely made out his "hello."

"Kenny? Kenny?" He was still trying to talk even as she was calling to him. "Wait, Kenny. This is not going to work. I can't make out what you're saying. What?" She strained to decipher his utterances.

"Gha Kel-i-gi-ion," he tried to tell her phonetically to look at the television but because of his condition, she could not understand him.

"What?" Oh, Kenny, be quiet. I don't know what you're saying. Just hold on and I'll come over there. You just hold on, okay? Listen, I'm trying to get dressed now. As soon as I get dressed, I'll be right over. You hear me?" She did, however, sense the excitement in his voice and let him try again to convey what it was he was trying to say but still to no avail. She just talked over the garble.

"Kenny. No. Wait. It's no good. Hang up. Hang the phone up and wait for me. I'll be there in twenty minutes." She heard Kenny mutter something else but ignored it. She hung up and went to her room to get dressed. By this time the weather report was on, and that's what she focused on as she dressed. She faithfully watched the weather report because she liked to be prepared before she went outside. She seldom was caught without her umbrella on a rainy day. She couldn't though, figure out what Kenny was so hyped about. She hadn't a clue.

"Maddelyn?" It was her mother calling. "Did you get that phone?" *What the heck was she talking about?* Maddelyn wondered.

"Yes, Mom. I got the phone." She knew her mother probably wasn't all the way awake.

"Who was it?"

"It was Kenny, Mom. I'm getting ready to go to the hospital now to see him."

"Somebody called earlier, but I don't have any idea who it was. Okay. So you're getting ready to go out now?" The voice was trailing off as she finished her sentence.

"Yes, Mom. I'll call you later. Okay?" Maddelyn was dressed and down the step as she spoke. She had decided to wear her big heavy coat, so she opened the closet door and pulled it out. She usually had to decide what to wear after she opened the door. She went to the kitchen with her coat draped over her arms and opened the refrigerator door. She had in mind to pour herself a glass of juice but saw it was behind the milk and a lot of other things that would have had to be moved to get it. So she let it go and went to the dining-room table where she picked up her keys and took a quick look at the obituary that was still lying there. Greg's smile hit her. He was always smiling. She thought that was a good picture of him. She quickly put him out of her mind and put on her coat as she proceeded out the door, taking care to lock and check it to make sure it was locked.

The weather looked menacing. It was cold. The car was cold, and she had difficulty inserting the key into the door lock. She couldn't open the driver's side, but she finally managed to open the passenger side. She entered from that side and slid over the cold leather seats. The windows needed to be defrosted. She turned the ignition on, pushed the heat and air control lever to heat, and defrost then sat for a few minutes before pulling off. "I hate this!" she remarked to herself aloud. She really didn't appreciate the winter period. Once the windows had defrosted and the heat was beginning to seep into the car, she pulled off. As she was driving, she noticed there was no music playing. She knew she had pushed the button but nothing was coming out. She looked. The tape had unraveled in the tape player and was hanging out. *Darn.* she thought. *How did that happen?* Things weren't going right already. Then she thought, *Did I thank Jesus for starting out my day?* No, she remembered. So she said a little prayer of thanks. And sat still for a moment. She felt better after that. That always made her feel a little better. She continued on to the hospital. As she entered the hospital parking lot and took her ticket from the machine, she couldn't help but notice that there were several cars with dents in them. This made her a little wary. After she parked the car, and got out, she took care to note that there were no dents or scratches on hers, as she knew these kinds of things happened in parking lots. Little baby accidents, she called them. You seldom catch the culprit in baby accident cases. You just have to grin and bear it. Satisfied that everything was in order, she went past the little shelter where the parking lot attendant was stationed, speaking as she passed. She entered through the hospital main entrance and to the ICU, which was on the same floor where Kenny was. He was waiting for her with his pad and pen in hand.

"Ooooo." At least he could say that good. "Gooog yaug gah hea quass." He was trying to say "Good, you got here fast."

"Oh please, Kenny. Don't you try to talk. I can't understand a thing you're saying. Lay back, chile. My goodness!! What are you so excited about anyway? I know you can't be thinking about getting out of here? Are you?" Kenny was beginning to write as Maddelyn calmed him down. He wrote on the pad, "MICHAEL IS DEAD. EVELYN KILLED HIS ASS."

Maddelyn was stunned, staring at the words in disbelief as Kenny sat propped up in the bed holding the pad to her face with outstretched arms. Finally, she said, "Oh, my Lord. When did this happen?" She obviously was very distraught at this news. She sat down on the edge of the bed. "Evelyn killed him? How? Why?" The questions just seemed to fall out of her mouth flatly. Kenny continued writing. "OPENED HIM UP LIKE A CAN WITH A CAN OPENER."

"How did you find this out?" She was looking at him quizzically. Kenny was writing. "I JUST SAW IT ON THE TELEVISION. THEY HAD BOTH OF THEIR PICTURES ON THE TELEVISION CHANNEL 6 NEWS. THAT'S WHAT I WAS TRYING TO TELL YOU TO DO WHEN I CALLED YOU THIS MORNING."

Maddelyn sat motionless for a moment, then reached for the phone. Kenny stopped her.

"IT DON'T WORK," he wrote. Kenny still was muttering all the while he was writing these notes, but he was not to be understood. She noticed that some of the swelling had subsided and his face was looking better, even with the bandage wrapped around his nose. His lips didn't look as big as they did last time and his cheeks were less large.

"I have to call somebody to find out about this. I don't think I got a chance to tell you this, but Evelyn had said that she thought he was involved—well, not involved with Greg's murder but that she thought he had done it. I wonder if she did it to avenge Gregory's death?" Kenny looked at her and began writing.

"NO BETTER FOR HIS BLACK ASS. IT DON'T MATTER WHY SHE DID IT. THE WAY HE TREATED THAT GIRL HE SHOULD HAVE BEEN DEAD A LONG TIME AGO. GOOD FOR HIM. PRAISE GOD. SHE LEFT TOWN AND THE POLICE ARE LOOKING FOR HER."

He was looking at her with a look reminiscent of someone mocking somebody, with his lips pursed and his eyes bulging and his arms folded in front of his chest. As if to say "I said it that's right!" Maddelyn couldn't help but comment on the absurdity of this facial gesture in view of the already distorted features.

She said to him, "You don't need to make that face, honey. You look funny enough." He took it in jest and lightly tapped her on the head with the pad. "Look, Kenny, I'm not going to stay long. I'm going to try to get in touch with Curtis or somebody to see if I can find out more about this. I can't believe all this drama that is taking place in such a short amount of time. Can you? I mean, first Greg, then you, then my mother, now Michael and Ev—" Her voice trailed off in apparent disgust. She looked down at him lying in the bed. "How are you feeling?" Her attention turned to him. "You do look a lot better. For real. When do you think they'll let you come home?" Her mind was still very much on the Michael murder and questions and bewilderment were still very much a part of that unconscious thought process, but she tried to convey a touch of sympathy to Kenny.

He muttered, "Awaiught, ah guesch," attempting to say that he was all right. She turned to look at him full in the face and leaned to hug him. They embraced for a minute, then she got up from the bed and looked around the room.

"Tch tch tch," she made a couple of those quick, sucking noises. "You don't have any flowers or anything in here. I never even thought to get you any either. Oh, you poor baby. It looks so depressing in here. I wish they'd hurry up and move you to a room! Well, I'm depressed enough as it is. I'm going to get ready and leave."

At this point when she turned to look at him, she saw something in his face that wasn't there before. He looked despondent. And in his hand was a note pad. A different one. One that he obviously had written in prior to her arrival. He began to write on the pad that she had seen earlier.

WAIT PLEASE DON'T GO YET. I WANT YOU TO READ THIS. I WROTE IT SOON AS I FOUND OUT ABOUT MICHAEL. I NEVER TOLD ANYBODY NOT EVEN YOU.

She slowly made her way back to his bedside while she was reading his note. He had the full pad extended in his hand, offering it to her. She took it and noted that it was quite full.

"What is it?" she asked in a playful manner.

He motioned to her to read it. She opened to the first page. It began:

I AM SO GLAD THAT HE IS DEAD. I HATED HIM. I FELT IN MY HEART THAT HE WAS THE ONE THAT KILLED GREG ALL ALONG OR THAT HE HAD SOMETHING TO DO WITH IT. MICHAEL HAS ALWAYS BEEN JEALOUS OF GREG AND I KNEW THAT HE REALLY DIDN'T LIKE

HIM AS MUCH AS PEOPLE THOUGHT. HE RAPED ME A LONG TIME AGO WHEN WE WERE IN SCHOOL AND AFTER THAT HE MADE ME DO WHATEVER HE WANTED ME TO DO. HE THREATENED TO DESTROY MY BUSINESS. HE TRIED TO INTIMIDATE SOME OF MY MODELS. HE WAS SELLING DRUGS TO 1 OR 2 OF THEM AND I WAS SCARED OF HIM. HE BEAT ME UP A LOT OF TIMES AND MADE ME GIVE HIM MONEY AND DO ORAL SEX ON HIM. I WANTED TO KILL HIM MYSELF ONE DAY BUT—

Maddelyn stopped reading. She was getting sickened by what she was attempting to put together from what he had written. She looked over at Kenny. He had been lying with his face away from her and was crying. The tears were flowing steady from his eyes as he lay silently weeping. It was contagious. She too began to weep. Together they quietly shared a very private moment of deep hurt and shame and caring. Kenny cried almost uncontrollably as he felt Maddelyn's closeness. Maddelyn held him close to her as though he were an infant in her arms. They held each other for a good five minutes. Then Maddelyn gently pulled herself away, took the pad, and tore the pages into small pieces, one at a time. She didn't even want to read anymore. She threw them all into the wastepaper basket near the door. She looked at Kenny with such concern in her teary eyes and said to him, "You don't ever have to worry about anyone knowing about this. Okay? I'm going to leave now. I'll be back in touch with you later today. Take care." With that good-bye, she exited the room, just as a nurse was entering with his meal. As soon as Kenny saw her, he began to mumble.

"Aw gno klease gnont—" the nurse began taunting him. They apparently were being playful.

"Shut that mumblin' up now. You know don't nobody know what you tryin' to say. You gon eat dis here food after I done mashed it all up. I know that much."

She allowed Maddelyn to pass as she was talking and winked at her as though to let her know that she had every thing under control. And she knew how to handle Kenny. Maddelyn smiled at her and peered back at Kenny who now has his arms folded and his head turned away from the nurse, appearing to shun her.

She continued down the corridor to the front door and the parking lot to Benny. It was still very cold out, but she had no trouble with the locks this time, as she had expected. She sat in the car and quickly turned on the heat and defrost. Michael entered her mind. *How could he have been so cruel?* she asked herself. Then she thought, *where is he now? What is happening to Evelyn?* She didn't have any answers, so she decided to go get some.

She cleared her mind of the ICU event and decided to stop past Evelyn's house since it was nearby. Pulling out of the parking space, she proceeded to follow the arrows that guided her through the security guard station so he could collect the ticket and parking fee. She turned right as she carefully entered the stream of traffic heading up Old York Road. Then she drove down Thirteenth Street to Clearfield. She saw that the area around Evelyn's house was cordoned off. The yellow tape also was around Michael's car, which she noticed first.

Police or at least people in uniforms and suits were standing in and around the house. It was clear she couldn't get down the street, so she turned and parked her car in the first available space nearby. She was thinking of how she was going to approach the situation as she got out of the car and began walking towards the area of activity. There wasn't a crowd of onlookers, but a few people were standing across the street, talking and pointing. She approached that group first.

"Excuse me, but isn't that Ms. Henderson's house?" she asked, pointing to Evelyn's house. The man she posed the question to looked at her with surprise.

"I don't know no Ms. Henderson, but I do know that a young lady used to live there. Somebody just got killed in there. Happened last night. I seen 'em take the body out bout a hour ago. I think they looking for her now from what I heard."

The other young man who was standing with him chimed in. "Yeah, I think her name was, uh Evelyn. I didn't know her last name, but I used to see her around here all the time. She ain't here now, though, I can tell you that much." All three were peering into the house as the door was wide open and suited men were seen moving about inside. A uniformed officer was standing on the porch as though on guard.

"Do you know what happened?" Maddelyn asked either of the two.

"Nope. I don't know nothin' but somebody got killed," one replied.

"Me neither," said the other. "They won't tell nobody nothin'."

Maddelyn assumed he was referring to the police being closed-mouthed about any details and decided she would try for herself. She alerted the two men that she was going to try to find out herself and began to attempt to go under the yellow tape. As she did so, the officer standing on the porch started for her, saying, "Excuse me, ma'am. You can't come into this area. This area is restricted." She stopped as he was nearing her.

"Oh, I'm sorry. This is my cousin's house, and I want to know what happened. Where is she? Is she in there?"

The officer responded by aiding her back under the yellow tape, explaining that he would not give her any information. He suggested that she go to the police station down the street. She saw that this would be fruitless and decided to heed the officer's advice.

"See. I told you," one of the men said. "They ain't tellin' nobody nothin'." She looked at them both.

"Yeah, I see. Thanks for trying to help me." She smiled at them and walked to her car. She sat in the car a few minutes before turning it on this time, thinking of what she would say at the police station. Once she was satisfied with her questions, she pulled off, headed for the police station. It was just down the street, as she was already on Broad Street. She merely had to turn the car around.

She parked across the street from the station, careful to feed the parking meter first. Looking both ways on Broad Street, she cautiously crossed. Broad Street is one of the biggest streets in Philly and the busiest. She knew to take caution before crossing. She entered the building and went to the window that had a sign taped on it. The sign read "STOP HERE." It was a sliding window that she was standing in front of, and both sides were closed. She noticed that there were two officers appearing to be engrossed in some type of paperwork at their desks and two other officers chatting and laughing and, obviously, ignoring her. She waited a minute or so before speaking.

"Excuse me!" she interrupted. The officer nearest to the window looked up.

"I'll be right with you, mamm." Then he went back to what he was doing. She relaxed herself on the counter and peered directly at him. He looked up at her again and said, "Miss? Would you take a seat over there, please?" pointing to an area to the side of her. As she moved to look at the area, he said, "Hold it!" He barked, "What is the name of the person you want to see?" She really could not understand why he was talking to her in that manner. She felt as though he were talking to her as though she had committed a crime or something.

"I wish to speak to someone about Ms. Evelyn Henderson. Is she here?" She was quickly becoming disenchanted with this unholy situation, and these people. They all stopped and looked at her when she mentioned Evelyn's name. The whole situation was making her feel as though she had done something wrong anyway, but these stabbing stares were even more convicting.

"Have a seat please. I'll get somebody to talk to you."

"How long will you be?" she inquired.

"Ma'am. Just have a seat please. I'll be with you shortly." The officer appeared to be getting annoyed at the question, and Maddelyn could not understand why but she didn't want to press the issue any further. She sought a chair, one apart from another person who was sitting and waiting.

"I don't know why they always got to be so damn nasty!!" It was the other woman who had already been seated who was speaking, but she didn't appear to be speaking to Maddelyn. "Just because we black they think they can talk to us any way they please." She turned to look at Maddelyn at this point. "I been here forty-five minutes and ain't nobody said nothin' to me since they told me to take a seat. They brought my son in here over three hours ago and ever since I been here they been tellin' me to wait. I'm gettin' sick of it." She had barely finished complaining when the officer closest to the window called to her.

"Ms. Jackson? Would you please step to the window?"

She gave a surprised look to Maddelyn. "Well!! It's about time." She then proceeded to the window. Maddelyn was left to wonder if she too was going to have to wait three hours. She prepared herself to wait fifteen minutes and check again.

She had heard how the police treat people who come into the station. But this was her very first experience. She did not cater to the feeling at all. She felt vulnerable. As though she had to remind herself that she had done nothing wrong. *Why are they so intimidating?* she wondered. She rationalized that they come in contact with the outlaws daily and that they feel anyone associated with them is just as bad. Or something like that. She couldn't put her finger on it. Well, she's not! She thought, oh, well. She decided to just grin and bear it.

She began to scan the environment that now surrounded her. It was cold and bleak. The floors were filthy. The walls were painted battleship gray, and they were filthy with names and obscenities written all over them. The air was stale and dank. And all the windows had chicken wire running through them. The lighting was emitted from fluorescent bulbs, but few were working. It was horrible. The whole scene was depressing, she concluded. This revelation prompted her to get up and walk to the window. She didn't even care how long she had been there already. As far as she was concerned, it was too long.

"Excuse me," she snarled at the officer at the window. He was engaged in a conversation that seemed to be very funny to him and the person he was talking to. But his laughter ceased at hearing the tone of her voice. Something wasn't funny anymore. He turned around to face her with a sneer on his face, which had turned a sickening blend of pink and white from laughing. She hated pink and his color pink was even harder to look at.

"Ma'am. Just have a seat please, we'll be with you in a minute." He tried to be authoritative and commanding this time. But she didn't go for it.

"No, I will not have a seat!" she angrily responded. "Look, Mister. All I want to know is whether or not you have a person by the name of Ms. Evelyn Henderson in your custody. Now I would like one of you to answer that question right now. And if you can't, then I would appreciate it if you got me somebody who could." And she stood there. The smiles disappeared from all the white faces and they all were looking at her as she defiantly looked each one squarely in the eye. The officer sitting in the far corner, who had been talking to another officer, stood up and leaned on the desk.

"Uh, Ma'am? Uh, I happen to have been one of the officers at the scene where I believe your, uh, Ms. Henderson lived. She did live on Clearfield? If I'm not mistaken. Is that right?" Maddelyn didn't answer. She was getting angrier by the second. *What were these people doing?* she thought. Were they deliberately trying to provoke her? She had sensed a note of facetiousness in his voice. Was he toying with her? She had a look of disgust on her face as she fought to restrain herself from getting loud and venting her anger verbally.

"Is she here?" Maddelyn demanded once again.

"Uh, Ma'am, I'm merely trying to establish if we are talking about one and the same people here. Now, if you are not going to cooperate with us, how can you expect us to properly satisfy you?" The officer looked around at the other officers who were beginning to smile. "Now, is—"

He stopped talking because Maddelyn had left. She could not believe what she had just endured. She was on the verge of tears as she walked. She was angry. Angry, humiliated, and frustrated. *How could they be so darned inept?* she thought. So rude. So darned arrogant. She strained to push open the heavy glass door that led to the outside and stepped briskly towards her car, which was parked across the street. She almost walked out into the street without looking, but a car sped past her and caused her to stop and take better precaution before taking another step. She waited until she could safely make it to the other side of the street. Her keys were already in her hand. She had been holding them the whole time she was in the police station. She pressed the code to her alarm and entered the vehicle. It was still cold outside. As she sat while the car warmed up, she pulled herself together a little more. She took a deep breath, held her head back, and expelled the air in her lungs. Jouscar popped into her mind. So she set out for his house.

When she got there, she was relieved to see his lights were on and his car was parked outside, indicating that he was probably home.

"Good," she said. She got out of the car, went to the door, and knocked. She was shivering as she stood waiting for him to answer. She looked at her watch: 5:24. The door suddenly opened and he was staring at her as if he wasn't sure who it was at first but quickly changed his glare to a broad smile.

"Maddie? Come on in, baby. I was just about to call you again." He was as anxious to see her as she was him. He had been trying to reach her all day. "Maddie, I know you heard about Ice? Well, guess what! I was there!" He took her coat as she was trying hard to listen to every word he was saying. He hung her coat up and they both sat on the long leather sofa.

"You won't believe this. I was there!! I was there, Maddy, when it happened. And he was just lying there dead and Evelyn—"

"Wait a minute. Wait a minute," she said. She wanted to slow things down now. He was talking too fast for her, and she didn't want to miss anything. She wanted details.

"Where is Evelyn now?" she asked calmly.

"Don't know!" He threw his hands in the air. He had been holding a shirt in his hands the whole time as though he was going to put it on. Maddelyn noticed his shirt and his sexiness but tried to overlook it. He saw her look, though.

"She just booked. Left us standing in the house." Maddelyn was frowning as he attempted to give a brief account. Her eyes kept being pulled to his nipples.

"You mean—wait a minute. You mean to tell me that she—wait a minute. What happened? I mean why did she have to kill him? How did she do it? Wait a minute. Hold it. This is too fast. I want to know every detail. Now you just wait, I'm thirsty. Do you have some wine or something? Lord Jesus. I need a drink for this before you start."

She had noticed that she might be getting a little turned on by this atmosphere. He had a very nice house, and the music was proper. She sat back a little and attempted to settle herself down. Jouscar stopped talking.

"Oh! Oh! Yeah, uh, sure. I know. You're right. I'm moving too fast. Hold on, uh, I mean, um, wait here. I mean I'll be right back." He stood up to go to the kitchen. She let out a low "ooooh" to herself as she tried not to look at the curves of his back and the cutoff shorts he was wearing. Jouscar, forever the indoor sportsman, had taken the moment away from her to recoup himself as well. It wasn't as though he hadn't seen that gorgeous body of hers as he slipped that coat from over her shoulders. Don't think he missed that brief glimpse of cleavage either. She was looking very good to him. He had not had her in quite a while, he recalled. No better time than tonight, he thought. This was a pleasant thought. Oh, yeah. He knew how to do her plus he knew that she wouldn't give it up if she didn't want to. So this was going to be fun. And tonight, he suspected vulnerability. This would definitely work out in his favor. He went for it. He leaned his head out of the kitchen to look at her. He saw her legs from the kitchen.

"Take off your shoes, honey. Relax. Make yourself comfortable. I'll be right in. I got a lot to talk to you about." She saw him look at her, and she saw what he looked at. She closed her legs tightly and shifted them around more to the side and looked into the kitchen, smiling a playful sort of smile. She relaxed against the back of the sofa and removed her shoes without thinking.

Smokey Robinson and the Miracles were on the turntable. "Bad Girl" was just beginning to play. Jouscar dimmed the lights as he brought a bottle of chilled Rosé and two glasses back to where they had been sitting. As he sat down, he sat closer this time and she didn't move.

"Why do we need the lights down low to talk? Look, Curtis, this is no time to be thinking about fooling around. There are serious things happening here. Can't we just talk??" she asked him, teasingly, yet still not moving from his closeness, her eyes being pulled to his smooth chest. She always was a sucker for a bare chest, and he knew it too. That's why he never bothered to put the shirt on. He saw her looking. What a game!!

"Oh! That. I, uh. You see, it helps me to relax cause I'm still all wound up from last night but listen, for real—." He talked and talked and filled Maddelyn in on all the details. By twelve o'clock, they had exhausted the grim details and were onto another subject. Equally as exhausting. Maddelyn spent the night. And not on his sofa.

II
REVELATION

Juice

Eleven years had passed since Evelyn disappeared. No one had seen or heard from her during that time. Much had changed in the way of life in that neighborhood and with that group of people who were involved with the tragic incidents of its past.

The Vietnam war had been over for some years, but Jouscar managed to catch the tail end. He enlisted in an attempt to avoid any involvement with Michael's death, but as it turned out, his four-year tenure as a captain in the United States Air Force actually served to catapult him into a very respectable standing in society afterwards.

The war had made it possible for some to become rich and for others to continue to struggle to survive. He was one of those who profited. His contacts and circle of friends he made as an officer had remained true even as he was honorably discharged from the military. He rubbed elbows with the very rich as well as with those who held high political stature. He, more or less, became a real estate mogul as well as a prominent investor. All of his investments in the blue chip companies were yeilding high monetary returns for him. He, in turn, reinvested his profits in commercial strips, of which he owned several. He also took advantage of multilevel parking lots of which he also owned a few.

He was fast becoming a proficient schmoozer. And during one particular shmooze, he managed to get invited to a senatorial inauguration in Washington, D.C. This invite would very well serve a twofold purpose.

It had been brought to his attention at this particular function that a friend of his was to be audited in the near future. He knew that already. So, it was not by happenstance that he was in attendance. Upon arriving in D.C., he went directly to work.

He'd been introduced to Mrs. Stanton twice, and had mentioned Ms. Burks name to her on one occasion. He managed to keep up with her whereabouts. He watched as she mingled. She finally sat down. He pursued. He was diplomatic and accommodating during this, their second encounter.

"I have been patiently waiting for the opportunity to speak with you. Do you mind if I join you?" She allowed him to sit with her. "Thank you. I'm going to cut to the chase here. I have a friend, in Philly. Her name is Maddelyn Burks and she is scheduled to be audited by Crass Int. Now, I certainly don't mean to impose, but I, 'we' would be most grateful if we could be assured that Ms. Burks agency would not have to be concerned about this up and coming audit. I do know Senator Vicks from Philly very well and—"

"I see. Uh, but, uh, just where do I fit into all this?" asked the woman.

"Well. You fit in because of your affiliation with the audit review board, as I understand."

"I see. As you understand. And just how well do you know Ms. Burks, Mr. Jouscar?" Jouscar looked at the woman for a moment. Confident, he smiled, moved closer, and placed his hand on the fingers of her hand as he posed his answer.

"Uh, a lot better than I know you. I'll tell you that much. As a matter of fact, Miss Stanton—"

"Mrs. Stanton," she politely corrected, her eyes on his hand but not moving from his touch.

"Oh. I'm sorry. Mrs. Stanton, as a matter of fact," he hesitated and leaned away from the woman, "well never mind now. Uh, Ms. Burks is a very good friend of mine. You might say we grew up together. I've . . . " The woman interrupted him again.

"Why the never mind? Up until this point, I thought we were communicating. I'm confused. Is there a problem because I corrected you? And where did that charming smile disappear to? Unless, of course, you were about to say something that was inappropriate, and if that were the case . . . then I'd like to hear what it was."

Jouscar's mind was racing. She had unnerved him. He hadn't expected her to respond with such directness. He was caught off guard.

"Okay. Well, now, uh, Mrs. Stanton . . ."

"Edith," she politely corrected him, knowing exactly what she was doing.

"Oh!" he quipped in a surprised tone. "Edith? Okay. Uh, Mrs. Edith. Now where were we?" Jouscar continued to be flippant.

"I was talking to you about my proper title. Where were you?" Jouscar felt inept. He could not compete.

"Oh, yeah. As a matter of fact, I was just wondering how I could make it possible to get to know you a little better." He was pleased with himself that he had said it. He sensed that she was testing the depth of his intentions. He decided to be as overt as he thought would be acceptable at this point in the conversation.

"Well, I see that charming smile has returned. But what exactly are you trying to say, Mr. Jouscar? That you would like to begin an ongoing affair? Or that you would like a one-night stand with me? Or that you would like to get to know me better? I'm not sure I understand where you're going with this."

Jouscar leaned closer to the woman, confidence at full throttle.

"Look, I know this is the eighties and all that, but I'm not one to bite my tongue, and I have never fallen prey to intimidation by male or female. Now, I know you've come a long way, baby, I can see that in your Virginia Slims, but where you've just arrived, I been there a long time before you. And where I'm going with this, and where I would like to go with this are two different places." The woman had risen from her seat as he finished talking. She placed a card on the table as she walked away.

"I see. Do you always have trouble saying what you want to say? Or is there an insecurity issue involved here? Well, when you figure out what it is that you want to say to me, you give me a call. Okay, sweetie? I'm a busy woman." At a loss for words, he felt lost with her. He had not been able to measure up. He lost.

Jouscar watched her walk away as his final comments continued to reverberate in his head. Gotdammit. *Why didn't I just say it?* he thought. He glanced at the business card that she placed before him, noting that there was an office phone number on the front of the card and another number written in pencil on the back. He secured the card in his wallet, knowing that he had failed to accomplish what he had intended, his initial intentions being to intervene and assure that Maddelyn's audit would have a favorable outcome. He was sure he would have no problem negotiating. He was not prepared for this. He was told that the name of the person he was to talk to was "E. Stanton." The affair he was attending was for the inauguration for "E. Stanton." It wasn't until their first encounter this evening that he became aware that she was a woman. And he, forever the indoor sportsman, got sidetracked and went for the game with her. He lost. He reasoned that he had failed, but now, it was imperative that he get back in touch with her. And soon. He needed a chance to recoup.

He sipped his Vodka Collins and looked around the room. A cursory scan of the tables forced his eyes to settle on yet another woman in the room. She was seated at a table with two men and two other women. As elegance was the order of the evening, this woman appeared to be drenched in it. She seemed to stand out from the others. From where he sat, he could see she was sparkling with jewelry and dressed just a little better than the other women. He concluded that it was the tiara that sat on her head that set her apart. He forgot all about his failure. She also happened to be looking in his direction when he noticed her. He felt compensation was on the way.

She was decidedly, a pretty woman. Her African-American features set perfectly into an ebony complexion. Her eyes were large and her lips aptly pursed. He just knew she was looking at him. He fixed his stare. The eye contact was sufficient to get his mind off E. Stanton and on to her. She affixed her stare momentarily to his before returning her attention to the gentlemen who had been addressing her at her table. He was anxious to see her up close. It was impossible to get a good body shot from where he sat, so he stood, fixed his bowtie, pulled his cummerbund in place under his jacket, and walked in the direction of the party. His attention was averted midway between his table and his destination.

"Juice!" A voice called out. He turned to his left and saw an arm motioning to him from a table approximately four rows in. He looked harder at the motioning figure. It looked like someone he knew, but he couldn't immediately place the face. He had quickly assessed that it was female and it didn't look bad. So he smiled and gave the table he was destined for a quick look. She was engrossed and not looking his way. He changed direction altogether and headed for the fourth row in. As he approached the table, he began to feel strange. What he was seeing was causing him to become disoriented. He stopped one row before reaching the table.

"Kenny?" Jouscar was stunned. He could only repeat the words. "Kenny?"

"Kyndra! Dahlin. It's Kyndra. Get over here and stop acting so surprised. Shoooot. You know me." The figure was moving towards him as she spoke. He was too astounded to do anything but allow himself to be drawn into her embrace. He looked deep into her face to assure himself that he wasn't hallucinating. She pulled back and gave him a good look, turning her face side to side and finally posing with her hands daintily poised on her hips.

"Well? Say something. You can't just stand there looking that good and not be able to talk. But then again, maybe that ain't so bad either." This brought a smile to his face and laughter from the table of women he was about to be seated with.

"Ken..., uh, Kyndra? Damn, girl! Damn! You look good. I mean you really... I can't believe it! I just can't believe my eyes." And he couldn't.

"Believe it, dahling. It's real. Ain't nothin' fake about it. What you doin here in D.C.? You a senator or something? I know you ain't no politician? Is you?" She seemed to be in extremely good spirits, he had noticed. Happier than he ever remembered.

"Wait a minute. Wait a minute. You got to let me digest you for another minute before I answer that." He looked at her face. It was slightly different from the Kenny he knew. Her nose was perfect, as thought it had been chiseled into the face. The lips were perfectly formed and the makeup was just right. This was undoubtedly the face of a woman. The body was adorned in a tight, silver lamé dress and revealed an almost perfectly shaped rear end. Her legs were wrapped in black silk stockings with butterflies and thick seams in the back. Her hair was long and naturally curly. She, indeed, was real.

"I know. We have a lot to talk about. First, let me introduce you to my 'entourage.' The one in the pink is Saleea and the one with the titties popping out of her dress is Eroka and this beauty here is Kelley." They all spoke as they were introduced. And Jouscar, back to earth, and fully saturated with the situation, responded to each in turn. His charm at the forefront.

"And, girls, this is a very dear friend of mine. We from the same neighborhood in Philly. We grew up together." She shifted her look to Jouscar. "We been through a lot together," she said as she gently grasped his arm.

"No doubt about that," Jouscar added. "We go back quite a ways. But it's so good to see you. Even though you've changed a little."

"You call this a little?" She brought the wide smile back to her face and looked around the table. "You better believe this was a change of a lifetime, baby. And it don't get no better than this. Tell him, girls." All laughed and agreed. "Oh! Let me get you a fresh drink ... and we can talk. Why don't you come on over to the bar with me and let's get reacquainted. Excuse us for about three hours, girls." They all laughed and made lewd comments as she and Jouscar departed.

The bar wasn't too crowded, so they easily found a table that wasn't occupied.

"What you drinkin' these days, honey?" Kyndra inquired. He looked at his cup of watered down Vodka Collins.

"I believe this was a Vodka and Tom Collins mix." She ordered two for him and two Remy Martins for herself. He rose to assist her, but she managed to get all four drinks to the table without spilling a drop.

"Now, Juice, I must say, you age well. How old you gettin' to be? Thirty-eight? Thirty-nine? Except for the gray at your temples and mustache, you look the same."

"Hey, thanks. I try. I eat the right foods and take a lot of herbs. You know they got one for everything. But look at you. You aren't even graying. Look, you got to tell me. I'm dying to know ... did you, uh. ... ?" She attempted to finish his question.

"Did I have plastic surgery? You better believe it, baby. Not only that, I had my sex changed too." That was the answer Jouscar was looking for.

"That's what I wanted to know. Really? Shit! ... Did you ... no, tell me this. How do they do that?" He had no idea what to expect as an answer.

"Easy! They just split that little thing down the middle, folded it up, and tucked it up inside me. And now it works better than it ever did when it was just hanging outside with those horrid balls clanging and banging around. Uh, yes, I experience orgasm and, uh, yes, I have sex. I have the best sex that any woman can have. I just can't have no babies. That's the only difference between me and the other women. Besides, between me and you, my little butt was getting worn out. I needed to get me a new hole." Kyndra thought that remark was hilarious. Jouscar was too overwhelmed with her explanation to be able to laugh. Or even think about what she was referring to.

"You mean they cut your penis in half, and wait a minute, where does this hole come from?" He didn't care how naive the question may have sounded, although he thought it a little on the ignorant side.

"Well, they sort of make your urethra your vagina and use your penis to give you the stimulation. So when another penis is inserted, you can feel it. And I just can't tell you how good it feels." She feigned a shudder.

"I'll be damned." He took a gulp of his drink. "But what did they do with your testicles? Your balls? Where did they put them?" This line of questioning seemed bizarre, but it was rapidly becoming okay to do and Jouscar was beginning to treat it as such.

"Oh. Those things. They ain't good for nothing but holding fluid and making up sperm and, who needs that? Certainly not a woman! She gets it from other men. And I don't need it at all." Kyndra was proud to speak of her transformation. And it was easy for her to joke about. This made it even more comfortable for Jouscar to be with her and talk about it. He could feel the happiness in her.

"I been a real woman for seven years now. And for seven years I have been happier than I have ever been in my life. Let me tell you, after I got out of the hospital, I was, oooh, I was so humiliated by what that damn hospital did to me. You should have seen me. I looked like some kind of Frankenstein or something. So I went out and got the name of a real plastic surgeon right here in Washington. And he redid my entire face. And I love him. And guess what else? Well, not all in one shot. I had to liquidate my business to get the money for the face, but it took me forever to beg, borrow, and steal for the genital changes. I got to like Washington. This place is even more corrupt than Philly. I got to know more people here in one month than I knew in my whole life in Philly. And people are more accepting here. Well, enough about me. What brings *you* to the Capital state?" Jouscar was still mulling over the genital surgery.

"Oh! Um, I came up for some business. I been looking at some property not far from here in Silver Springs. That's not too far from here. And while I was up here, I took advantage of this invitation to Congressman Stanton's inauguration. But I seemed to have pissed her off."

"Her?" Kyndra chimed in. "He ain't no woman. If you talking about Ellis, he's a man, and I can attest to that. And don't even worry about pissing him off. I see him just about every day.

"Oh no. You mean to tell me. . . . Edith Stanton is not the one?"

"No. Hell, no. That bitch ain't nobody since they separated." Kyndra took pleasure in divulging that tidbit. And Jouscar was more grateful than she could have known.

"Man! So she's not him, huh? That's funny. That's really funny. You just don't know how good that makes me feel to hear you say that. Hey, why don't we just go back over to your table with the other young ladies and enjoy the rest of the evening. I still have a little time before I have to get to bed." Jouscar had finished one drink and had almost finished the second one. His words were beginning to slur.

"Sure, baby. Hold on, though. Let me get you and me just another little drink."

The night wore on, and the party at their table got wilder. The inauguration was held in one of the hotel's rooms and the bar had closed. Kyndra's table was among the last tables that was still alive and flowing with booze. Others had joined them and they had pulled tables together to accommodate the growing number of people.

Jouscar never got to meet with the congressman that night. But he did get to meet Eroka up close and personal. She seemed to gravitate to him as soon as he got back to their table. She was not at all bashful about her intentions.

She liked him and she wanted him. And she went straight for him. He spent the better part of the evening sprawled in her arms. He was content with that. He was having a good time. Nay. A great time. He was getting drunk, to be sure. Eventually, he had to be escorted to his suite by the core group.

While they were waiting for the elevator to arrive, he managed to become engrossed in a very long and passionate kiss with Eroka at which point he passed out. It took all four of them to lift him onto the elevator and then into his suite. Once inside, they dumped him on the bed and took advantage of any food and liquor that was available in the room. They seemed to handle their booze with little effect, as none of them appeared little more than high. The suite was a double suite and easily accommodated the troupe. Eroka landed in bed with Jouscar. Kyndra, in the meantime, made a phone call. And inside of five minutes, there were two men at the door. She knew one of them and she took him. Saleea and Kelley were left with the other. All beds and couches were occupied.

Morning came at 10:30 for Jouscar. Noting this, he sat straight up on the side of the bed and began to try to put the evening together. There was no one else in the room with him. He remembered being with other people. He assumed, correctly, that they had left. *Hope we had fun,* he thought.

He showered, shaved and dressed, and left the suite. As he entered the lobby, he was addressed by the manager.

"Good morning, Mr. Jouscar. I trust you had a satisfying evening here at the Blake?"

Jouscar thought it strange that he would be remembered by the manager. He hadn't met him before that moment.

"Yes. Uh, yes, I slept well, thank you." He continued toward the revolving door.

"Excuse me, uh, Mr. Jouscar, but may I have a word with you?" The manager again forced Jouscar to look in his direction. Jouscar stopped and turned towards him.

"Are you the manager?" he asked, as though annoyed.

"Pardon me for stopping you, but yes, I am the manager." He pointed to the name plate on his jacket. "I won't be long at all. I just would, if I may, sir, advise you to be a little more discreet in your social affairs here at the Blake. I have been informed that the party you were with last night was not the most noteworthy. And may I add, prostitution is not something that is taken lightly here at the Blake." With that said, he glared directly into Jouscar's eyes. "I'm aware of the calls that were made from your room last night. A word to the wise, sir." The manager continued to stare him in the eyes before starting to walk away.

Jouscar stopped him. "Hey. Hold on a minute. What are you talking about?"

"I'm talking about your guests last evening, Mr. Jouscar." Now it was he who was annoyed. "I'm talking about having other guests solicited to your suite for the purpose of prostituting the four 'women' you were seen cavorting with at the congressman's inauguration. I'm talking about them escorting 'you' to 'your' suite immediately after. I'm talking about discretion! Mr. Jouscar." The manager turned to walk way again.

Jouscar was perplexed. "Wait a minute Mr. uh." He leaned forward to get a closer look at the name plate. "Mr. Walker. Look, I appreciate your advice, but I don't need it. I had no prostitutes come to my suite last night. They were friends of mine, thank you, and they didn't even stay." He actually had no idea what happened.

"Very well, sir. Have a nice day." The manager bowed slightly, and smiled as he walked away, leaving Jouscar standing. Jouscar quickly tried to recount the events of the evening. It was a blur. He remembered being with Kenny and enjoying the other people at the table, but everything else was a blur.

"Mr. Walker." He wanted to know more. "Hold on for just a minute. Can we discuss this a little further. I seriously don't know what you're talking about. Maybe you could help me."

"Mr. Jouscar, I don't have time to play games." He stopped and stood at attention in front of Jouscar.

"I ain't playing no game with you, man. Look, I don't even remember what happened last night, if you really want to know the truth." Jouscar tried to smooth over the moment. "What happened? I mean, uh, who told you I was soliciting prostitutes? And are you sure it was my suite? I'm in—"

"I know what suite you occupy, Mr. Jouscar. If I may? I happen to know all of the 'women' you were with last night. Most of the politicians and wealthy men here in Washington do, too. I know that you are from Philadelphia, but I assumed you knew as well. Your 'friends,' Mr. Jouscar, are highly paid call girls. Okay? And last night, after you and your 'friends' retired to 'your' suite, several visitors, subsequently, were called to come to your suite throughout the morning. Last one leaving at approximately eight thirty-five, and your friends leaving at approximately nine-twenty. There were six male visitors total. To be exact. You see, one of the visitors was not pleased with the 'service' in your room and he told me about it. Your 'friends' generally work out of the Constitution, which is down the street. Room service here at the Blake is quite different from room service at the Constitution. If you get my meaning.

Now, will that be all, Mr. Jouscar? Oh. And pimping is not taken lightly here in Washington. Understood? Mr. Jouscar?" Jouscar listened and learned.

"I . . . uh, see what you mean. Uh, I just didn't know . . . uh, I just . . . uh, look. Sorry I caused any problems, but look, I am nobody's pimp. I don't have any idea what happened after I left the party . . . uh, inauguration. But I would appreciate your understanding." He folded a fifty-dollar bill in his hand and extended it in a handshake to the manager who graciously accepted.

"You needn't worry about any further comments from me, Mr. Jouscar. I hope you have a pleasant day. And, a word to the wise, Mr. Jouscar, this town's full of 'em!"

Jouscar allowed the conversation to end and left. He was more amused by the situation than confused. *That damn Kenny*, he thought. *I should have known.* He smiled to himself as he went about his business. As he drove down Constitution Avenue, he passed by the Constitution Hotel. It didn't look like a dump, he thought. As a matter of fact, it looked rather swanky. He stopped, parked across the street from it, and went in. He walked directly to the clerk and inquired if there were a person by the name of Kyndra Bailey on the register. The clerk checked the register and advised him that there was no person by that name registered at the hotel. He left, not sure how he would get back in touch with her. He figured that she would not register under her real name. He didn't even know her real name at this point.

He drove to Silver Springs and completed his business. Upon his return to his hotel, he was informed that there were two messages for him. One was from Kyndra, the other from Maddelyn. He immediately called the number. There was no answer. He then called Maddelyn and she was not available.

It was three thirty-seven and this was his last night in Washington. He figured he would relax a while and try to reach them both a little later. Instead, he went down to the indoor pool and exercise room. On his way to the pool, he was pleasantly reminded of the face he had looked at in the inauguration. The one with the tiara.

"Hi, there," she said to him. "I see you're still here."

"Oh. Yeah, I'm still here. I've been staying here for a couple of days. I'm just going to take a dip and relax for a while." He assumed she had already been since she was coming from that direction with a towel in her hand and her hair still damp. *She looked gorgeous*, he thought.

"You already been in there, I see. How's the water?" Jouscar was hardly able to concentrate on the pool now that he had seen her body. She was clad in a very revealing bikini bathing suit, and it failed to hide very much of her full figure. She was short in height but solidly built. Her face was radiant with natural beauty and color. Her skin was even darker than he remembered. More like toffee colored. Smooth, contoured legs and ample back. He was not about to let her get away.

"Oh. The water's great. It's heated, you know? Well, it was nice seeing you again. I'll be seeing you around." She started on her way, but he stopped her.

"Excuse me, but, uh, I didn't get your name."

"I didn't give my name," she said as she continued walking.

Jouscar was at a loss for a come back. He drew a total blank. He could not take his eyes off of her butt. She never looked back.

Jouscar lay in the pool's shallow end. His mind had wandered to Maddelyn. They had been married going on two years now, he thought. And here he was still trying to play the bachelor role. Could that be the reason he wasn't faring very well in this game? Should he not be doing this any more? These thoughts crossed his mind. If not a stark realization, it was indeed an eye opener for him at that moment. He seemed to have come to some sort of crossroad. It felt good. Maybe it was time for him to stop it. He was distracted by a splash in the water next to him. It was a little girl who had jumped into the pool. He smiled to her and then to himself. It was time to get out of the water, he thought. It's too deep.

He was waiting for the elevator when the clerk at the desk called him to give him a message. It was from Kyndra, and it was requesting him to call her at five o'clock. It wasn't the same number he had earlier. He went to his room and fixed himself a drink. It was four-forty. He lay across the bed, resting until five. At five o'clock on the nose, he called. She answered.

"Juice? Good I'm so glad you called. Look, I got to get out of here. When you going back to Philly?" Jouscar had planned to leave the next afternoon, but he really didn't have any more business in that area. He was free to leave whenever.

"Hey, you. Just hold on there for a minute. I got a bone to pick with you. What do—"

"I know, I know. Look, Juice, I'll explain everything to you when I see you, okay? But for now, please, I got to get out of this one-horse town now. When are you leaving? I'll wait if you're going tonight, but I'll see you in Philly if you leaving any later. So when are you going?" Jouscar didn't particularly like being rushed.

"I had planned to leave tomorrow afternoon. I can leave any time I want. Why? What's—"

"Good. Stop asking questions. I'll tell you everything. Now, you can pick me up right outside your hotel. I'll see you when you come out the door and when they bring you your car around, I'll come over. Now what time?" She was really pushing it, he thought.

"Damn, Ken. Kyndra. Whatever your name is. I guess I could be ready by about six o'clock."

"Great! I'll see you then. I got to go." His head was still spinning from the conversation after he hung up. It had all happened so fast, he thought, now he had to get ready to leave.

Six o'clock came and he was waiting for the valet to bring his car to the hotel front. He was looking around the area as he waited, expecting to see Kyndra. But not until the keys were given to him and he was about to seat himself, did he see her. She seemed to come from nowhere.

"I'm so glad you was here on time. I don't know what to do," were her first words.

He was even more shocked than the first time he saw her because at this meeting she was not dressed as a women. She had on a man's suit and tie and an overcoat that may have been too big, he couldn't be sure. She/he also wore a Stetson hat. Masculinity abounded. No makeup.

"What the...?" Jouscar attempted to disarm himself of his suspicions, but Kyndra interrupted him immediately.

"Juice. Please. Just be quiet and move the car. Please," she demanded. All the time her attentions were divided between the street behind her and the building directly across from where they sat. Jouscar obeyed her directive to move the car and they sped toward the beltway. As they put a few miles between themselves and the hotel, Jouscar felt that maybe he was allowed to talk again.

"Is it all right if I talk now, Kenny? Huh? Can I say something now?" Jouscar was slightly perturbed.

"Okay. Okay. I know I owe you an explanation. So why don't you let me explain first. Okay?" She softened her eyes as he spoke. Although dressed in male clothing, she still had an alluring voice and her mannerisms were still very feminine. Jouscar shook his head and continued to drive, once again submitting to her overwhelming dominance of the situation at hand.

"Well, first of all, let me apologize for not telling you that me and my friends were 'working girls.' I mean, after all, I hadn't seen you in ages and I didn't think it would be appropriate. I hope you can understand that. Next, I had no idea that the men we had in your room were connected with Mr. Andrews. I know you don't know him, but he is not to be trusted and I didn't know that at the time. Well, he had so much money on him that I just couldn't resist. He was stupid drunk, trying to do cocaine, and trying to be fresh at the same time. I gagged him out of every gotdamn dime he had. Plus his blow. Shoooot! He had no business following us. You don't remember because you fell out at the elevator. But him and his dogass friend kept trying to talk us into coming to their room while we was helping you. You know? We didn't know them, so we decided to take them. Eroka got they number to they room, but we thought it would be much safer it they came to our, excuse me 'your' room. You know? They was drunk and couldn't do nothing nohow, so we took the money and sent them on their way. I really didn't even think that they would remember the room number to tell you the truth. But just as we was leaving, we saw them talking to the night manager. We snuck out and they never even saw us leave. Look!" At that point she reached into her pocket and pulled out a wad of hundred dollar bills. "Fuck em! You know what I mean. So anyway, that's why I had to leave town so fast. And before you say anything, this getup is just a disguise. I will be pretty in pink before we hit Phillytown." She smiled an alluring smile and turned to face Jouscar. Jouscar could not think of a thing to say. He drove on in silence.

Maddelyn

Maddelyn, on the other hand, had been expecting Jouscar to arrive a day later. She was as much surprised to see him as he was to have had to leave. He immediately told her about his experience with Kenny. She didn't seem at all surprised. It was as if she knew already.

"Oh. That ain't no big thing. But how did it go with the auditor? That's what I want to know about." She was sincerely concerned about the audit, as she had just been informed of some very distressing revelations about the industry.

She, too, had become successful in her endeavors. She was, as it turned out, a visionary in the field of surrogacy. One of the pioneers in the field. And now, all of that was being threatened.

It had been thirteen years since she started. She began as in independent procuror of potential surrogate mothers with an experimental program using government grant monies and doing business under the name of Surrogate, Inc. She conducted business under contract with the government for a good while, but as time went on, she found out how lucrative the business was and became less and less in need of government funding. She eventually broke ties with them entirely. But not without a fight.

She'd been in continual litigation and legal hassles. And had spent a good bit of her time and money dealing with the legalities of the divestiture as well as with the inherent legalities of the business itself. Meanwhile, a multitude of problems had begun to plague the industry.

Historically, a combination of hard work, accumulated experience, and ambition had played a major part in her success and the attainment of a few milestones in her life. But it was the upholding of the Surrogate Mothering Act by the U.S. Supreme Court that catapulted her into the mainstream. It helped her gain financial stability and establish legitimate credibility within a system where there had been, up to that point, extremely little understanding of this unique concept in child-bearing. There had been virtually no ground rules. Other than what the federal ruling body tried to enforce every once in a while.

Surrogacy was previously associated with monkeys. For the past twenty or twenty-five years, people had haphazardly engaged in the practice, hoping to fill a void in their childless lives by having a child through someone else. A child they could call their own and raise it as though it were their own. It was because of Maddelyn's uncannily accurate perception of people and her interest in the surrogate movement that she became prominent in this field. She learned very early that the most natural and sacred virtue of child bearing, which all were supposed to be blessed with, was denied to many people, for many years, from all walks of life. She had grown to care. She also had seen there was a profit to be made.

Once in the business, she learned quickly. She came to know her business inside out. She managed it competently and responsibly. Coping with the problems well. And the range of problems she had dealt with were many and varied. It was all so new then.

She had been inured with the devastation of people, young and old, newlyweds, lovers, single women alike, who had tried in vain to reproduce a living being by God's method of procreation, the act of intercourse. The sexual act. She saw that this act of unparalleled pleasure and satisfaction had become, to some, an agonizing, futile struggle to prove the doctors wrong. She knew that some couples viewed each attempt to have sex with skepticism and fear. Or as a failure. A failure that followed every union where infertility was eventually diagnosed. She saw the frustration in the face of homosexual couples who were rebuffed time and time again until some sympathetic, more likely, desperate woman would agree to undergo the artificial insemination process for them. Her instincts grew sharper and her wisdom had deepened as a result of all she had endured over the years. She had become wise to the tricks of the trade.

Somehow, though, her organization had gotten too big and was beginning to get out of hand. Things were getting more and more difficult to control now. Accountability was going out the window. She had set up several satellite agencies around the city and suburbs to be closer to the public but maintained the mother company headquarters in the newly constructed Liberty One Building downtown. It was the satellite agencies that were her biggest problems. She had to hire over two hundred employees. They just weren't running the agencies efficiently. For one, they were loosely run and the quality of service was getting increasingly poor. She was in the process of fixing that when the government stepped in.

A recently performed state audit of other facilities had revealed some disturbing information that was critical to the survival of her agency.

For example, through the audit, it was discovered that in some instances the surrogate carriers weren't even qualified. They were given positions because they were friends or family members of employees who had forged entry papers just to get them on the payroll. She learned that still others were getting paid without carrying legal full term. What they were doing, she learned, was aborting the child in early stages of pregnancy and feigning as though they just weren't "showing" for a while, only later to have a doctor confirm that they had miscarried. Under the terms of the contract, money would still be paid them due to the "short-term carry clause."

Still others were making money on short-term carries merely by claiming pregnancy and not being pregnant at all. They were using corrupt physicians to certify that they were pregnant. And they really weren't. Then they would get the doctor to later claim miscarriage. Or that an accident had prevented them from carrying full tern. Under this scam, everybody was getting paid illegally. Payment for short-term carries varied according to the amount of time the child was actually carried. But she knew that even a four-month carry could conceivably provide enough money for a person to live off of long enough not to have to worry about where their next meal was coming from for a while. For instance, if the full-term contract provided for a twenty thousand dollar fee, if realized, then, a predetermined percentage of the twenty thousand would be set based on the length of carry or a mutually agreed upon settlement would be awarded to the surrogate carrier depending on the circumstances. Subsequently, large sums of money could be acquired through this method. Legitimately and illegitimately. And since there were so many contingencies and legalities involved in the settlement process, the carrier frequently came out on top. It was easy to see how this method became so popular. It was easy to pull off and hard to prove.

Maddelyn knew these kind of things took place all the time and all over the world. But now, something had to be done about it. And quick. She had to find a way to put a stop to this madness or she was going to lose. These were just some of the problems that she was faced with. She had others to be sure.

The audit also uncovered the possibility that still other girls would blatantly disregard the terms of the contract, forego the money, and attempt to sell the child that they had carried for nine months. Even though penalties were stiff in most cases, if they got caught, there was a market for that also. And Maddelyn knew good money was paid for children, depending upon where the child was sold. Maddelyn had her lawyers working on it. And Maddelyn's attorneys were among the best in the field. She realized the importance of maintaining competent lawyers to complement the cadre of lawyers representing the various levels of government. She also knew that the outcome of the cases were left solely up to the judgment of the judge who presided over them. So she had made it her business to wine and dine a few of them over the years. She was a businesswoman. A good shmoozer. And smart.

And, she was among the first to pick up on the newly devised language of the civil/surrogate laws. She was fluent. And she spared no cost learning how to speak it and how it was spoken. She had made her mind up that her agency would flourish. No matter what.

The surrogate industry on the whole is low key for the most part. It goes on unnoticed until something happens to make the public aware that it exists. But, as it were, this field of law dealt solely with litigation of surrogate issues that were rapidly cropping up all over the world. The field attorneys were referred to as civil surrogate attorneys. Some were more reputable than others, but as is with most lawyers, money was the driving force for case acceptance. And being that the field was fairly new, each case more or less set a precedent that was to be used as the basis for future cases. Only after a case had been heard for the first time would they be able to determine what might or might not be adjudicated right or wrong legal or illegal. So whatever settlement amounts came out of them usually set the precedent for future awards as well. To say the least, civil surrogate law was very popular among the young and aspiring law school graduates. And most importantly, the field had not yet been saturated. Maddelyn was at the point where she was bound to fight for her agency and she made sure she had the best of everything. But she had problems on the homefront that she had to deal with too.

She and Jouscar had been married two years now. She was aware that he was strongly considering moving to Silver Springs. And she knew that he was anxious for her to get through this audit. She knew that he hoped that they both would make the move together after that. He felt good about it. She was undecided but leaning toward staying because she was so well established in Philadelphia. And it would mean starting all over for her if she were to remain in business.

They lived together in a suburb called Lavroc. Split-level home with about two acres of land. Swimming pool, the whole bit. They lived well. He had replaced her dear Bennie with a Jaguar that she named "Jake." He drove one also. Hers was candy apple red and his was jet black. They had a two-car garage and car ports for each. The house itself was eyecatching. It was positioned so as to be slightly on a hill overlooking the small suburb. It had a winding path leading to a cul de sac in front of the door with a garden patch in the middle. A separate path lead to the carports and garages. An indoor pool that could be opened to flow into the outdoor pool. There was an atrium overhead in the sitting room that could be remotely opened and closed. They designed the house together. But it was

Jouscar who used all his resources, and very little out of pocket cash, to finance its construction. It was pleasing to the eye and had a warmth about it that made it very comfortable to live in. Maddelyn did most of the indoor decor herself except for the pool decor. Jouscar handled that. Nice soft cushiony sofas with large billowy pillows, love chairs. A surround sound system with speakers in every room. Exotic art lined the walls. Plants and flowers strategically located throughout the house. Nothing hard. Everything soft and flowing. Warm colors evenly spread throughout the house. The bedroom was magnificently arranged with a four-post, king-size bed made of very heavy mahogany wood. And you had to step up on a raised portion of the floor to get in it. Mirrors overhead. It truly made you want to get into it. There was also a fireplace in the bedroom that was made of quartz rock. And it was topped off with a heavy wooden mantel. It was cozy, to say the least.

The best thing about the house was that it came free of a mortgage. There were only annual taxes and utilities to pay. The worst thing about the house was that it had no love in it. Love had spilled out of the bay windows and sifted through the cracks of the woodwork during the first year. After he got caught with Ellena at an affair and after she, herself, was accused of having too many men friends. They merely coexisted together as well as they could. They got along okay, but it wasn't what one could call a good relationship. They both attempted to keep up the image. The sex was still good, but they only did it once or twice a month. Maybe slipping up in between times only to end up having the biggest arguments ever. They both were strong personalities and they both were responsible, aggressive people. But it was something in there that just didn't make them conducive to one another.

She admitted she hated his neatness. He seemed to be obsessed with cleaning up and keeping order. He kept his nails polished with clear nail polish and was always trimmed about the head. Maybe he was just too neat. Too anal.

He'd always been like this, though, and she knew it prior to their marriage. But to live with it was different. It was becoming more than she wished to bear. She was somewhat like that as well, but not to the degree he was. She could at least overlook a messy room for a while or leave the dishes in the sink overnight or something like that, but not him. If he saw something like that, there'd be attitudes all around. Another thing she didn't like was that he was always correcting her or somehow making her feel she was wrong a lot. Or she didn't know what she was talking about. She was always wrong. It got so she didn't really like talking to him anymore. She knew she was a smart cookie, and she didn't take his advice or corrections without challenge. Right or not. She questioned why she had married him in the first place. She never had a good answer. Steady sex?? Maybe. She thought she may grow to love him because she always liked and admired him and she thought they shared similar interests. Not exactly. She found out that they were two very different souls. She found that she was too independent to need to be around a man all the time. And that's a good part of the reason why they were still together. She was home when he was not and he was home when she was not.

At least it worked. It sort of let her lead a life of her own, as she had been accustomed to living it as she pleased. She found it was harder to adjust to the thought of being with the same person all the time and feeling as though she had to be there all the time. She wasn't cut out to be a wife. That wasn't good. She did try, but it didn't come across too well. She knew she was definitely part of their problem. At first she couldn't put her hands on what it was, but as she talked with her mother and her girlfriends, she slowly came to this realization. Actually, she knew she would be forcing herself to change when she first got married. But she thought it would happen over time. It was taking too long and she wasn't happy. She automatically assumed he would not understand if she told him how she truly felt about the marriage thing at their first argument's end, when they vowed to tell each other everything and not hold anything back. So she didn't. She held back. She did say something like "This marriage ain't all it's cracked up to be" or something to that effect. She rationalized that he should have caught on from that statement that she didn't like it. And truth be told, she just flat didn't like it. It was too confining. Too restricting and demanding. Unecessarily so. She wondered how her parents did it. Although she sort of knew from what they used to say, "grin and bear it," that it was true. That wasn't acceptable. Even though she felt that was 90 percent of what you had to do to make it last for real. These truths didn't help things either.

Then, she never really forgave him for his night with Elena. She never even tried to forget it. She was more mad at herself for getting herself into this mess. But as far as she was concerned, he had really violated. And it wasn't so much the hurt as it was that he had lived up to what she had always expected of him. He had told her he was finished messing around. That he'd had enough. She should have know better. She allowed him a lot of freedom, and in return, she got a lot of it too. This helped a little. But as it turned out, he just couldn't handle it. She was not stupid, but she could be so very trusting. She didn't even care if he had other girls in his life, but he didn't have to have sex with them. That was a violation. But she knew he did. And she knew there was more than just Elena.

She had always known men couldn't be trusted. Why? She sees other men even now. Goes to lunch, dinner, and out with them. But she doesn't have sex with them. She may have wanted to once or twice, but she didn't. Why did he? Maybe it's just as well. She honestly didn't want to even think about moving to Virginia or wherever it was he was contemplating. And be trapped down there with this man. She knew it was just a matter of time before things had to come to a head. He was acting like nothing had ever happened. Like he was trying to put things behind him and get on with the marriage. Trying to be friendly and loving like he used to be before they were married. She went with it sometimes and didn't at others. It all depended on how she was feeling at the time. She couldn't act like nothing ever happened, because it did. And she wasn't about to forget it.

Kyndra remained in Philly and visited one night they happened to be getting along pretty good. He hadn't been as successful as they. And he talked about how things used to be. Before he got shot. Before he lost his natural good looks. He talked about his happiness in these days since his sex change. He talked about everything. He comes out raw when he's around Maddelyn. He liked them both. Always has.

They were talking about old times as usual and how popular his modeling shop used to be. A record by the Four Tops was playing when Kenny stood up from the floor where he had been sitting drinking wine.

"Aw, shucks. That's my record." He began to sway to the music. "Man. That record always reminds me of the first time I heard it. We was in the shop and we all just went off. Lawd, he sound so good. Uhm. I remember when yall used to come through there all the time. I always had music playing. Girl, we was grooving. Remember? And you used to have that Mercedes Benz." He was dancing around while he was talking and had now directed his gaze at Jouscar and pointed at him.

"I remember when Juice used to come into my shop sometime. Girl, all the models would be wanting to know who he was and stuff and they be asking me to get his number and stuff. I would tell them, shooot, you better ask him yo self."

"You never told me about all this!" chimed in Jouscar.

"Yeah, I bet," said Maddelyn. "He always told me." Jouscar threw up his defenses.

"No, for real. I never knew any of them chicks was talking about me."

"No, honey," added Kyndra "I ain't talking about no chicks. I'm talking about my queens. They the ones."

Maddelyn enjoyed that one. She knew Jouscar didn't like to be associated with homosexuals.

"Oh. Well, the hell with them. I don't care what they thought. I thought you was talking about some of them fine women that was in and out of there."

"Yeah, I just bet you did, honey. But they was on Maddy's ass too. Shooot. Them shonuff good-lookin' men that use to be coming up there? Shooot. She looked better than some of my models. Don't you think so for real, Juice?"

Her back was to Jouscar, so she had to swivel her head around to address him but was back talking to Maddelyn before Jouscar could even answer.

"But you know what, Maddy? For real though, you was about the best-looking one around that way any way. Mostly all them other ones was mostly skanks. Wouldn't even comb they hair and stuff. At least you would comb your hair." Maddelyn sneered at him because she could tell where this was going.

"Oh, come on, Kyndra," emphasis on Kyndra, "there were a lot of nice-looking girls around our neighborhood. Remember that real pretty girl? Uh, Oh, darn, I can't even remember her name now, but she had real long hair and—Oooh, tch. What is this girl's name?" She directed the question to either.

"Verna?" Jouscar tried to guess. "Was that her?"

"No," Maddelyn snapped. "She didn't have no long hair.

"I know who you talking about, but I can't think of her name either, but yall remember this skank named Bernadett?" Kyndra was back in the conversation.

"This record remind me of her. That girl was plug ugly, but she could dance her butt off." She was laughing and getting a little high from the wine she had been drinking. She did that. Maddelyn had expected her to begin to talk about people.

The record went off and another began and Kyndra went into yet another frenzy. She was, if nothing else entertaining for them both. She was good company for them as well.

Maddelyn thought to herself that it did feel good to think about those good ole days. If only Greg could have been there to share them with her. The night ended.

Not long after their little gathering, one day when Maddelyn was walking from her attorney's office which is across the street in the 5 Penn Center Building, she saw her. It had to be her. She thought. The woman was heavier and had more hair than Maddelyn remembered, but she knew that face. It was Evelyn. And she was walking straight towards her. Her mouth dropped open as she drew nearer. The woman was the first to speak. She stopped directly in front of Maddelyn.

"Maddelyn?? You still look the same." She looked good. She had an aura around her. Healthy, well dressed. And, she had a young boy with her.

"Evelyn?? Oh, my God! Evelyn?" They both stood and looked at each other before they embraced. "Oh, my God. You look so good!!"

"So do you, Maddy. And this is Gregory. I named him after your brother." She was looking at the boy who was as tall as she was but still very young looking.

"Hello." The young boy spoke. He favored Michael. She saw that right away. He had Michael's nose.

"Hello," Maddelyn cheerfully reciprocated. "Is this the baby?? Well, I can see he's not a baby, but he's so handsome." She studied the boy's face and looked up at Evelyn's. "Oh, Evelyn. How are you? I can't get over you. I just can't believe it. How long you been back? I mean when—?" Maddelyn was talking, but Evelyn broke in.

"I been back in Philly about two months now. And me and Greg live with his father who we're on our way to meet right now. We're staying in Southwest Philly right now. But . . . I can't get over you either. You really look good. Girl, you haven't changed a bit. Haven't gained no weight. Nothing. I'll tell you what. Give me your number and I'll get in touch with you. I know you don't know what's going on or anything, but I been doing real good.

I'm saved now and I just let God tell me what to do and I do it. He hasn't steered me wrong one time!" She said this very proudly. Maddelyn stared in stark disbelief at what she was seeing and had just heard.

"I am sooo happy for you." she said, "Oh, here take my card." She reached into her pocketbook and produced a business card that had her work and home number on it. 'Oh, Evelyn, I am so glad to know that you are all right. It's been at least ten years. Hasn't it?"

"Yeah! A little more. Eleven. It's been eleven years and an awful lot has changed since then. God has been good to me and my family. But, look, Maddy, we're late. I got your number and I will call you this evening and maybe I could come over and we could talk. You still live over on, uh, I can't remember the name?"

"Bouvier Street?" Maddelyn helped out.

"Oh, yeah! That's right," Evelyn quickly responded.

"No. No, I moved a couple of, well two years ago. I live in a place called Lavroc, now. It's just a little community right off of Cheltenham Avenue as you're going—oh, it's easy to get to. I'll give you directions when you call me." She saw that Evelyn was ready to get moving. "Be sure to call me, Evelyn?" she pleaded. "I just can't believe it's you. And this beautiful boy?"

"He is beautiful. Isn't he," Evelyn agreed. "Well, I'll be talking to you. Bye now."

"See ya," the boy said.

"Bye-bye, Greg. It was nice meeting you!"

They continued on their way and Maddelyn continued walking toward her building. She had been stunned beyond belief. She stopped to look at them as they made their way through the crowd. Mouth still agape. She had never in a million years expected to see Evelyn's face again. It wasn't as if she and Evelyn had been best friends back in the day. They hadn't even been good friends. But it was largely her contribution to the mystery surrounding her brother's death that brought them close together. And during that time, they talked more than they ever did.

The events that led to her disappearance were still rather sketchy. They never did confirm who killed Gregory or why. Or who shot Kenny, either. Those events were still sketchy too. But that was something she avoided thinking about. Back to Evelyn, she thought. She couldn't wait. Couldn't wait to get to a phone and call Kyndra.

Saved?? She thought this was inconsistent with her understanding of being saved. After all, she did take a life. That's one of the Ten Commandments—THOU SHALT NOT KILL—could someone commit murder and still be saved?? Got to ask somebody about that. She thought. It was puzzling.

She continued into the building and through the bustling lobby, past the guard's desk to the elevator, speaking to various people as she walked.

"Hi. Hi you doing?" she repeated over and over again. She really didn't like doing that as much as she did, she did it any way to be polite. She reached the elevator and as she stood waiting for the up light to flash, she smiled to herself as Evelyn came to mind.

The elevator bell rang, signaling its arrival, she moved to let people off and then she herself stepped in. Pressing the button to her floor, she heard someone say, "15th please?" She pressed the button and backed away to stand and wait for it to stop on her floor.

"Excuse me. Aren't you Maddelyn Burks?" the voice asked. She turned to look. It was the guy who did the audit on her firm.

"Oh! Hi. How are you Mr. uh—"

"Emerson. Herbert Emerson. Remember? I was assigned to your place of business to conduct an audit? Uh, Surrogate Incorporated, I believe?"

"Oh, yes. Now I remember," Maddelyn said as she turned her face away. "I guess I should be asking you then ... how *are* we doing? Huh?" She smiled up at him.

He didn't return the smile. His reply was, "Well, we don't know just yet. I'll be in touch." The elevator stopped on his floor. Maddelyn took note.

"Good day," he said as he brushed past her. She didn't respond.

"Well, it won't be because of you, buddy," she muttered under her breath. The doors closed, leaving her to ponder yet another surprise. What was he doing in this building? She glanced at her watch: 2:48. He must be making somebody else miserable, she concluded and returned back to reality just as the elevator bell sounded for her floor.

She was headed directly for the phone, picking up messages as she walked.

"Mr. Jouscar called while you were out, Maddy. He said he would probably be late coming home and he left a number where he could be reached." This was her administrative assistant talking to her. She had practically helped Maddelyn start the business. And had been with her forever.

"Thanks, Henrietta. Is this it?" She kept on walking as Henrietta held up a memo with a number on it.

"Yes. That's the one."

"Okay, I got it," she told her. Henrietta returned to her work. Maddelyn entered her office and closed the doors. She dialed Kyndra's number and waited until she picked up.

"Chello?" she answered.

"Hi, Kyndra? It's me, Maddy. You'll never guess in a thousand years who I just ran into."

"Maddy, what you doing callin' me here. I told you my boss don't allow us to stop working to answer no phone. This better be good. Now. Let me see. Guess!! Uh. Is it a man?" She tried a guess but was truly stymied.

"No. It's not a man. You'll never get it. Evelyn?" She blurted out the name and waited for her to respond.

"Whaaaat? Evelyn is back in Philly? Get outta here, girl. When you see her?"

"Kyndra, I almost thought I saw a ghost. I was shocked to no end. She's back."

"Do the police know? I mean, is she running? Do she look bad? How do she look?" Kyndra always wanted to know the dirty laundry part. "Tell me the nitty gritty."

"No. No. She looks good, honey. I have never seen her look so healthy. And guess what else?"

"She's pregnant!" Kyndra said, jokingly.

"No. She had her boy with her and guess what his name is?" She told her before she could even try to guess. "Gregory! Is that something? She named him after Greg."

"She did have that baby then? Huh? Who he look like?" Kyndra was just being plain newsy.

"What do you mean, who does he look like? Michael!" she said convincingly. "Why would he look like anybody else? Michael. He looks just like him. Got his nose and everything."

"So what's she doing in town? Is she going to stay or what?"

"Yes," she told him definitively. "She told me. She's been here two months already. And she's with somebody too. Because she said she was downtown because they had to meet the boy's father. I guess she got somebody to adopt him or something. I don't really know, but she's going to call me later. Why don't you wait until she calls and I'll come get you. I'll tell you what. You go over to your mother's house and wait because that's closer to us. And I'll come pick you up and you can be here too."

"Wait a minute. You mean she's going to call you tonight? 'Cause I'm supposed to be up there anyway tonight. I got choir rehearsal. What time?"

"I don't know. But I'll call you. I'll tell your mother if you haven't gotten home by that time. Okay?"

"Okay. Look, I got to go. Just make sure you call me. Bye." She hung up. Maddelyn thought about it for a minute, then picked up the phone again and dialed the number that Curtis had left. It was busy. She made a mental note to try it again later. She got busy with the business and stayed engrossed in it until 6:45. When she did notice the clock, she panicked. She thought she might be late for Evelyn's call. She thought better of it and slowed down again, put her papers in order, and left for home.

Once there, she was surprised to see Jouscar was already there. He apparently had been exercising and had just stopped because he was out of breath and sweating.

"Hey. What's happening?" He didn't look up. He was never sure how to receive her. So he tried different approaches. This time it was the "I'm trying to be okay with you, but I don't know what kind of mood you're in" approach. "You didn't expect me home, did you?" He hadn't let her say anything yet. She was a little excited that he was there, but she couldn't show it. That was good because that meant that he could see Evelyn too.

"No. Not really," she said in a quiet voice. "I thought you said you were going to be late or something? You had something to do or something." She was taking off her coat and hanging it up as she spoke to him, not looking directly at him.

"Yeah. I did. But I didn't feel like it. I changed my mind. I figured I'd spend the night coolin' out here with you."

Was he trying to drop hints? Well, do tell, she thought. She was caught off guard with this action, so she tested her theory.

"Why tonight? You don't do it any other night?" She still was curious what brought this on. She had stopped and was looking at him with a homemade grin, half hoping to hear the right answer.

"Aw. Come on. I just thought me and you could sit home together tonight. We haven't done it in a while. That's all." He was looking up at her with the puppy dog eyes now.

"Yeah, well, I hope you aren't smelling as funky as you look." She had decided to invoke a spark of humor into their exchange. He picked it up right away.

"What? What you mean? I don't even smell. Here." He had gotten up and was walking towards her with his arm raised, smelling himself as he did so.

"Get out of here. I don't want to be smelling your funky underarms, boy." She moved quickly out of reach and on to the bedroom. He was right behind her.

"Don't come in here funkin' up the place," she warned playfully. He stopped just as she put her hands out to prevent him from coming any closer.

"No. Wait. Here, smell. I don't even stink. For real!" He was not as pure as he would have had her to believe. At first he thought he didn't smell, but upon closer inspection, he really did detect a faint odor, but now he wanted to try to trick her into getting a whiff. She didn't fall for it.

"Get out of here. Go wash. Go," she persisted. She leaned a little closer anyway.

"Peeeuuu. Yes, you do too. I ain't playing." He was laughing now but had surrendered and was headed for the bathroom.

It had been a long time since they had even come close to playing like that. It felt sort of relieving or something to Maddelyn. She decided to go with it. She was changing into her swim wear, preparing to take a dip in the indoor pool.

"Don't think you're going to try any funny stuff either when you come out," she said as she walked past the bathroom on her way to the pool area. He heard her and was rushing to get out. He hadn't heard that tone in a long while, but he still recognized it as the green light tone. He was just a-smiling, smiling, and singing to himself. He opened the door and heard her hit the water. He knew the sounds. *Oh, boy*, he thought. *Fun time in the water*. He couldn't even finish drying himself off for rushing to get in there with her. He was tipping sneakily up on her when the phone rang. "Shit!" he exclaimed. His stealthy attempt to surprise her was foiled. She heard him.

"Ooooooo. You were trying to scare me. Where are your clothes?" She was surprised to see he was naked. "You better go put your trunks on. You ain't getting in here with me like that. Now. You got caught. That's just what you get." The phone rang.

"Get that phone, boy." She laughed. "You think you so sneaky." She smiled to herself and dove under the water. He submitted but couldn't take his eyes off her butt and shapely legs as they disappeared under the water. He watched her swim under water for a second before turning to pick up the phone on the table that was next to the pool. He had already begun to get an erection. She emerged from the water, splashing and flailing. She had just remembered. Evelyn.

"Wait, wait." She was trying to stop him now, but it was too late.

"Hello? Sure, hold on. Here, it's for you." He was handing the phone to her as she exited the water with her finger to her lips.

"Shhh. Who is it?" she asked in a whispery voice.

"I don't know. Some woman. Here." She reached for the phone, but he took her hand and placed on it on his partially erect penis. She snatched it back and pushed him into the water. She took the phone and pressed it close to her body so as to muffle the sound of her voice.

"I didn't get a chance to tell you. Evelyn is back in town and this is probably her." Her eyes were bulging as she spewed the news. His eyes opened just as wide as hers upon hearing it.

"Shhh. Hello?" she said. It *was* Evelyn.

"Maddy? Hi. This is Evelyn." She motioned to Jouscar to confirm that it was her.

"Oh. Hi, Evelyn. I was just taking a swim."

"What? You guys have a pool in the house?" Evelyn asked in astonishment.

"Yes, we do. And it's great. You are welcome to get in when you get here. It's heated!" She was feeling a little like she was showing off, but she realized it was true, so why try to hide it?

"Boy, I don't know what to say. You guys have gone and got rich on me."

"Well, not quite. But we're working on it," Maddelyn said.

"The reason I'm calling is to tell you that I won't be able to make it over to your house because you live too far from where I'm staying. And we would have to take public transportation to get there. But you would be more than welcome to come out here if you like." She waited a moment to see if there would be an immediate response from Maddelyn.

"Uh, sure. Um, we could do that. When? Now? Tonight?"

"Yeah, if you'd like to or if not, we could make it some other time?"

"No. No. Tonight's fine." She looked at the clock: 7:38. *Not that late*, she thought. "Look, uh, would you mind if Kenny came along?" She wasn't sure how Evelyn would feel about bringing someone else.

"Kenny? The one who got shot? Oh, God is so good." She seemed very pleased at the request, and this made Maddelyn feel a little more at ease. "Not at all. By all means. I had simply forgotten that—" She stopped mid sentence. "Oh, there is so much that I have forgotten. Please, please let him know that he is welcome to come too. I am looking forward to seeing him. Let me tell you where I live. Are you familiar with—" Maddelyn cut her off.

"Wait a minute, Evelyn, let me get a pen and a piece of paper to write on." As she said this, Jouscar got out of the water to retrieve them for her. He gave them to her and remained up close to her.

"Okay. I'm sorry. Now where is it exactly?" She looked at Jouscar as though he were disturbing her.

"I was about to ask you if you were familiar with Southwest Philly?"

"Yeah. Pretty much. Whereabouts in Southwest Philly?" Maddelyn knew Philly pretty well and had never been afraid to travel.

"It's right off of Woodland Avenue. It's a street called Greenway Street. Do you know where that is?" Maddelyn did.

"Yes, as a matter of fact, I do. What hundred?"

"It's the 2100. It's the only house on the block painted green. You can't miss it." Maddelyn was getting antsy now. She was ready to go.

"Okay. Uh, 2100 block of Greenway and green house, got it. We should be there in about an hour. Okay?"

"That's fine. I'll be looking forward to you coming. Bye now!" And she was gone.

"Come on. Hurry up. They can't get up here, we got to go down there," she told Jouscar who was right in her face. "Oh, do me a favor? Call Kyndra's mother's house and tell her we're on our way." She deliberately pushed him back in the water as she headed for the bedroom.

Evelyn

They left the house, picked up Kyndra, and arrived at Evelyn's door in forty-five minutes. She was right. You couldn't miss it. It was the only house on the block that was still occupiable. The remaining houses on the block were all boarded up with plywood or metal sheeting. It was green, too, just as Evelyn described. But the green paint was so dark and old that it didn't look green at all. The paint was peeling heavily everywhere on the house. They approached the house with caution, not knowing whether is was safe or not. Besides, the neighborhood was known to be one of the most treacherous neighborhoods in the city. Notorious for its burglaries, it had a drug-ridden and murder-riddled history. The people who still lived in that sector appeared to have lost hope. And one would just assume that they are trapped. Victims of "lack of money to move." They seem to have succumbed to the pressures of society, and it would appear that they just didn't care anymore.

The group studied the environment carefully and decided that it was not a good place for humans to live. The entire section they rode through to get there was an eyesore. Blight was the most prominent feature of the streets. Once they finally got up the nerve to emerge from the car, they all wondered if it would even be there when they returned. Or if it would have tires on it and still be drivable. They were actually scared. But the fact that they had come all this way made them keep moving. And, besides, they truly did wish to confront Evelyn on several pressing issues. They pressed onward toward the house. The screen door still had the screens, or what was left of them, hanging on. In the dead of winter, this was hardly practical for keeping in the heat. Nor was it economically prudent. It was falling off the hinges and leaning open as if to invite them to reach in and knock on the inside door. Jouscar did. As they waited, they had their eyes looking about them as though they were in a war and had to maintain a constant vigilance against a surprise attack. It was horrifying just standing there in the cold and dark doorway, not knowing what was going to happen. They heard a noise up the street, which caused them to huddle even closer together and move closer to the door, so close they were leaning against it and squashing Jouscar who had taken the lead.

"Dag, y'all. Y'all squashing me!" Jouscar squealed in a low whisperlike voice.

"Sorry, but it's cold out here and I'm scared," said Kyndra. "Did you hear that?" The torn and tattered shade was moved to the side, and Jouscar peered directly into a man's frowning face. It looked like he was terribly angry to Jouscar and the others. They pulled back from the window. Kyndra started to run back to the car but stopped when Maddelyn caught her coattail and pulled her back. The man pulled back too, as if startled, and Jouscar began talking. Fast. More out of fear at being in the wrong place than anything else.

"Uh, excuse me, but we are looking for Ms. Evelyn Henderson? Does she live here?" He didn't realize it, but he was talking loud enough for the entire neighborhood to hear. He was ready to bolt from the door if she didn't live there. The door opened and the frowned face turned friendly with a warm smile.

"Come in. Come on in. I'm sorry if I had you standing there in the cold so long, but I didn't know who you were at first. You can understand my hesitance, I'm sure? Come right this way. Evelyn will be right down. She's upstairs doing something, I don't know what." He was holding the door open as they filed in past him, each with his eyes scanning the house for who knows what. But after their adventure with the outside, they didn't know what to expect inside. Everything was suspect.

To their dismay the house inside was clean and orderly. And it smelled good. It smelled of roast beef and gravy, it was almost tantalizing. This helped them to relax. Just a little. Once the three of them were in the house, the man pointed towards a well-lit room and invited them to continue in that direction. No one said a word except for Jouscar. And that was hardly audible. Once in the well-lit room, the man, who had been behind them, excused himself as he made his way to the forefront.

"Here, let me take your coats." All of them were still a little leery of the surroundings and were checking out the furniture, the floor, the stairs. Everything. Kenny had the feeling that a rat or something would jump out any minute. A quick scan and a quick assessment assured them that it was all right. The house was warm. Just right, as a matter of fact. And the smell of that food was overpowering. The man collected their coats and they were about to pick seats and seat themselves when they heard footsteps on the stairs as Evelyn descended. She stopped before she reached the bottom and looked directly at Jouscar. They were standing still and were now looking up at her. It was a heartwarming moment. For some reason this reunion felt exceptionally good. The feeling of relief came over them all as the smiles grew across their faces, Jouscar's especially. He was quite pleased at what he was looking at. He remembered that he and Evelyn had been what you might say were lovers or something in junior high. They went back a long way. And to him, she looked just as she did then. He could easily see past her aged face.

"Curtis!" she said, softly. Her face softened even more as she studied his face and smiled the most pleasant and reassuring smile he had ever seen. It sent goose bumps up and down his body. He held his eyes on her.

"Ev? Come on down here and give me a hug, girl." The way he said it didn't fit. It was as if he was trying to sound like he used to talk, but it didn't come out right. The reality of it was that he was overwhelmed with nostalgia, and he actually didn't know how to greet her. Something was prompting him to go to her and hug her, but he didn't move. Her face had a glow to it like she had just greased it with vaseline. Her skin was smooth. You could hardly notice the scars that were so prominent when she was younger. And there was a sparkle in her eyes from the light. Her hair was singed in gray around the edges and in the front. It was neatly tucked into a French curl in the back. So she actually did show some signs of aging, but it only served to enhance her natural attractiveness. She didn't look sexy or anything close to it. It was just becoming. She looked settled and peaceful. Seasoned. There was a calm about her that they had never seen before. She still hadn't moved off the step. Her eyes moved to Kyndra, and as she settled her smile on her, she too attempted to "try to be himself."

"I was wondering if you was gon try to act like you didn't know me?" She had a small lump in her throat as she spoke. It didn't quite come out as she wanted. She was almost on the verge of tears. She was sucked into Evelyn's gaze. You could feel the power she had over the three of them. She looked at all three again, and then she broke it off as she turned her look to the steps beneath her feet before continuing down the steps still with that knowing, tranquil smile gracing her face. It seemed as though they had been standing for a long time. As if they had been in a trance or hypnotized or something. Evelyn walked to Maddelyn and embraced her, then to Jouscar, then to Kyndra. She was telling each of them how happy she was to see them. She had released her hold on them and was acting a little more "normal" now, so they all got back to normal, but no one had sat down yet, Evelyn saying nothing about Kyndra's new look.

Evelyn turned to the gentleman who had been standing with his elbow propped up on the mantelpiece of the fireplace. An unlit pipe dangling out of his mouth. He was of average height, about 5 foot 10 with a stocky build. His head was balding on top, but hair remained in the back and on the sides. He had thick, dark features. Reminded one of an Australian Aborigine.

"This is Jason," she said proudly, as she introduced him. "And this is Maddelyn, Kenny, and Curtis," she said to Jason. They spoke in turn, saying "Hi" to Jason.

"I've known these people a long time, Jason. These are the people I told you about years ago." She looked at him, but he just smiled. "Jason and me have been together almost since I first left this town." She looked at him again and playfully scolded him. "Well, aren't you going to say anything?" He snapped out of his pose.

"Oh. Yeah. It's a pleasure to meet you all. Why don't you have a seat and make yourselves comfortable? We got some homemade apple cider and some crackers and stuff ya'll can chomp on if you'd like. All the roast beef and potatoes gone. She saw to that," he said, insinuating that Evelyn ate the last of the food.

"Oh, stop it, Jason, I did not." She playfully tapped him as she turned to look at the group and they at the couple. A little playfulness can always be counted on to help break the ice in a group. And it worked wonders in this group.

"That would be nice. I'm thirsty," said Maddelyn.

"Me too," said Kyndra. "And I hope you got more than just apple cider 'cause it's cold out there and we gone need something to help keep us warm once we hit that door. You know what I mean?" They all were smiling and Maddelyn was almost laughing. They all knew he was hinting for some alcohol. Evelyn and Jason both looked at Kyndra. Jason kindly told him, "We don't drink anything that has alcohol in it. It's not good for you." Evelyn agreed and she started for the kitchen. A hush came over the three visitors, and Maddelyn and Jouscar were pleased that it had not been either of them to have made the request.

Kyndra, although slightly embarrassed, bowed her head and peered up to Maddelyn slyly and muttered, "Well, shut my mouth!" She thought she had covered her mouth so as to appear as though she wasn't talking, but Jason heard her.

"We just don't believe that drinking alcohol is a good thing. We try to do what's right. I hope I didn't offend anyone?" He dropped his arm from the mantel piece and put both his hands in his pockets as he looked each one in the eyes. No one responded immediately. Maddelyn had the feeling she was a child again and that she had just been scolded by her father. She sat quietly. Kyndra spoke up.

"Oh, no. I didn't take offense or anything. I can dig that." She tried to mend the moment with a hand gesture that is commonly seen in the streets. But that didn't go over well either.

"Good," said Jason. Evelyn was walking in with a tray. The tray had five glasses and a pitcher of apple cider on it.

"You want me to get the crackers, hon?" Jason asked Evelyn as he had seen she didn't have them.

"Yes. Would you, please? They're in the bottom cabinet. And bring the spread and knife also, would you?" She placed the tray on the coffee table, which was within reach of all of them and she sat down in the reclining chair that they all had purposely declined to sit in. As if they just knew better. She leaned her arms on her knees, hands folded in front of her, looking at the three in turn. She breathed in deeply and expelled the breath as though she were gently blowing out candles on a birthday cake.

"Well!" she said, and paused. "Here we are! After eleven years. Here we are in the same room. It makes my heart smile with happiness. I know all of you have been wondering what happened to me. What have I been doing and such. Well, I want you to know I have often thought of you as well. Especially you, Juice." She said that teasingly and with emphasis on Juice. "Because you were one of the first people I met when I moved here and you were one of the last people I saw before I left."

"Yeah, that's right. I was there all right." Jouscar lamented.

"And I'm sure you were told of the horrible act that took place that night in the house where I used to live?" She directed her eyes to Maddelyn, then to Kyndra. Maddelyn, indeed, was aware of every gory detail. Kyndra had heard the story enough times too.

Satisfied that they were all in tune, she continued with a story. She sat back and allowed both of her arms to rest on both arms of the big, tufted chair. She carefully crossed her left leg over her right and looked up at the ceiling. There was a very loud silence that preceded her first words after she settled into the chair.

"After the funeral, Gregory's funeral," she clarified, "I was led to believe that I was to 'lure,'" she intentionally put emphasis on the word *lure*, "Michael to my house later that evening. And that several people, including Yvette, Glenn and his wife, Rose, Phil and Curtis, were to come at some point and we were supposed to, uh, how should I say it? Uh, get Michael to admit his guilt in Gregory's murder." She had everyone's undivided attention as she spoke. She spoke slowly and precisely, articulating each word carefully, deliberately. Eyebrows were furrowed as they strained to hear every word and see every movement Evelyn made.

"What actually did happen was that Michael came earlier than planned. He surprised me as I was about to bathe. I was in the bathroom running my bath water when I heard someone come into the house. So I went to see who it was. As I made my way down the hall, Michael came up on me so fast that I had no time to respond. He proceded to accuse me of having had an ongoing affair with Gregory, which I thought was ridiculous, but nonetheless real in his mind. He began beating and kicking me. He got me down on the floor and threatened to harm the baby.

"At that point I changed. I don't know what happened to me, but I changed. I felt responsible for guarding my baby's life. I can't explain it exactly, but it was as if I became another person. I had no fear of Michael. And I had feared him all my life. I was scared to death of him. But at this point as he was threatening to hurt my unborn child, I forgot all about my fear and I stood up for my child. I looked him deep in his eyes as he picked me up to beat me some more and that was the only time I had seen fear in his eyes. I saw something that was almost demonic in those burning eyes. Something inside of me told me that he must be destroyed. He must die or me and my baby would die. The next thing I know I had picked up a can opener from the floor and had torn his eye open with it and ripped his throat apart. I had not fully realized what I had done until minutes later. I guess I was so caught up in what I was doing that I didn't really think of the consequences. I never looked at his body again. Not once did I set my eyes upon his dead soul after I killed him. I don't even remember what made me stop or why I stopped attacking him. I just remember feeling relief. It was as if a heavy burden had been removed from my body. I felt exalted. Redeemed.

"The next thing I know, I'm on a bus headed for God knows where and I wake up on the floor of the bus terminal in Kansas. And the first face I see is that of Jason. He was standing over me, asking me if I was all right. I remember that very clearly. He took care of me from that moment on. He told me that he was on his way back home and he asked me if I would go along with him. I said yes, and he took me with him. I haven't been without him since.

"He nursed my wounds and healed my spirit. Jason taught me things that I had never knew about before. Most importantly, he taught me about Jesus. He taught me life and a way to live it that I had never even thought possible. At first I tried to take advantage of his kindness. I would let him preach and I would act like I was listening, but as soon as I could sneak away, I would. I would sneak out and try to find some drugs or get a drink or something, thinking that he didn't know what I was doing. But he knew. He just let me keep on trying to be slick until I finally gave into the truth. After a while, I really was listening.

"I started reading the Bible with him and going to church and little by little I gradually forgot all about the things that I used to want to do. I no longer craved the taste of alcohol. No longer felt that sex was so important. Didn't know the meaning of drugs. My arms and legs were healing from where I had abused my body with a hypodermic needle. I had only the scars to remind me of the hell I had endured prior to my meeting him. He was my Angel. And when my baby was born, he was there for me. He raised little Gregory as though he were his own. I can't say enough about this man. He is truly my angel. My guardian angel. I love him dearly.

"One night as we sat on the back porch of our house, I heard a coyote howling. It was very close to where we live. I remember thinking. Closer than I would have wanted. So I asked him what that coyote was doing. I thought it was strange. He explained to me that there comes a time, when the female gets in heat, and the pack is hungry, that it is her job to mate with them and get them food. He told me that this female coyote will assume the responsibility to have sex with the aggressive males in the pack, then she will go out alone and attempt to get a dog or a stray coyote to follow her back up onto the desert. And once she had done this, the other coyote in the pack will be lying in wait for the unknowing, unsuspecting animal she had brought with her.

"They attack the poor creature and use it for food. I was amazed. I was simply amazed at this. I automatically related to that female coyote. It was as if I saw myself doing the same thing as that lone female coyote at one time or another. I too, had felt like I was responsible for giving myself sexually to men. I thought I was needed for that purpose. I too, had been used at various times to set up drug dealers. I used to bring these unknowing, unsuspecting men to places where I knew they were going to get hurt and their drugs and money would be taken from them. I did it for the drugs and money. It was the same thing as she was doing. Only she was doing it for their survival and I was doing it for drugs. Thinking that I needed them. That I was helping us survive. But I wasn't, we didn't really need those things. That revelation made me know just how closely the behavior of us humans resembles the behavior of animals at times. We all need air to breathe and nourishment for our bodies and we do what we feel we have to in order to continue surviving until God sees fit to bring us home. We both have the same basic needs. I began to realize that there is a big difference, though, when it comes to surviving and living. Then, I was surviving. Now, I am living. Living in the Word of God." Evelyn had been talking for over an hour. She had hypnotized her audience. Captivated them to the point where they were not even aware. Jason had gotten up and refilled their glasses with the apple cider and had spread the hors dourvres out before them. It was time for a break. They all seemed to notice at once now and reached for their glasses.

Kyndra stretched, exhaled deeply, and asked where the bathroom was. Maddelyn merely sat there and stared at Jouscar who had been equally stunned and quiet.

"I know I've said quite a bit already, but please, bear with me, there's more. I've waited eleven long years to tell what has been in my heart and I appreciate the fact that you will listen." She picked up her glass and took a short drink. "Um, my mouth was getting awfully dry. That tastes pretty good. Don't you think so?" she asked Maddelyn.

"Yes. Uh, yes, it is very good. This is the real apple cider here." It was definitely homemade. You could still see particles of apple floating in it. It was thick and rich with pulp. Naturally sweet. Kyndra returned and excused herself as she repositioned herself back into the dent she had made in the cushion.

Evelyn looked at her captive audience. Jouscar was still holding onto his glass. Kyndra and Maddelyn had replaced theirs in the exact places they had picked them up from. Evelyn began again.

"Well, I remained there in Wichita, Kansas, for eighteen months before I got the courage to come back to Philly and turn myself in. I had no idea about whether or not I was considered a fugitive or what. Jason and I had just agreed that it would be best to 'face the music,' so to speak. So we boarded a train bound for Philly one summer day. I didn't exactly know how to go about it, but we both decided it would be best to contact a lawyer first. Which we did. I chose not to have any contact with anyone I knew while I was in town then, so that's why you never knew I had come back. Though, I did speak with Yvette while I was here then and I told her what I was doing or rather, what I was about to do because I hadn't done it yet. She was glad to know that I was doing that because she told me that it had been weighing heavily on her conscience as well. She had told me that she felt obligated to go to the authorities herself, but she never did. I don't know how things would have turned out if she had. I just don't know. Well, it ended up that the lawyer told us that I didn't have anything to worry about. The police apparently didn't care anything about Michael's death or who killed him. That case was closed. I couldn't believe it. We paid him $500 dollars for that information and it was worth every penny. Well, anyway, Yvette had told me that she was preparing to move to Virginia. Apparently she did. Because I haven't been able to find her here in Philly."

Maddelyn chimed in at this point. "She did. She moved about three years ago. I believe she got married and is managing a retreat-type resort down there. That was the last I heard."

"Oh? Is that right? That's good to know. I'll have to look into that. She was another person who helped me in my dark days. I'll forever keep her in my heart no matter where she is, I'll never forget what she did for me. I guess it was because she knew of my early teen years and what had happened to me that she showed so much love and caring for me. No matter what I did to her, she always stuck with me. She had faith in me.

"You see, when I turned thirteen, I lost my virginity. I went wild. I was living in New York then and I was having sex with anybody who wanted to have sex. I was addicted. I was masturbating when I wasn't having sex. Sex, sex, sex. That's all I knew. No concern for my reputation!! No protection from pregnancy or disease. Nothing. I didn't care. I just knew that it felt too good to be true and I liked it. I liked it a lot. It was easy to get. And I didn't have any trouble giving it away. My mother had passed and I was living with my father. And he didn't half know how to handle me nohow. He drank a lot. I too, began to drink. I hadn't found out about drugs yet, though. I was just drinking. I found out that I liked that too. I started out drinking Thunderbird wine. It was cheap and easy to get. Wine and sex seemed to go together automatically. I would get so drunk that I didn't even know what I was doing. I would have sex with anybody who was around. Women included.

"Well, one day, or one night, I should say, I came stumbling into the house. It was pretty late and my father was still up. I remember, he was sitting on the sofa. And as I came in the door, I saw him moving to zip up his pants. He was frantically scrambling to fix his clothes. Mostly, zipper his pants and buckle his belt. He only had on the pants. No socks or shoes or shirt. I noticed that there was a bottle of Scotch sitting half full on the floor next to where he was sitting. I tried to act like I didn't see anything. I had been drinking, of course, and I wasn't feeling any pain either. As I started up the steps to my bedroom, I was distracted by the sounds of people having sex. You know. Heavy breathing and moaning and groaning and whatnot. I looked to see he had a pornography movie running. He had a 16-millimeter motion picture projector that he would shine on the wall. And I put it together that he had been watching it and fell asleep while he was masturbating. I figured that I had surprised him. I thought of it as I stood there. It struck me funny. My father masturbating. So I asked him.

"What he was doing? 'Daddy, don't tell me that you are doing what I think you are doing?' I said to him. He told me to mind my business and go on upstairs. I did. But I could not get the image of what I had in my mind to go away. I stayed up there about fifteen minutes. I got undressed except for my panties and my bra. I laid there till I could resist no more. I tippytoed to the top of the stairs and peeped down to see if he had turned off the projector or not. He did and was back to sleeping. But I decided I wanted to watch it. And besides, I knew that scotch was down there too. I eased back down the steps, got the liquor away from him, and found the film, which he had called himself hiding. I knew how to work it from school, because it was just like the one we had in our classes. I put it on and turned the sound down so as not to disturb him. Poured me a big glass of that scotch and proceeded drinking. After a few minutes of watching this porno film—they called them "smokers and stag movies" in that day—well, I got so hot I didn't know what to do. I cannot, to this day, account for my actions afterward, but I live to regret it daily. I don't know if I felt sorry for him or what. I guess I thought that it was a shame for him to have to masturbate because he didn't have a woman. I don't know. I remember thinking, I guess I must have been drunk. But I thought that I could help him with that. I was wrong. So wrong. It was a dreadful mistake that I made."

Evelyn was beginning to be overcome by emotion and tears were running down her face as she spoke. Her voice was quivering and she was notably upset, but she kept talking. Her listeners attempted to comfort her and make her take a break from the story, but she persisted she could go on. So they allowed her to continue through her tears.

"What happened was..."—she paused to let out a burst of crying that went on for a few minutes. They just let her cry it out. Nobody moved to console her this time. Maddelyn herself was touched by this confession and so was Kyndra. Jason had left the room. Jouscar had his head in his hands, covering his face. When she finally got the strength to continue, she wiped the tears away and sat up straight in the chair.

"I'm sorry. I didn't mean for that to happen." She exhaled deeply and continued. "So. Uh. What happened next was I, uh, made my way across the floor...and...as my father lay there...sleeping...I opened up his pants ...and I took his penis...into my mouth." She paused to look each one in the eye as she waited. "He awoke but he never really resisted me and we ended up—we ended up having sex right there on that sofa. It was more like I seduced him." Her head was bowed now. She waited a couple of minutes before going on with the story.

"After that, I knew what I had done was wrong. I felt ashamed. But I could never admit it to myself. And after that, he wanted to continue doing it. I didn't want to let him do it any more, but then he started making me do it. He made me have oral sex with him and he had it with me and he had his way with me when he wanted. I was beginning to hate it. I was beginning to hate him. But I blamed myself for starting it and I didn't know how to stop it. I hated the thought of going home. So I ended up running away from home before I turned fifteen, and I have never looked back. I came to Philly and stayed with my aunt. And it just got worse from there. Drugs. Sex. Stealing. Lying. Cheating and finally murder. I had reached rock bottom. There was nowhere for me to go but down. And any further down would be in the very ground itself. Then I'd be dead, I guess. Or? I could go Up!! And thank the Good Lord, that's what I did. My Angel took me up with him." She smiled softly as she turned her eyes to Jason who had returned and was listening just as intently as the others.

"And that's my story. I'm finished. Any question?"

Her audience was simply drained of emotion. You could see it on their faces. What was there to question? She had bared her soul to them. Any questions, it seemed, would be totally irrelevant. She had just about answered them all anyway. Nobody answered. They all sat there digesting what they had just heard. Not exactly knowing what to make of it.

"You all right, honey?" Jason asked of Evelyn.

"I'm fine, dear. I'm just fine. Thank you," she reported slowly. She had put that smile of wisdom back on her face. Her back straightened up. That look of understanding returned to her eyes.

"God is good!" she said.

With that, Maddelyn spoke. "Yes, He is! Evelyn, I don't know, but I believe you are truly blessed. I mean, after what you've been through—I-I-I-I just don't know what to say!!" She was completely at a loss for words. So were the others.

"Well, I've learned that you should say what's in your heart," Jason answered. "If you feel the need to say something, then say what is truly in your heart." They were all looking at him now.

What profound words, Maddelyn thought. She already knew that, but the way he put it it struck home. Spoken with such assurance and confidence. She knew he was right.

"Well, I guess I don't have much to say then. I can only feel my heart beating very hard. And I feel such sympathy for her and what she's gone through."

"Well, don't say anything then, sweetheart," Evelyn said, "As I look back on my life, if you could call it that, I see it as a twenty-eight-year nightmare that seems like it never really happened. I am almost forty now and I know that it did happen, but I'm still alive. And I have a whole new way of life. I have a wonderful man and a beautiful son in my life. You may be right. It may be that I am blessed. I don't know. Although I may have gotten past serving any time man may have given me, I don't believe I've served God's time yet for my crimes. I don't know. But I thank Him daily for giving me the rest of my time to serve Him. And I will serve Him with all of my heart until my last dying breath. So don't go feelin' no sympathy for me. Please. That's a useless word with me." Evelyn was looking at Jason as she spoke to Maddelyn.

Jason smiled as they looked into each other's eyes. He knew she was referring to a conversation they had had about sympathy some time ago. When Evelyn sought it. He knew that she knew about sympathy and that there was, indeed, a place for it. But it wasn't with her. He had taught her that sympathy was to be given to the sick. The helpless and the poor. But he had made her see where she was no longer sick, or poor, or helpless and she had no need of such a word. He had fortified her with the Spirit of God. He tried to permeate her very being with the Spirit through the Word. Once she caught on and began experiencing God's goodness, she was like a sponge. She soaked up all she could and craved for more.

It was a rather somber departure. Evelyn and Jason were accompanying the visitors to the door when Maddelyn turned to her.

"Evelyn? Just one thing. Did Michael kill my brother?" she asked with sincerity. Evelyn locked eyes with her.

"Honestly? I think that that is something that we may never know. I feel that he died senselessly. But all I do know is what I believe in my heart. I really don't know." With that they all turned their attention to the car and were relieved to see that it was still there and in one piece. The door still hadn't been opened yet and Jason was standing with his arm around Evelyn's shoulder.

"Oh. One more thing. How long will you be staying?" Evelyn looked at Jason before responding. Jason had his pipe in his mouth as usual, and took it out to say, "Don't look at me!!" He kept the pipe in his mouth, but he never lit it. It was just a reminder of his smoking days. His sinning days. Those days without Christ.

"I can't say for sure. We actually just came up to sell this house. And we were going to go back to Kansas City as soon as we found a buyer. But it doesn't look too promising that it will bring any money, considering the condition of this neighborhood. We should be heading west directly." Jouscar perked up then.

"I'm in real estate. You know that, don't you? I'll see what I can do to get it off your hands. What are you asking?"

"Anything we can get," was the reply.

"Well, let me see what I can do. I'll get back to you on it by next week. Is that okay?"

"That may be a little late," Jason said. "We really want to get moving before next week. I'll tell you what. Let's do it by mail. Give me your address and whatnot and we can go back home and take our time waiting. It's not really all that big a rush."

"Okay. That's good."

They moved back into the room and exchanged contact information, said good-byes, and commenced to leave again. This time it was Evelyn who stopped them.

"Whatever happened to that guy Phil? Has anybody heard from him?"

"He's in jail doing big time, last I heard." Kyndra knew because he cruised the bars every once in a while.

"Oh. I'm sorry to hear that. And how is Rose doing?"

"She got married too and moved. Nobody's seen or heard from her either." Kyndra knew about Rose too.

"Well, God bless her. And how are you doing?"

"Just fine. I was waiting for you to get to me," Kyndra said.

"Hopefully, God will get to you before I do," Evelyn responded and embraced her.

"May God bless you all and let me just thank you all for listening to my tale of woe." They all embraced her and told Jason how good it was to meet him and they finally made it out.

Once in the car, the stunned looks came again.

"That was deep!! Wasn't it??" Jouscar said.

"Oh, Now you have something to say. In there you didn't say a word." Maddelyn was taunting Jouscar for his lack of words during the visit.

"Shit. I didn't know what to say. I couldn't believe what I was hearing. She got away with murder. Sucked and fucked her father, then found Jesus. My God!! It was like in a movie or something. Jeez! I was flabberghasted. I never knew she went through all that, though. She's a strong woman, you could say that about her." Maddelyn pulled off and began to figure out which way to get out of this godforsaken neighborhood.

"Which way is best? Up here or turn around and go back the way we came in?" The question was directed to anyone who answered.

"I'd turn around and go back the way we came. I ain't too sure what's up that way," answered Kyndra. She made a U-turn and they headed for Cobbs Creek parkway. There was mostly silence as she drove. Maddelyn went through the park and got to Kyndra's house rather fast.

"Well, folks. This is where I get off. Maddy, I'll call you tomorrow, baby. We got a lot to talk about."

"All right, Kyndra. I'll see you later,"

"Yeah, take it easy, Ken . . . uh, Kyndra," Jouscar said. They sat and watched as she went inside.

It took them about twenty minutes to get home. Using the remote, Maddelyn opened the garage door and pulled the car in. Neither of them had much to say. "That house will never sell. I really don't see much that can be done with it. I'll try a few tricks, but I don't know." Jouscar was merely making conversation while they were going up the steps. "Did you reset the burglar alarm?" he asked Maddelyn.

"Oooo. No, no, I didn't. I'll get it right now." Maddelyn was trailing, so she went back to do just that. She stood for a moment and reflected on the night. It was, after all, a very different night. An enlightening night. She remembered what Evelyn had said about Greg and nobody knowing who killed him. *Does it really matter now?* she asked herself.

Satisfied that she didn't have that answer either, something clicked inside her head at that precise moment. A realization that she had not heard the voice of God in years. She used to know how to pray. She used to go to church. Maybe she'd find the answer to some of her questions. She turned the lights out and went upstairs to bed. For the first time in thirty years, she got down on her knees and clasped her hands together in front of her face like she used to do as a child. She laid her head gently on her hands and she prayed.